His Fantasy

by

Sheila Kell

HIS Series

His Fantasy

Cover Art by *Lea Schizas*

The Wild Rose Press, Inc.
PO Box 708
Adams Basin, NY 14410-0708
Visit us at www.thewildrosepress.com

Publishing History
First Edition, 2025
Trade Paperback ISBN 978-1-5092-6193-2
Digital ISBN 978-1-5092-6194-9
Previously Published by Cunningham Publishing 2018

HIS Series
Published in the United States of America

Dedication

To my valued readers
You keep the joy in writing

Chapter One

A chill slid down Madison Maxwell's spine and froze her thoughts. That unwelcome feeling didn't happen often, but when it did, something terrible usually happened and had affected her in some disastrous way. *What's coming my way now?*

"Maddie, are you still there?" her sister, Rylee Hamilton, asked through the Bluetooth car speaker.

Giving herself a mental shake, Madison smiled at the thought of seeing her older sister again. Granted, they were step-siblings, but they were closer than most sisters and shared their hopes, dreams, and secrets. Her smile grew. Lots of secrets. That secret sharing tapered off as they became adults, though. Lately, Madison hadn't shared all her secrets with her sister. She still held a big one in her pocket from when she'd attended Rylee's wedding in Vegas. That was to say, her second wedding for the family nearly a year and a half earlier. In a nutshell, Madison had slept with one of Rylee's brothers-in-law—the one who'd turned into an arrogant asshole. Madison adored the rest of the family, even though she hadn't seen them since the night she'd lost all common sense and slept with Brad Hamilton. She was too embarrassed to face anyone.

What if they knew how foolish she'd been? Had Brad bragged that he had a supermodel in his bed? After his words to her, she wouldn't put it past him.

He'd done enough of it when next to her on the mattress after they'd had sex. Madison still didn't know whether his boasts had been playful or his true character. She didn't take the chance at the time and had got the hell out of there.

She mentally slapped herself for her idiocy. *That's what you get for going to bed with a man you don't know that well.* In fairness, she hadn't just met him. He'd all but kidnapped her when Rylee had been in trouble, forbidding her from helping search for her sister. Of course, he said he was there to protect her and then told her he couldn't participate in the rescue operation because he had babysitting duty. She hadn't been any happier about the situation. While housed together, they'd only exchanged hostile words and glares before he'd released her when Rylee—and presumably Madison—had been safe.

For the love of the bride and groom, she and Brad had tried to be civil at the wedding. The alcohol afterward had helped. She'd met an entirely different man. It had been like going to bed with someone she'd just met, which she'd never done before, but they'd been drinking, ignoring their brief past, and getting to know each other, and one thing had led to another….

Thankfully, Rylee hadn't said anything about Madison's indiscretion. Either she was playing it cool, waiting for Madison to bring up the topic, or she truly didn't know the truth. Nodding to herself, Madison went with the second possibility because it put her mind at peace.

Unfortunately, she'd probably see Brad on this trip—her final trip from New York City—and she still wasn't prepared to face him after she'd cowardly run from his room. As a strong, independent woman, Madison turned into a wimp at the thought of seeing the man who'd rocked her world, then treated her like a celebrity to be awed by instead of the real person he'd had his hands all over. He'd told her that she was his fantasy come true. That's when she'd realized he'd taken the supermodel to bed and not Madison as his sister-in-law, of sorts. Her heart sank at the memory. She'd been such a fool.

"Yeah, I'm here." Madison pushed the entire drama away to focus on her driving and the conversation.

"You're sure you want to turn PYNK into a lingerie boutique? I know we are not interested in running the club, but our manager is good, so there's nothing to worry about. If you don't want it, we could sell it."

A wave of panic surged through her at the thought of losing her dream of running her own business and not the club. "Do you want to sell it?" *Please say no. Please say no.* Madison didn't know what to do if her sister made that choice. Although financially sound, Rylee had contributed most of her nest egg when they purchased the place. The last thing she wanted to do was lose it for her sister. Sure, Madison could buy another place—smaller even—to open a boutique, but she'd planned out every bit of space in the current location of their small, exclusive women's club.

"Only if you do. I'm excited about the boutique, but I wanted to ensure you want to take on that much space."

Too much space didn't bother her. Heck, what business owner wouldn't love extra space? The great thing was that she and Rylee had purchased the place outright several years ago as their fallback for when they decided it was time to change careers. Only later did they realize that Rylee wasn't interested in managing a nightclub and neither did Madison. It had been a steal they couldn't pass up at the time. In the beginning, Madison had thought it would be exciting, but she'd changed and wanted something else. Something without drunken women and then men trying to crash the party. And the protesters. God, she'd had enough of that. Why couldn't women sit and watch male strippers without going to hell?

"Are you kidding?" Madison said with a laugh. "I have all kinds of ideas for space utilization. I can't wait to show you the line Javier has created. The best news is it will be exclusive to our brick and mortar store and online stores." As a designer, Javier ranked in the top five in the US and was a friend in the cutthroat fashion industry. True friends were few and far between in that business. She'd been lucky to collaborate with him early in her career, and he'd eventually become a true friend.

"Didn't you help him design the pieces? Wasn't that why it's in your store?"

"First, it's *our* store. Second"—her smile grew with excitement at her accomplishment—"I did. I may not have the fashion design degree, but after years of modeling for top designers, I know fashion and lingerie."

"He's in love with you," Rylee chuckled.

"Don't even think it. Javier is happily engaged to a nice man named Justin. Javier just believes in me. He's always been my biggest supporter, even when a photographer was on my ass during a photo shoot. What gets even better is that once the line takes off, he said we'd talk more about other pieces—we did limit it to a few items since I'll be the only one selling them—and expansion. Imagine, there will be a line of clothing called 'Madison.'" She almost squeaked out the words with delight. For some reason, she was happier than when she'd made *People* magazine's most beautiful people list. There was satisfaction in this emotional storm she felt. Satisfaction and joy—lots of joy—yet fear lurked deep in there.

Could she make the boutique a success? She was hoping her name would bring people in the door. Would it be enough to entice them to come in and meet her and then buy merchandise? She hoped so, but always in the back of her mind, she worried. "It won't be the only line we carry, but it will be the cornerstone of the store."

"I'm so proud of you, sis. This is big. We need to celebrate. Wear your cocktail dress. We're hitting the town."

Laughing at her sister's sudden thirst to party, she wondered if Rylee's husband, Devon, took her out often or if she just missed girls' night out. Madison did miss those fun times that seemed so long ago. "No. I'm tired, and I'm not even sure if I'm in Maryland. How about dinner at home another night? Maybe we can pop some champagne or something." She hoped her sister didn't ask how she could be so tired with only a three-and-a-half-hour drive. Sleep had eluded her the last few nights. She'd been too worked up over the change in her career and move. It had been hard leaving a lucrative modeling career for something so uncertain.

"Done. Day after tomorrow since we're meeting already."

"Done. What're you cooking?"

Rylee laughed. "That's an excellent question. I may have to pull Devon into the kitchen. He cooks better than I can."

Madison wouldn't say one word about her sister's cooking abilities or lack thereof. Rylee had been learning from her brother-in-law's wife, Kate, but her sister had vented her frustration at not making successful meals every time. Maybe she'd be pleasantly surprised since it had been so long since she'd had Rylee's cooking. She crossed her fingers on the steering wheel.

"Actually, Brad has been my guinea pig lately."

Madison started at the mention of Brad. "Really?"

"Yeah. Single guys need to eat, and he's been great in trying out what I've made. He's nicer about it than Devon." Rylee chuckled.

Nice? Brad? She'd seen that on him briefly, but her other experience with him hadn't been so pleasant. He'd been demanding and dominating. He'd been a true alpha. Could she be wrong about him? Had he just shown the wrong side of himself to her?

Out of the blue, Rylee assured her, "You're doing the right thing, Maddie."

"I know," Madison said. "I'm ancient in the modeling world. I've had my turn, but times are tough." When she'd lost her multi-million-dollar cosmetic contract to a younger model, she'd known it was time to begin a new path. She couldn't blame the company but didn't have to like the decision. It's not like she didn't know the day would one day come, but no one liked being put out to pasture.

Finding herself gaining on a black town car, she checked her speed and noticed she'd been driving fifteen miles over the limit, so she eased off the accelerator some. Being pulled over for a ticket while leaving her old life behind and embarking on a dream wasn't something she cared to experience. Of course, she never wanted to experience it. She didn't need an omen like that to begin her new life.

"You're not ancient. Christ, you just turned thirty-one."

Madison laughed, but it was stilted. "That's ancient in the modeling world."

"They don't know what they'll be missing," Rylee stated in support of her sister. "Would you do even one shoot if they called you?"

Thinking for a moment, she glanced in the rearview mirror. Empty except for woods and green fenced fields. Would she accept a job? She'd decided to leave her entire life behind—constantly starving herself and always being on display—but if Javier asked her, she'd do whatever she could for him. But only him. "Maybe," she said hesitantly.

A loud sound ripped the air, and the town car flipped over the small bridge it had been approaching. Dumbstruck and watching with wide eyes, Madison's breath caught in her throat and seized her voice. One minute the car was driving and the next it was airborne before landing in the water upside down.

After a moment's hesitation at the scene, she sped up to bring herself to the embankment near where the vehicle had left the road. "I have to go, Rylee. The car in front of me just crashed." She hung up without waiting for a response from her sister and hit the SOS button on her rearview mirror. Never having used it before, she had no idea if it even worked, but BMW was renowned for their quick response. "Come on, come on," she muttered, ready to physically help the car's occupants in the water, but she knew she had to get help to them. Thankfully, it was a small creek and didn't look deep. But still....

After she relayed the accident to the calm voice that boomed over the car speaker, Madison stepped out of her car, then, as an afterthought, reached in and grabbed her emergency tool from the glove box. Her mind briefly flittered to when she'd purchased it from a department store some time ago. It guaranteed an emergency escape from your vehicle with six different options, including a seat belt cutter and a glass breaker, to name a few. With it in hand, she left the car and skidded down the incline by the creek. Her high-heeled boots weren't the best footwear, but she refused to go barefoot in the underbrush. Hell, there could be snakes for all she knew. She shuddered at the thought of confronting a snake. With her determination to aid the passengers, something as small as a snake wouldn't stop her.

No one had exited the overturned vehicle, and with its tinted windows, she couldn't tell how many occupants it held. Her pulse raced at the thought of someone injured. She had no medical training.

Had their tire blown? That would explain the loud noise. Then, the driver must've lost control and hit the small bridge railing that boasted "Bridge ices before road."

Sliding down the last of the slope, she landed in the

cold water. Her jeans automatically soaked up to nearly midcalf. Thank God it wasn't deep where the car had landed. Making her way to the upturned vehicle, her stomach lurched at what she was doing and what she might find. She could only hope the emergency vehicles would hurry. It wasn't like they were in the city. The two cars had been on a long stretch of country highway. A shortcut she'd learned from Rylee to get to her sister's house in Baltimore.

Madison internally crossed her fingers when she reached the vehicle and yelled, "Hello. Can anyone hear me?" There was no response. She rushed to the driver's side door and tried to open it. It didn't budge. *Stupid,* she told herself. She'd watched enough television to know the door wouldn't open when partially submerged in water. That's why she had the emergency tool.

As the blood pumped fast through her veins, her heart pounded loudly in her ears, adrenaline rushing through her, giving her strength.

Madison held the tool in her right hand. Turning her face away, she bent down, even with the window, then swung hard at the glass on the rear-door window and hoped the tool did its job. Pain reverberated up her arm at the impact of the metal tip on the glass. She knocked at the spider-webbed glass around a small hole to clear the window for access, fear and dread pulsing through her. She didn't know what she'd find, but her heart beat faster, hoping the occupants weren't injured.

Ignoring the biting cold, she kneeled, shivering as the water covered her legs to nearly mid-thigh, and peered through the opening. Her eyes landed on an unconscious woman in the back seat, hanging upside down, her seat belt holding her in place. A sweep of the front showed the only other occupant was the driver, who was also unmoving.

The water lapped over the top of the woman's head, her hair lost in the current, but not high enough to interfere with her breathing. Yet. Well, Christ. Should she move her? She had no idea if that would make any injuries worse. But what about the water? That couldn't be good. If Madison waited and the water rose, she wouldn't be able to help both the woman and the man, and then one would drown. She wouldn't allow that.

With an uneasy breath, she crawled toward the woman and froze. Her heart skipped a beat when the car skidded further into the creek. She searched frantically, listening hard for sirens, but there was nothing but the lap of water filling her ears. That and her still pounding heartbeat. Once the car settled again, she exhaled shakily and focused on the woman. With a trembling hand, Madison released the woman's seat belt. "Shit," she gasped, when the unconscious passenger dropped into the water. Madison hurriedly turned her to keep her face out of the water, praying there'd been no injury. Not daring to think of anything but making the woman safe, Madison refused to acknowledge her achy muscles or her shaking limbs as she tried to keep the woman from drowning.

With a grunt, Madison dragged the woman to the opposite bank, pulling her up on mud and rocks, ensuring she was entirely out of the water. Dropping on her butt, Madison breathed hard and steeled herself for what it would take to remove the driver. He had to outweigh the woman by a good eighty pounds. She had no idea if she could even manage it; her muscles were already screaming. Knowing she had no choice,

Madison stood on her shaky legs. Then, taking a deep breath, she looked at the car and took a determined step forward.

"Anyone else in the vehicle?"

Madison spun at the firm, deep voice. When her eyes fastened on the dark-haired, jean-clad man, panic skittered through her, and her breath caught. "You."

Chapter Two

Brad Hamilton slipped when his foot hit the muddy embankment. He then wrenched his ankle trying to regain his footing. When he looked up, he did a double take at the woman dragging someone through the water. He needed to make sure he was right. For far too many nights he'd been wishing to be near her. Realizing his eyesight hadn't failed him, he tightened his jaw against the sudden rush of anger at her. Of course the fucking cosmos would throw her in his fucking path.

Madison Maxwell. Even though he hated doing that "talking thing" women wanted, they had a lot to discuss, but first, he had a more pressing matter to deal with than the woman who'd run away from him.

He hurried past her into the water with a tire iron gripped in his hand. His body reacted sharply to the freezing cold of it. Water slid into his black tennis shoes, immediately soaking them and his socks. The lower parts of his jean-clad legs followed behind, making them heavy to lift. He considered if the water was too deep for a passenger to survive. Come to think of it, when he'd called out to Madison, she'd never responded, apart from her surprised "you."

He raised his voice and asked her again, "Was there anyone else in the car?"

Madison nodded, her face pale and dirty. "Yes, the driver."

With a nod, Brad turned and smashed the front passenger window with the tire iron. After using the tool to clear the space, he got down on his hands and knees, crawled into the vehicle, and cursed at the cold water soaking the arms of his shirt. At least the water hadn't risen over the driver's head.

With the man's sharp black suit, Brad surmised that he must be a chauffeur. Not that it mattered in a rescue operation, but it registered in Brad's mind. A curious snip wondered what had happened for the car to end up overturned in the muddy water.

Assessing the man, he reached out with two fingers, searching for the driver's pulse at his neck. When he didn't feel that steady beat, Brad adjusted the position of his cold digits, despite knowing he had the spot right the first time. Still, he checked. This wasn't something to be wrong about. After a minute, he removed his hand and sighed. Nothing.

He turned the driver's head toward him, and Brad's blood ran cold, but it had nothing to do with the temperature of the water. A slice of fear crawled through him. He'd left the women alone and undefended on the creek's bank. With dread urging him on, Brad backed out of the vehicle faster than he thought he could move.

Exiting the vehicle, he yelled to Madison, "Get down!" Sloshing his way through the water to the bank, he cursed at how heavy his steps had become. *Fuck. Fuck. Fuck.* His pulse rate accelerated as adrenaline spiked through his system. He didn't have his weapon. Although, if he happened to be competing against a sniper rifle—which was what he suspected since the driver had been shot cleanly in the forehead—his weapon would be useless at that range. Plus, there was no cover on that side of the bank.

When Madison didn't move, he pushed through the creek faster, screamed and waved his arm at her. "Get the fuck down!"

It took her a moment to react, and those few seconds felt like a lifetime to him. After the confusion left her face, she dropped into a squat and looked around. Her paleness seemed more of fear than that of a few moments earlier. Before Brad could reach the bank, he heard shots reach them through the air just as mud flew on the bank from the bullets. Who the fuck were they shooting at? Madison? The passenger? Him? It had to be the passenger since the shooter had already targeted the driver. Then, who the hell was the passenger?

Uncaring if the shooter struck out again, Brad left the water and launched himself on top of Madison, knocking her flat on her back. He registered her "Oomph" before covering her body with his, her wet sweater soaking his long-sleeved T-shirt. Christ, she could've been shot, and he hadn't been there to protect her. His gut wrenched into knots at the thought.

She clawed at his arms, panic lacing her muffled words.

"Shh. Someone's shooting. Be still." Brad could only hope the passenger didn't suddenly wake up and sit. Although, something told him that was what the shooter hoped would happen. He and Madison had just been in the way. Now they were caught, and there wasn't a damn thing he could do about it at this point.

Madison stilled underneath him, but her body shook. Her fear broke his frigid heart. Was she shaking with fear of the shooter, her cold clothing, or the closeness to him? He'd never done anything to make her fear him, but she'd been pretty pissed at him when they'd parted. Both times, come to think of it. As for the second time, he'd never had an opportunity to apologize—not that he was sure an apology was due, but the man should always apologize because chances were he'd done something wrong at one point in time— but now didn't seem the time to rehash their brief history. Although it might be the only time he could pin her down.

"What about the driver?" she whispered, her words trembling.

"He's dead."

"What do you mean he's dead? The accident wasn't that severe, was it?"

How much to tell her? Hell, they'd already been shot at, so there was no use pretending. "He was shot."

Her breath caught, and she paled even further.

Instinct told him to hold her tighter, but reason told him to leave her to deal with it. He wanted to be there for her even though she'd been the one to walk away, and it was difficult not having her in his arms while she dealt with what was happening.

When no further shots were fired, he lifted his head and scanned the woods surrounding the creek once again. Would the shooter come closer to make sure he made his kill? He had to have noticed they were unarmed. Brad weighed how long it would take him to retrieve his weapon from his truck, but that would leave the women alone, and he couldn't do that.

Blessed sirens sounded as emergency vehicles approached, and Brad took a deep breath of relief. He didn't, however, get off the top of Madison. Not until he was sure it was safe.

When the first sheriff's deputy arrived, Brad relayed there'd been an active shooter, which sent the deputy quickly back to his car, squatting behind the open door with his weapon drawn.

"You can get off me now," Madison whispered.

"Not yet. We don't know for sure the shooter left." Although his gut told him he'd departed before the police arrived.

The unconscious woman moaned lightly. Fuck. That was all he needed, another person to try to cover. Thankfully, the woman didn't wake. She needed an ambulance, but they wouldn't come through until the shooter was neutralized or confirmed on the run. The last was where Brad's money sat.

Whoever the shooter was, he was a professional. He'd hit the bulky driver right between the eyes while the car had been doing, he'd guess, at least seventy miles per hour. No one just cruised on this stretch of road. Then again, the shooter had missed hitting them on the bank. Had that been a warning to them for protecting his target?

Time slowly passed while Brad and Madison waited for the next move by either the shooter or the deputies. The seriousness of their situation brought the Maryland State Police into the mix. After what seemed like forever, the state police pieced together a four-man team and sent them into the woods to check for the shooter. Brad guessed they didn't have much choice unless they stayed in their positions forever. While the thought of Madison underneath him again was something he'd hoped to happen someday, he didn't want it because of these circumstances.

Feeling her trembling beneath him, he silently tried reassuring her that it wouldn't be long before they could safely move. When his eyes met hers, he almost fell in deep. Even frightened, she had the most gorgeous eyes he'd ever seen. He'd love nothing more than exploring the connection between them. The strong connection he felt in their gaze. But now was not the time or the place. "It's going to be okay," he quietly reassured her.

She nodded, and he couldn't tell if her daze was from the situation or their shared moment. Either way, he was there to soothe and protect her. Being in the water and unable to cover Madison had ripped at his inner being. He'd never felt so helpless, and he'd been in plenty of tight situations.

The law enforcement officers returned from the woods, frowning and shaking their heads. Brad was given an all clear, and he grudgingly lifted himself from Madison.

Before he could offer her his hand, on her hands and knees, Madison crawled to the passenger of the car. "She's still out," she said, worry tingeing her voice.

Cupping his hands together, Brad shouted to the law enforcement parked on the road, "We need EMTs. We've got an unconscious woman." Next, he kneeled on the opposite side of Madison and felt the woman's pulse. Although it could be stronger, he wouldn't classify the beating as weak. On her temple, he noticed some drying blood. "Looks like she might've hit her head on the window in the crash."

Madison leaned over to see the wound and frowned. "I think I know who this is."

Giving the passenger's face another once-over, Brad grimaced. She looked familiar with her short blonde hair, but he couldn't place her. Maybe it was the wet hair or the slightly streaky makeup that he guessed came from her tumbling out of her seat into the water. "Who?"

"Senator Sharon Walden."

Stunned, Brad remembered meeting her when he'd been a Secret Service agent. Her husband was a U.S. Senator and had needed protection for the presidential campaign he'd just kicked off. While the extra security wasn't necessarily standard, it wasn't unheard of. When an agent had been sick, the senator had demanded the position be filled, and Brad had been placed on temporary assignment with that detail. At the time, the senator's wife had been a brand-new senator, but her popularity had already outshined her husband's. It never made sense to Brad why she'd run a senatorial campaign when he'd been planning the presidential run so soon after. Supposedly, she would resign if he won and be just the First Lady.

Brad shook his head. He'd never understand how his father had navigated the craziness of politics for so many years.

Looking over his shoulder, his gaze focused on the car with the dead driver. "You mean the woman whose name is on the primary presidential ballots?" he clarified. Her husband had lost his bid for the White House but promised to run again. Word was his wife was running, and he'd willingly accept the post of First Gentleman should she win the presidency. Something about that niggled the back of his mind, but it remained out of reach.

"Someone was really shooting at us?" A nervous lilt lifted Madison's voice as she asked the question.

"My guess is they were shooting at her." He nodded to the senator.

EMTs made their way down to them, carrying a backboard and a large bag since the gurney needed to stay at the bank's top. He and Madison moved away to allow the EMTs access and climbed the embankment, but not before informing them, the sheriff's deputy, and the state trooper, who'd come toward them, of the dead body in the vehicle. At the top of the rise, they were met with more law enforcement and were compelled to remain and provide their statements. It wasn't like it mattered. The shooter was long gone, and Brad would bet his next paycheck they wouldn't find out who it was.

His blood boiled. The bastard had shot at Madison, whether she was his target or not.

"I heard a loud noise, like a tire blowing out, and then the car swerved off the road, hit the bridge incline and flipped over in midair, landing upside down in the water." Madison spoke matter-of-factly, almost woodenly, like she wanted to get it out and over with. He couldn't blame her; he wanted to get out of there.

He still couldn't believe of all the women to be put into his path on this trip, it'd be Madison. He wouldn't complain about his luck. He just had to figure out how to use it to his advantage to get to know her better. Even if that involved just soothing her while the horror of the incident sank in for her.

"That was probably the shot that killed the driver," Brad offered, as if the deputy couldn't figure it out for himself.

The deputy, who'd been all but salivating over Madison, gave him an evil eye. What the fuck?

Because he liked to piss off people for no apparent reason, as his twin brother, Matt, liked to remind him, he said, "You can see none of the tires are blown out or flat, so it only makes sense." He wanted to add dickwad, but thought that might be pushing it.

Uh-oh. The man turned on him. While that couldn't be good for Brad, at least his eyes were off Madison. "How many shots were fired when you were"—he flipped back through his notes like it'd been an exhaustive interview—"in the water?"

"Three. A single burst of three." He pointed to the disturbed spots near where the senator had lain. Christ, the shooter had only missed hitting her by inches. He wanted to pray to the gods—any of them—and thank them for allowing the bullets to have missed Madison.

Thankfully, his assertive, exact answer took the bluster out of the deputy. Good.

While they completed their statements, the senator woke and, after the EMTs explained what had happened, she insisted on seeing Madison, who then began to notice her messed up appearance. Sure, her dark hair was an absolute mess, but it was an attractive mess. To clean her sweater, she swiped a hand down the front and made it worse. Not that he wanted her to look bad, but her fretting made him smile. Until today, he'd always seen her looking perfect, from the top of her head down to her cute toes. The camera always captured an image of her that made him want her with every fiber of his being.

"She wants to see you, too," a tall EMT informed Brad.

Fuck. Drawing the senator's attention was the last thing he wanted. What if she remembered him? They'd never been introduced during that week he filled in for the other agent. He didn't want to be dragged back to that time in his life. Things had been good with the Secret Service until…. Even now, years later, it remained out of his reach.

"Come on," Brad said to Madison, with a hand to the small of her back, turning her toward the ambulance, "let's go over together."

Nodding, she stayed beside him on the road where the ambulance had parked. They approached the vehicle and stopped at the gurney outside the open doors. He wondered if his discomfort—and not just from the cold clothing—showed on his face.

"Did you save me?" Senator Walden asked Madison.

Madison visibly gulped before she answered, "I only pulled you from the car."

The woman reached out a trembling hand. "What's your name?"

Shaking the woman's hand, Madison seemed to gather herself and answered firmly, "Madison Maxwell."

Studying Madison for a moment, the senator nodded. "The model?"

With a small smile and a slight cock of her head, Madison nodded. "Yes."

"Thank you." The senator squeezed Madison's hand and released it.

"And you," the woman had focused on Brad, "helped?"

The intense scrutiny by the senator bothered him.

"Not really."

"I know you, don't I? What's your name?"

Oh, here the fuck it goes. "Brad Hamilton."

After a brief moment, her eyes lit up with surprise. "Secret Service."

"A long time ago," he said, hoping that'd be the end of his past. He only prayed she hadn't heard about his departure from the agency and what had happened to him to facilitate it. He didn't remember everything that had happened to him, but he had enough memory to make him jaded. In his heart, he knew someone had set him up. He just hadn't been able to prove it without his entire memory.

The senator nodded, and he refocused on the conversation around him. "I want to thank you for this. There's a dinner I'm hosting in a few days. I'd like you to be my guests."

Not only no, but fuck no. He couldn't go to the Lion's Den of DC and run into his old colleagues, who'd surely be guarding some of her esteemed guests. Not with that cloud over his head. Hell, they might not even allow him entrance. Wouldn't that be fucking grand? As for going to the dinner, his resounding answer was still no fucking way.

Madison's eyes brightened. "Yes, thank you," she said, as if answering for the both of them. Well fuck.

"Good. I'll have someone send you the information."

Utterly dumbfounded—an expression he'd not prefer to wear—Brad stood and stared at the two women who'd just decided for him. Had his not speaking first and Madison accepting had him somehow agreeing to the dinner? Hell, he'd just not go.

They couldn't come after him for that. Madison would be fine on her own in the den of vipers. Shit. She wouldn't be safe at all with the sleazy politicians—his father excluded—and others in the political arena who attended such events and preyed on young women. Young hot women. Like Madison. She'd be great arm candy for one of the men she needed to avoid. Yet, she was so much more than that; his little time with her had proven it.

Christ, he'd have to go to protect her. That'd mean facing a past he'd put far behind him. All he had to say was that she'd best appreciate his monumental effort.

Chapter Three

By the time everyone had asked their questions, and Deputy Waters—who she'd wanted to reach out and slap—had stopped trying to see through her damp, dirty sweater, Madison was freezing enough her teeth chattered. Although it'd been near seventy earlier in the day, the temperature had dropped, and it was closer to fifty, if not lower. Not only was she wet, but she wasn't wearing a jacket. She hadn't needed it earlier so she had just tossed it in the car. More than likely, she could've retrieved it before she spoke with law enforcement, but she hadn't wanted anything to prolong the event. Her nerves had been frazzled enough dealing with the aftermath of the incident. She'd had enough of this scene.

Someone frickin' shot at me. Someone killed the driver. Those thoughts slid into her body and stole her breath. Why did her body suddenly feel so weak? Her legs shook, as did her body, and dread slipped down her spine. It was over. Panic nearly set in as her body tried to shut down on her. She fought it and, with a deep breath, held herself steady.

Someone frickin' shot at me, she thought again. She couldn't get that out of her head. Sure, they were probably shooting at the senator, had shot the driver, but she'd been there in the thick of it, and they could've hit her. Or Brad, who'd charged in like an avenging angel set on covering her. His method of getting her to the ground could've been gentler, but he'd run headlong into danger to protect her. She absently rubbed her behind that had taken the brunt of the impact of their bodies when he'd tackled her to the ground.

Then he'd lain on top of her, covering her, ensuring her safety. Having his warm body—albeit wet—against her, so snug, set her body spinning in a pool of lust that had been completely inappropriate for the situation. She'd felt the heat creep up her neck at her embarrassment.

She stumbled, and a hand grabbed her arm to steady her. Even though she knew she was safely ensconced in a law enforcement barrier, she started at the touch, her heart hammering. Turning, her gaze collided with Brad's concerned one.

"Are you okay?" he asked in a caring voice that reminded her of when they'd first made love. He'd fooled her, and she wouldn't let him fool her again, despite how brave he'd been, or the fact that he'd probably saved her life.

Attempting to yank her arm back, she lost her footing again and found herself pulled up tight to his chest. His rock-hard chest that she'd pressed kisses all over that one night. "I'm—I'm fine," she finally got out in a throaty voice, one she didn't mean to use.

A chuckle escaped him, and she wanted to smack him for it. It was just anger, not just at the situation, which wasn't fair to either of them.

"Oh, Maddie." The use of her nickname sent an unexpected spark of warmth through her. It sounded so loving coming from his lips.

Regardless of the comfort she was beginning to

feel, she insisted, "You can let me go now." When he did, she stumbled back before regaining her footing. On shaky legs, she turned back to trek to her car. She wasn't trying to be ungrateful, but the whole situation was a mess and disturbing. She needed to work through everything—alone. She took two steps and nearly collapsed from the maelstrom of emotions and feelings that swamped her. With a speed she wouldn't have believed if she hadn't seen it, Brad was there and caught her in his arms. Fleetingly, her anger with him evaporated.

"You're not okay. Let me help you." He pulled her to his side and wrapped his arm around her so she could walk on her own accord, or he could assist her with his strength. "Where are you going?"

"My car," she said, confused by his question.

Brad shook his head. "No, from here."

Oh. That made more sense. "The Ivy."

"I'll drive. We can pick up your car tomorrow or have one of my brothers pick it up and drive it into town. Safer to have someone pick it up tonight."

Leave her car? With all her samples in it? The thought gave a jolt to her stomach at the possibility of losing anything from her car. She'd just have to find a way to drive herself. She shuddered from the adrenaline dump tormenting her body. Who was she kidding? She couldn't drive. "Would you drive my car? I have things in there that I need." While she didn't need them immediately, they represented the new life she created for herself. She couldn't let the items out of her grasp.

He studied her with an intensity that saw right through to her soul and almost knocked her wet socks off. Oh, she couldn't wait to get dry. And warm. The idea of getting warm with Brad turned her insides to jelly. No matter how he'd acted before, she'd once seen the good side of him, like she had today, and that man stirred her both emotionally and physically.

Rubbing her arms to generate heat, she thanked him and repeated her question. "Thank you for protecting me. Thank you for helping me now. If you wouldn't mind, would you drive my car into Baltimore?"

As if just noticing she was cold, he turned toward her vehicle. With his free arm, he pulled out his phone, swiped and tapped until he put the phone to his ear.

"I need a favor. Can you get someone to drive you to pick up my truck?"

He relayed their location as best he could since they were in nowhere.

Madison eavesdropped as, in a crisp tone, Brad explained what had occurred to whoever was on the other end of the phone line. It amazed her that he could detail the incident without any emotions. She feared she'd break down trying to explain everything, especially about the dead man who she'd never met.

After a bit more conversation, which included where to find his spare key, he ended the call. "Taken care of. AJ and Jake were already headed in this direction and should be here shortly. They'll pick up my truck and deliver it to The Ivy for me."

Maybe it was the waning sun or the day's adventure, but the thought of lying in bed, in his arms, at The Ivy set her blood afire. The idea of him in her hotel room while they waited for his truck to be delivered conjured up images of their hot night together. Lying naked in each other's arms like there was no tomorrow. Her body heated just thinking about his large hands on her again. Yet, no matter how much he fanned her flames with only a smile, she couldn't allow them to return to bed without more to their relationship. The term "more" confused her about what she wanted, but she knew it had everything to do with Brad Hamilton.

They reached her car, and he opened the passenger door for her, settled her in, and latched the seat belt.

"I'll be right back."

Nodding, she watched in the side mirror as he jogged to his black truck, reached in and pulled out a small black duffel bag before he jogged back to her car. Opening the back seat door, he tossed the bag inside. Then, he slipped into the driver seat. He turned to her and caught her staring at him. "Are you sure?" he asked.

No, but she didn't have a choice unless she waited and had AJ or Jake drive her, increasing the friction between her and Brad. She'd rather not get into an accident and hurt herself or, heaven forbid, someone else. "Yes. It's fine." Did her voice betray that it wasn't fine? She hoped not because he was being super nice and helping her when she needed it without being the arrogant prick she knew he could be. At least at one time.

He adjusted the seat. With her long legs, he hadn't had to scoot the seat back far, then adjusted the mirrors before he put his foot on the brake and pushed the Start button. Her key fob, located in her purse on the passenger floorboard, was close enough for him to ignite the engine successfully.

On the nearly hour-long drive into town, they

didn't speak as the miles passed them. Not a word, except when he waved at an SUV and told her it was AJ and Jake.

The brittle silence in the vehicle attacked her nerves. On the one hand, she worried about Brad in her hotel room and keeping them out of bed, but on the other hand, the events that had unfolded had her almost biting nails. She'd never been in such a situation. While it might be second nature to Brad to run into the spray of bullets and dead men, she didn't deal well with the concept.

"So," she said, breaking the silence, "do you really think someone would've killed the senator if we hadn't been there?" It was the only safe question she could think of. She didn't want to know if he thought the shooter would kill them like he had the driver. She shuddered for the dead man who'd only been doing his job.

Brad glanced at her before returning his eyes to the road. She had a feeling he was struggling with what to tell her. The truth or some semblance of it. Finally, he nodded. "Probably."

Her shudder deepened. "I know I said thank you once before, but I really mean it. I've never been so scared in my life." The honest words slipped from her mouth, and she didn't care if it made her appear weak.

"I'd be worried if you hadn't been." His soft voice calmed her jumbled nerves, and they lapsed into companionable silence for the rest of the trip. She put the thought of someone being murdered as far back in her mind as she could. It didn't work as well as she'd liked, but with Brad near her, she felt safe.

By the time they arrived at valet check-in at The

Ivy, Madison felt herself again. The weakness had seeped itself from her bones. Getting warm had helped immensely.

"Suite One is all ready for you, Miss Maxwell," Margaret—the clerk on duty—said as she handed her the key card—two of them. Great, the clerk assumed Madison would be sharing her room. Well, she guessed that looked rather obvious since Brad had carried in his duffel bag.

To remain a much sought-after model, she'd worked hard to maintain her clean image in public. She'd watched whom she associated with, watched what she did, and watched who was watching her. The paparazzi would have a field day with this tidbit of information, regardless of the truth of the situation.

Accepting the key cards from Margaret, Madison said, "Thank you," then turned her suitcase to roll it to the elevator, Brad following at her heels.

The elevator ride was awkward. With each passing second, the walls seemed to close in on her. Not only were her nerves shot from everything she'd witnessed, but being so close to Brad was all too much. Since their encounter, she had tried desperately to avoid him, hoping to ready herself for the inevitable moment when their paths would cross once more. The terrifying events from earlier had seen to that.

Madison was a mess of emotions. Her heart warred with her gratitude for the man who'd saved her, which heightened her lusty thoughts, leading to her confusion. Among all that, a bubble of anger remained unsettled beneath the surface.

She'd have to admit he could do more to her without a word than any other man she'd known.

However, not all of it was good.

Arriving at her room, she slipped the key card in the slot, opened the door, and walked in.

She rolled her suitcase to the bedroom and called over her shoulder, "I'll change in here. You can change in the bathroom." Although she wished she'd been alone so she could take a hot shower and warm her bones.

Once changed, she walked barefoot into the living room where Brad lit the gas fireplace. The heat slowly reached her, bringing warmth to her weary bones. He'd changed into another pair of jeans and a red, long-sleeved T-shirt that molded to his exquisite frame. She caught her breath and chastised herself for her unruly thoughts about the gorgeousness of the man before her. *Remember what the man said to you.*

"Thank you for helping me earlier," she said again, unsure what else to say. Someone had to break the silence.

"Listen, Maddie"—he stepped toward her and stopped—"I'm sorry."

Her stomach fluttered, and she gulped at his words. "For what?" Why, oh, why did she ask that question? She didn't want to rehash anything that had happened between them. They'd had a little too much to drink, had sex, he'd been crude, and she'd left. End of story.

"I was only joking with what I said. I didn't mean to upset you."

She jolted. It was as if he'd read her mind. That was very unsettling. He seemed to know what she needed to hear.

I finally banged a supermodel. I can check that off my bucket list. Those were his exact words.

Getting to know Brad at the wedding reception, she'd foreseen he could be special. However, with his words, she'd seen that idea tossed aside. He'd slept with her not because she was Madison, Rylee's sister, but because she was a model and he'd wanted to "bang" one. She'd been such a fool, and bringing up his words made her almost forget how tender he'd been when they made love or during this afternoon's incident. It was nothing like the first Brad she'd met when they'd been stuck in close quarters, each angry at the situation and unable to help Rylee.

Her heart beat a staccato rhythm in her chest that pounded in her ears as she absorbed his apology.

While stepping closer to her, he continued. "I didn't sleep with you because you're a supermodel. I slept with you because I'm drawn to you, and we had incredible chemistry."

Her breath hitched at the thought of how drawn they'd been to each other—that time. She'd never slept with a man while under the influence of alcohol. Now she knew why that wasn't a good idea. You never knew the man behind the sexual appeal. She stepped back at his closeness. "Okay. So, you didn't mean it." Something inside her broke, and she felt the belief down to her soul. How could she ever have doubted him?

Nerves skittered through her bloodstream when he kept closing in on her. She'd backed up enough that her knees touched the couch.

"Maddie," he said in a low, gravelly voice before his hand reached out and gently touched her cheek.

Heat surged through her body from his touch down to her fuchsia-painted toenails. This was a bad idea. Yet she struggled to ignore the pull of him and even hoped he'd kiss her like before, when they'd been all over each other at the hotel in Vegas.

"Maddie," he whispered this time. She had a split second to decide whether she'd let him kiss her or push him away. With her heart pounding, she chose, and he lowered his head, touching her lips gently.

Electricity arched its way through every nerve ending in her body and had her wanting to throw her arms around him after ripping off his clothes. Like before—before he'd opened his mouth and spouted those words that cut her to the core—this felt right. She figured the first time they'd been thrust together was foreplay of sorts, even though neither had seemed to notice how that interlude had fed into their desire for each other.

He drew back, and his eyes darkened as he looked down at her, a question residing in his mesmerizing golden-brown eyes.

Breathless and against her better judgment, she said, "Don't stop kissing me." After listening to her sister, deep down, she knew he wasn't the crass guy she'd had a glimpse of that once, but she really didn't know him, so maybe it was wishful thinking. Come to think of it, she never did hear a story in the *National Enquirer* or other ragtag magazines about them sleeping together. All she knew was that her body heated with the desire for his touch…his loving…his caresses. At that moment, she wanted it more than her next breath. How could that be wrong?

With a sly grin, his mouth covered hers again. She opened immediately, and his tongue swooped with the same force as when he'd tackled her on the bank. Her palms went up his biceps, and she felt the rippling muscles in her hands and the strength he held in them. Continuing her trek, she wound her arms around his neck where her fingers played with the short, dark hair. She kissed him back with all she had as her body trembled with desire. Their tongues brushed, then dueled, and she felt each warm, wet stroke throughout her body.

Brad's hand left her face and wrapped itself in her hair behind the nape of her neck while his other hand reached to the small of her back and drew her hard against him. Her emotions and desire went into a whirlwind. The hard length of his erection told her that he wanted her, the mess of a woman standing in front of him, not the pin-up girl he'd joked about.

His mouth lifted ever so slightly, and she tried to pull him close again. "Maddie," he breathed against her lips.

Sensations rocked her body. She was so hot that fire should've been shooting from her veins. She was lost in him…his kiss…the moment.

With a groan, Brad pulled her even closer and devoured her mouth with his, his tongue all about domination. As he deepened the kiss, his arms slid down to her butt, and he pulled her up, lifting her feet off the floor. She'd been ready to wrap her legs around his waist when a knock sounded at the door, and they sprang apart like a couple of teenagers caught making out on the couch.

"It's AJ," they heard from the other side of the door. "With Brad's truck."

Brad glanced at his watch. "Dammit. I should've known he'd speed to get here." He frowned at her. "It's best I go. I've been up here long enough and don't want to ruin your reputation." His words startled her as he touched her cheek again. He then placed a light kiss on her lips and left her suite.

She wasn't entirely sure she knew what had just happened. He'd considered her reputation, and she'd been ready to toss it to the birds. Her heart did a pitter-patter at his thoughtfulness to keep her image clean. She'd worked hard to stand out positively in an industry rife with scandal. It'd helped her career, and she needed it just as much now to open the boutique.

No matter what happened, she could no longer pretend she didn't want them to be together, at least not sexually, because her actions and her body betrayed her every thought on keeping her distance from Brad Hamilton. But no good could come of a hot, torrid affair with him, except awkward moments with the family when their fire had burned out. So, her mind told her to stay away from him, and she would.

Chapter Four

After a shitty night's sleep with nothing but images of Madison—naked and in his arms—Brad showered then dressed. He might need to pull up his long sleeves later in the day, but for now, he wanted to stay warm in case they had any outside training.

On the drive to work—Hamilton Investigation & Security, co-owned with his brothers—he thought about the incident with the senator. Something niggled at the back of his brain, but he couldn't pull it forward. The memories of what had happened to him in Colombia that cost him his career as a Secret Service agent were lost to him. It frustrated him to no end that he couldn't remember the events leading up to what had happened. Although a small part of him wasn't sure he wanted to remember. What if he really did hire the prostitute? It wasn't in his character, but maybe he'd been drunk…or drugged. It wasn't the first time he thought he'd been drugged, but he couldn't prove it since he'd been sent home before he could have any blood work done. When he was in the States, it was too late to test his blood. It seemed asinine to believe one of his brethren would drug him. Maybe a local Colombian had. That could've happened. But why? It all made no sense.

Arriving at Jesse's home and HIS headquarters, which was now its separate building on the large acreage of land his brother owned, Brad noticed a group congregating around the field where an outdoor firing range had been established so they could hold in-house weapons practice. They had plans to build their own indoor range in a few months, so everyone must be taking advantage of the fresh air today. Not wanting to miss out on whatever was happening, Brad hustled over to the group, stopping where AJ and Devon stood apart from the large group of HIS men and women—from law enforcement or military careers.

Catching his breath in the crisp morning air, Brad asked his brothers, "What's going on?"

"Shootout at the O.K. Corral," AJ told him, without looking his way. His gaze remained on the paper targets several hundred yards downrange.

"Shootout? We're way back here, so I take it Jesse and Neftali are taking the shots?" The two sharpshooters on the team, snipers in the military, were constantly trying to outdo each other. It also provided entertainment for the team.

"The new recruit challenged both of them."

It took him a moment to grasp whom AJ had meant. Samantha Milton had been a recent hire, straight from a SWAT team, as one of the best—if not *the* best—sharpshooters in Baltimore. It was ballsy of her to start her employment with the team this way. As far as he knew, she'd never seen Jesse or Neftali shoot. "Who's your money on?" he asked curiously.

"Jesse, of course," AJ said without hesitation.

"Neftali," Devon chimed in.

"Pity Matt and Trent are missing this type of fun."

AJ's words hit home like a sucker punch, and the fun of the event left him in a whoosh. Trent—their half-brother—had moved away for the love of his life and had cut ties with HIS, preferring to be a rancher. But Brad's twin, Matt, who'd also moved away for a woman, met with them via video conferences and calls unless they were face-to-face on a mission. He missed his best friend something fierce. The phone calls they shared weren't enough. Yet, his brother had finally married the woman who'd stolen his heart in college, and since she, because of her charitable organization, couldn't move to Baltimore, Brad let go the hurt of his brother moving away and separating them. It was bound to happen, but selfishly, he'd have preferred Matt to have found a local girl.

Pushing himself back into the fun unfolding before them, he decided to mix things up. He liked to fuck with his brothers. He figured they'd come to expect it from him. And, well, because someone had to do it. Why not him? "My money's on Sam."

Heads swiveled his way in surprise. He'd always been an avid supporter of Jesse's and boasted when he'd win these matches and call them rigged when he'd lost. Thankfully, his eldest brother had won more than he'd lost. Jesse stood as the reigning champion sharpshooter on the team, but Neftali didn't quit trying to one-up Jesse. "What? We hired her because she's good. I have the utmost faith in her."

Samantha walked by with her sniper rifle slung over her shoulder and her blonde hair, pulled back in a ponytail, flying in the light breeze. "Thanks, Brad. At least *someone* has faith in me."

He noticed Ken Patrick—a former army Ranger who'd served on Jesse's team—grumbling in her wake that it was too soon to challenge the others. What the hell? Ken, their field team leader, didn't have faith in her? That was unlike Ken and could be a problem they didn't need. Sam, as she preferred to be called, was the first woman they'd hired who wasn't one of his brothers' wives. Did that have something to do with it? Brad was sure she'd earned her spot with the group. Hell, she'd made SWAT, and that shit wasn't easy by any means.

With a smug smirk, he prodded his brothers. "Twenty bucks?"

Based on their gazes and expressions, AJ and Devon seemed to have the same concern about Ken and Sam. Yet, they nodded in agreement.

Come on, Sam. Show them what you've got. That's forty bucks in my pocket and a great way to start your time on the team.

The three competitors found a prone position while everyone moved back to give them space. Not that they worried about stray bullets, but they worried they'd be distractions. Not that a distraction would really bother the shooters either. The three were solid professionals.

"So," AJ started, "what's happening with Madison?"

Brad stiffened, not sure where his brother was going with that comment. One look at Brad yesterday and AJ had to have known something was going on between them in the hotel room. Brad had been more gruff than usual when he'd opened the door to a grinning AJ, who'd assured him his truck handled ninety like a gem.

No one could know that he'd had a one-night stand with Madison and that she'd been the one to end the night. He'd never had a woman walk out on him. Never.

Yet, even with his mantra of love 'em and leave 'em, he'd never had a woman leave his bed and not look back unless he cut ties. Maybe it wasn't just the mind-blowing sex he'd had with her, but that he'd felt a connection with her that he hadn't felt with anyone else. She was a challenge he wanted to tackle.

"Nothing that I know of," he finally responded, no doubt adding to the intrigue in his brother's mind by his delay in responding.

After a shouted warning, they covered their ears as shots fired.

Removing his hands, Brad heard Devon, a former CIA agent, say, "Bullshit," but it'd been hidden in a fake cough.

"That's what I was thinking," AJ said with a laugh.

"I don't know what you think happened, but it's simple. I came upon the incident behind her. She was too shaken to drive, so I drove her into town. I left when AJ, the speed demon he is, arrived with my truck." His back was up by now, and he narrowed his eyes at his brothers. "Now, what the fuck is the problem?"

Devon held his hands up in an "I give up" gesture. "Whoa. No need to get all defensive with us." Then he grinned like a schoolboy with a secret. "Or is there?"

A sudden thought occurred to him. Did Devon know the truth? Did any of his brothers besides Matt? He thought he and Madison had been discreet in Vegas, so no one would ever guess they'd planned to spend the night tearing up the sheets. At that time, it'd been assumed it was a one-night stand, so he shouldn't have been so upset when she'd left. The reason she had left dropped stones to his gut. He'd been joking and hurt her feelings. He admitted it hadn't been his finest moment. It'd been his fantasy for many years to have her naked beside him, and he'd screwed up any chance with her outside the hotel room.

He didn't need any crap from his brothers. "Fuck you." If they knew, they'd keep it secret. At least he hoped so because he was sure Madison would go ballistic if she became the talk of the break room at headquarters. And he'd have to kick some ass with his brethren if that happened because he wouldn't want her reputation tarnished or her sister to hear about it and want to kick his ass for allowing Madison's name to be slung around.

"Yep, something worth talking about." From beside him, AJ slapped him on the shoulder. "It's okay. We'll make up something."

The urge to do something he hadn't done in a long time—deck one of his brothers—was fighting its way out of him.

Three HIS team members retracted the targets from downrange with the pulley system they used to keep them from entering the field of fire.

"I'd be careful if I were you making up something. Rylee will have your ass on a platter." Rylee, the mother to his five-month-old nephew, hadn't mellowed with motherhood. If anything, she'd become more protective of those she loved. And she loved her stepsister, Madison. Maybe more than her husband, Devon, who shouldn't be joking around like this about his sister-in-law. "Especially you, Dev."

"I didn't say I would make shit up." Devon jerked his thumb toward AJ. "That's dipshit here doing that. I know better than to test my wife where her sister is concerned."

"Have you heard anything more about the shooting?" AJ asked.

Shaking his head, Brad answered in the negative. "I doubt I'll hear anything." However, going to the dinner with the senator might change that.

"I haven't told Rylee yet," Devon said. "Madison had best do it soon, or she'll hear about it from someone else and, knowing those two, Madison wants to be the one to tell her."

"I'm not sure what you want me to do about it," Brad said. "That's between the two women."

To steer the conversation away from him, he nodded toward where a group was evaluating the three targets and the location and closeness of the shot each sharpshooter fired. They allowed only one shot because they said if you needed more than that, you sucked and needed to have your sniper rifle repossessed. "Are you ready to pay up? I'm going to win."

"No fucking way," AJ taunted. "Jesse'll win."

"Fuck both of you. Neftali's going to take it this time. I have faith."

With a shake of his head, Brad chuckled. "I'm about to be forty dollars richer." He grinned mischievously. "Do you two actually have the money or do you need to beg for an allowance advance from your wives?"

"Doesn't matter because we won't be giving you the money. You'll be paying me," AJ boasted.

Typically, he'd agree with AJ, but today, he felt bold and a bit reckless. Betting on the newbie not only poked at his brothers but showed him as a rebel, and he tried to do that whenever he could.

"Whatever," Devon stated. "You both know you'll owe me, so you may as well get your money ready. Rylee would love a dinner out. We haven't gone anywhere alone since Mitch was born. Except work."

Sighting Rylee in the mix checking the targets, Brad asked, "Is she ready to return for missions yet?" The teams relied heavily on Devon because of his superb computer skills, so he didn't really take a break when his son was born, but Rylee, a former FBI agent and HIS team member, took maternity leave— something Brad didn't know they fucking offered—and still hadn't come back to work for missions. She came to train, though, like today.

"The Belgium assignment. She'd wanted six months to not be away for more than the day, but the trip was close enough. I have a feeling it's going to be hard for her. She's pretty attached to Mitch. So am I," he added.

A tightening in his gut settled at the talk returning to babies. He was happy for his brothers and their families, but they needed a life outside of young ones— something they could share in with him.

Loud groans echoed among the group surrounding the targets, telling Brad what he needed to know. He held out his hand. "Pay up." He knew the groans were from all who lost and probably only one or two—if that—placed their money on Sam. The team would not be the same now that they had a new best of the best, and she was a woman. Not that they begrudged women—they worked side by side with them with trust—but being bested by one still crushed a man's pride.

He wondered what Ken would say about Sam and

her abilities now.

"Damn," AJ said as he slapped a twenty-dollar bill into Brad's hand. "I can't believe she beat Jesse."

When Devon placed his twenty into Brad's hand, he held it there. "Make things right with her. Whatever you did, make it right. Madison refuses to come to any family dinners or events"—he lowered his voice—"and I know it's because of you. I know, Brad," he emphasized. Devon released his hand and returned his wallet to his back pocket. "Let's go congratulate our new champion." Slapping AJ on the shoulder, they moved to the group about fifteen yards away.

Devon knew. *Fuck.* Brad couldn't be the reason she wouldn't do shit with her sister's family. He wouldn't believe that. He needed to see her and set things right. Say what he wanted to say yesterday but couldn't because of her fragile state. Although their kiss had shown her strength and had only whetted his appetite even more for her. They'd settle this between them. He knew there was more than sex attracting them to each other, and he wanted to explore that with her and see if a relationship was possible. And if they ended back up in bed, he wouldn't complain.

Chapter Five

Madison exited the elevator at The Ivy and entered the luxurious lobby. Inhaling the clean, fruity scent that filled the common areas, she could never get enough of this hotel and the magnificent spa. Sure, it only had nine suites and nine rooms, but the atmosphere alluded to much more. As she walked by one of the many seating areas with the fireplace lit, she noticed two men watching her from a gold-toned sofa. When they stood to approach her, her heartbeat sped up as it always did when people approached. Some wanted to tell her how much they loved her modeling while others went into a lecture on not eating enough and how she should be ashamed as a role model. In reality, she wasn't quite as thin as the other models. It frustrated the designers to no end, but she had always been determined to stay a healthy weight.

Two men intercepted her. "Miss Maxwell?" the large, bald, African American man with a graying soul patch asked. She ensured her face remained neutral as she eyed the soul patch she was certain had gone out of style.

She had no recourse but to stop unless she wanted to plow into the second man with mocha-colored skin and a sprinkling of gray in his beard. His wire-framed glasses did nothing to hide large, dark eyes that seemed to reach out to her, and not in a good way. They didn't appear threatening, but she knew looks could be deceiving.

"Yes," she answered with as much confidence and poise as she could muster at being approached by one husky man and one who looked like he was the brain behind their operation. Whatever that was.

"I'm Richard Casden, and this—" He turned to his companion and nodded. "—is Jeremy Rogers."

He stopped like those names were supposed to mean something to her. When she didn't comment, Richard asked, "Can we take a seat? We've got something we'd like to discuss with you."

She wondered briefly if this could be about a job. She'd had small business owners approach her before but then walk away when they found out her fee and restrictions on the type of business and their reputation that she'd represent. If she'd wanted to keep her sterling reputation in the modeling world, she'd had to be tough. Something about these men told her that they weren't approaching her about a job though.

A frisson of fear shot through her. Her nerves were still frazzled after yesterday's terrifying encounter, and being approached in a lobby by men who had clearly been waiting for her did nothing to calm her. As she looked around the open lobby, her heart sank. It was deserted. What could these men want with her?

"Please, Miss Maxwell, we won't take up much of your time."

She eased a little at their politeness and that they wanted to remain in the public place. She offered a slight nod. "I don't have much time, but I can give you a few minutes." She expected to meet her realtor in half an hour for a viewing. Since she planned to live in

Baltimore, she wanted a place of her own, and this time, unlike her rental in New York City, she wanted a home where she could paint the walls.

"That's all we ask." Richard gestured toward the cream and gold seating area, allowing her to precede them.

Choosing a cream striped chair facing the sofa, Madison sat and crossed her legs, then uncrossed them in case she needed to rush away. It was a reaction she'd been aware she'd developed since learning of the harsh reality of kidnapping after her sister had been taken.

Once the men sat, she took a better look at them. Richard had to be in his fifties, and his tweed sports jacket appeared to be a size too large across his broad chest. The man looked like he'd been a bouncer in a nightclub for years. On the other hand, Jeremy, in maybe his thirties, could've been an accountant looking immaculate in his dark business suit and soft pink shirt opened at the top and without a tie.

"We wanted to talk with you about our offer on PYNK," Richard began.

Shocked, she was at once at a loss for words. She and Rylee had agreed and weren't selling their business to anyone. There was no way her sister had gone behind her back and put it up for sale. No. She wouldn't believe it. That funny feeling returned. Something wasn't right. "I'm sorry, gentlemen,"—she started to stand—"there must be some mistake. PYNK isn't for sale."

The men jumped up with grim expressions on their faces.

"We know it isn't listed for sale, but every business has its price, and we have a very generous offer, Miss

Maxwell," Jeremy finally spoke, although it came through clenched teeth.

Her ire rose at his comment. Her business definitely didn't have a price. Besides, they were changing the type of business. Surely these men didn't want a high-end lingerie shop. "PYNK is not for sale." She moved to exit, but Jeremy was suddenly there, crowding her. Her pulse spiked, and her breath caught as Richard also moved closer. So much for a quick exit.

"What do you want for it?" Jeremy ground out. "We'll entertain your request."

God, they were serious about buying her business. What the hell? It was a successful nightclub but not worth all this attention. She wished now that she'd seen what they'd offered for the business. With no desire to sell, she'd not asked Rylee anything specific about the offer they'd received. She'd discuss it with her sister this afternoon. Until then, she needed to get rid of these men so she could leave.

"Like I said, PYNK is not for sale, gentlemen." Her grin remained fixed on her face as she spoke. The men were too close for comfort, but she was determined not to let them see how uneasy she was.

"Like I said, every business has its price," Richard said.

She shook her head. "Not PYNK."

"Even PYNK," Jeremy added.

Her heart beat erratically, wondering if these men would hurt her in public. All for a piece of property. If intimidation was their tactic, they were doing a damn good job of it. But she wouldn't hand over the club due to intimidation.

"What's going on?"

The air released from her lungs in a relieved sigh when she heard Brad's voice. It didn't matter that she'd not wanted to see him again. He'd just become her savior. Again.

Irritation settled on Jeremy's face, and rage crossed Richard's. She took the opportunity while they were distracted and slipped by them to Brad. "You're just in time. Thanks for picking me up today." She hoped he played along.

Searching her face as she took his arm, he read whatever she was broadcasting and nodded. "We don't want to be late." They turned to the entrance, and she didn't even look over her shoulder to see if the men followed. She didn't care. She had Brad at her side. No matter what she thought of him or their tumultuous relationship, she knew he'd protect her at all costs. It's what he did. It's who he was.

Brad's truck was still waiting for valet parking at the entrance, so he opened the passenger door. She didn't want to get into his truck. When she glanced back and saw the men walking that way, any hesitation Madison had was gone. She climbed into his vehicle without a word.

Coming around the hood of the truck, Brad slid into the driver seat, started it up, and then drove away from The Ivy as if that had been the plan all along.

The tension in the vehicle was thick. After a few moments, her racing heart calmed down enough for her to speak steadily. "Thank you. I'm sure the men wouldn't hurt me, but I appreciate you helping me get away from them." She mulled over how to continue. Flashes of last night's kiss made her want to climb him like a tree. She swallowed hard. "Honestly, you can turn around now and take me back so I can get my car." She forced a smile on her face as she finished, not quite sure she was doing a good job of convincing him, or herself.

Appearing to chew over her words, he worked his jaw. "Who were they, and what did they want?"

She released a pent-up breath and decided to go with the truth. "They wanted to buy the club."

"I thought it wasn't for sale."

"That's what I told them."

"Who were they?" Brad asked again.

She gave him their names, and he went rigid, his hands tightening on the steering wheel until his knuckles turned white.

"You're not going back there," he stated flatly.

"What?" Confusion dipped her brows. Was he seriously going all caveman on her?

He slowed, pulled to the shoulder of the road, and stopped the truck before turning to her. The morning sun beamed in the front windshield, almost blinding her.

"Maddie, people who cross those men die. Sometimes horribly."

She blanched.

"Their names are notorious. They own most of the strip clubs in downtown Baltimore. They don't play around. If they want your club and you're not giving it to them, they could take that as a slight, which would mean your life could be at risk." The tension in his large frame radiated in waves to her. The tightness of his palm still gripping the steering wheel got her attention.

Madison didn't want to believe what he was

saying. There had to be a mistake. The men wouldn't kill her to get the club. Wariness laced its way through her senses. With a churning stomach, she tried to put everything into perspective. They might try to intimidate, but that was all. Besides, men who killed as much as Brad described didn't walk around as free men. "If they're responsible for killing people, how come they aren't in jail or something?"

"They're smart enough not to get caught, or they have someone do it for them. It doesn't mean they aren't responsible. I don't like this at all. This is serious, and I need you to take it as so," he added.

She sat stoically, unsure what to say. She'd been back in Baltimore one day, and now, she'd seen someone killed, been shot at, and, according to Brad, her life was in danger. This couldn't be her life. It was like walking into the damn twilight zone or something.

"We'll come back later and grab your stuff. You can stay with Dev and Rylee."

Madison's eyes widened in shock, and she shook her head. Was it truly so serious that she had to go into hiding? That couldn't be what he was suggesting, right? As if on autopilot, she responded, "No, I can't. They used their second room for the baby and their third for an office for Devon."

Brad narrowed his eyes as if in concentration and stayed quiet for a moment. "Then you'll stay with me. Matt's old room is still empty."

Stay with him? Was he out of his freaking mind? The last thing they needed was to be in close quarters where beds were involved. She could just see that disaster without a crystal ball. "I'll just get another hotel."

"They found you at this hotel," Brad reminded her. "Don't you think they'll find you at another one?" he asked incredulously.

They had found her and fast. Though she honestly hadn't been in hiding. Nor had Madison noticed any paparazzi around when she'd entered The Ivy, broadcasting her every move. Reality slammed into her. They'd tracked her down somehow, and it had to be illegally because hotels didn't just give that information out to anyone. She'd stayed off social media since she'd arrived, needing time to decompress from everything. Besides, since she wouldn't be modeling any longer, her fans were sure to abandon her for the next hottest model. But staying with Brad…that had trouble written all over it. Where could she stay that would keep her low profile so they couldn't find her?

She wondered if those men would really hurt her because she wouldn't accept their offer to purchase her club. If so, what about Rylee? If what Brad said was true, her sister would be in danger too, and she had a family to concern herself with. Foreboding slithered down her spine, even though she desperately hoped Brad and his reaction were going overboard. But if Brad were right…. Her mind spun to the possibilities of protection. Rylee had her alpha husband and was a badass in her own right. Madison needed someone, and Brad was offering. Why did it have to be him of all people?

With no alternative, she'd accept help from Brad until she could convince her sister to find her another protector more suited to Madison's personality. Admittedly, it had nothing to do with personality. She just needed the support of someone she didn't want to jump into bed with. She may be signing her emotional death warrant with this decision, but she had to do something. Fear had swamped her around the two men, and they'd done nothing but stand there. With Brad's characterization of them, she could readily see one of them pointing a gun at her, sending her senses reeling. She shivered at the image and voiced her decision while her gut clenched. "Okay. I'll stay." Then she added, "For now." The last thing she wanted to sound ungrateful because she truly was thankful, but even displaying the hint of any emotion, she was terrified it may mislead him, or even worse, she may give in to her attraction.

"Until we clear this up," Brad intoned.

She bit her tongue to keep from arguing with him.

"Now, where were you going this morning? To see Rylee?"

"Oh." She checked her watch. "I'm meeting with my realtor." What to do now? She didn't have any transportation and wanted to see what her realtor had put together for her. She craved a place of her own so badly she could taste it.

"Okay," he said. "Where to?"

"Brad, this could take most of the day. I can't tie you up like that." She almost choked when he smirked.

"Princess, you can tie me up anytime."

She squinted, narrowing her gaze at the endearment.

"Now, where to?"

Defeated, she rattled off the address where she'd been scheduled to meet her realtor for the home tour. What bothered her was that she was a little giddy about touring potential homes with Brad at her side, ready to ask his opinion on the choice. It bothered her a whole lot.

Chapter Six

A chilly wind blew in through the door behind Brad and Madison as they entered his house. Not wanting to take her back to the hotel right away in case the two men were staking out the place, Brad had suffered through house hunting and exploring luxurious homes with the size and amenities he could never imagine. At least not nothing possible on his salary. He earned an excellent salary with even better bonuses and profit sharing, but he'd never made the kind of money Madison had made as a model. She told him she'd banked most of her earnings all those years with a plan to purchase a home outright, so she never had to worry about a mortgage payment. She wanted to be able to do what she enjoyed, whether it made her wealthy or not. Her dedication to her goal impressed the hell out of him. It couldn't have been easy for her. Her patience and professionalism while they toured the homes set up a certain warmth inside him that rivaled any he'd ever felt for a woman. There was something about Madison that made him look beyond sex. And, he liked what he saw.

It almost embarrassed him to bring her to his modest two-bedroom, two-and-half bath starter home he and Matt had purchased years ago, after the three homes they'd toured earlier. She'd only been scheduled for the first one, but her realtor decided there was another one she had to see and then another. Damn if the mousy realtor hadn't been right. Madison had fallen in love with the third home, which had its original hardwood floor, marble accents, granite countertops, and heated bathroom floors, and a price tag worth more than he'd be able to afford in many years. Madison hadn't balked and had made an immediate offer on the property.

She'd been serious about setting down roots here, and he liked the idea, as long as he could tangle in her life.

Entering his home, his eye glanced over the plain look of his living room and, to his other side, dining room. No type of tablecloth or place settings on it. Just a wooden table and four chairs. Sniffing, he decided, after smelling the other homes today with their scent to attract a buyer, his could use an air freshener.

"Matt's bedroom is the second door on the right." He added, "It has its own bathroom."

As she wheeled her suitcase down the hallway with stiff shoulders, he watched her magnificent ass. Perfectly rounded and ready for him to take a bite. He shook his head to clear it. His job was to protect her.

"Thank you," she softly tossed over her shoulder before she entered the empty bedroom.

He worried a bit because he hadn't touched it since Matt moved all his personal items from the house to live in Kentucky with his wife, Caitlyn. He grinned. She was expecting twins. Matt as a father seemed odd. Not that he thought Matt wouldn't be a great father; it was just since they looked alike, he saw himself in that position and enjoyed the rush of pride and love that shot through him. He never saw himself as a parent. He liked to play too much to settle down with a wife and rug rats.

The bedroom door closed, breaking into his crazy thoughts. Okay, her smile from house hunting had turned to a frown when she walked through his door. So, he'd been a bit overboard earlier in the morning before they'd toured the homes. After she'd agreed to stay—albeit reluctantly—she'd tried to find other avenues of escape. She'd tried the hotel route again, but he'd nixed it. If he were any other man, he'd be taking that shit—her trying to be away from him—personally. But they'd got on well while touring houses. She'd shown him features and even asked his opinion a time or two. As far as he'd been able to tell, she'd been enjoying herself with his company and putting aside the danger. However, it was never far from his mind.

Hell, he couldn't say for sure if Richard or Jeremy would come after her, but he wouldn't chance it. The two men had worked hard to establish a reputation of domination in their world, and there had to be some truth to some of it. Madison—and Rylee—didn't need to be made an example of. The question was how to end any possible retribution and ideally stop their interest, with the women safe and keeping their club.

While Madison had spoken with the realtor, Brad had called Devon to tell him of the development. Apparently, Rylee hadn't shared the names of the men who'd made the initial offer with Devon. She hadn't known the significance of their names. Brad figured that during this instance, Devon had her wrapped up tight even though she could hold her own. She'd proven that time and again.

Devon hadn't been too keen for Madison to stay

with him. He even said he'd turn his office back into a bedroom. Brad thought that was overkill to get her away from him. When Devon had invited them to dinner, Brad had declined, knowing Devon and Rylee would try to talk her into staying with them instead of Brad. He couldn't have that. He wasn't sure why, but he couldn't.

Considering it was dinnertime, he entered the kitchen and pulled a glass casserole dish from his refrigerator. Uncovering it, he was glad that last night Kate had sent him a pan of lasagna as a thank-you for making the trip to New York City for Jesse to settle things with a new client. A trip that put him back in the path of Madison Maxwell.

With the oven warming, he searched his refrigerator for anything edible to go with the dish he wasn't sure she'd eat. Didn't models eat nothing but salad? He couldn't help her there. He'd been gone too long. He did have the bread Kate had also sent, but didn't models avoid white foods? Christ, how was he going to feed her? Granted, she could stand to gain a few pounds and keep her model figure.

He paused when he heard the shower start. Images of her wet and naked flashed through his mind. He groaned and adjusted his growing erection. Maybe having her stay here wasn't such a good idea after all. He wanted her, yeah. She was gorgeous, and he begrudgingly admitted to himself that the more he got to know her, the more he liked her. Something about the woman drove him fucking insane, though.

With the lasagna in the warm oven, he was at a loss of what to do, so he stood in the kitchen. Normally, he'd grab a beer and sit and watch *SportsCenter*, but he wasn't alone now and didn't want to exclude her from the evening. Hell, he'd at least do it until she came out of the bedroom.

Settled on his worn, leather couch, he turned on the television and found the channel he needed. With football season over, and the Ravens losing season, *SportsCenter* just wasn't the same. Sure, he loved all sports, but football, after playing in college, was his love.

Trying to think ahead, he decided to channel surf and find a movie they might watch after dinner. Would she want action? Romance? Comedy? Please, not some sappy story that would make her cry. He didn't think he could stand that. Hell, he couldn't stand any woman crying, but the thought of Madison crying tore at his gut.

Madison entered the room and blood shot to his groin. She wore a snug long-sleeved T-shirt and tight jeans, with her bare pink toes peeking out from underneath the hem. This was nothing like the classy dress slacks and cashmere sweater she'd had on earlier. This was the real Madison. The one he'd protected while her sister had been kidnapped. This was the Madison who liked to get comfortable. He wondered if he could get her in sweats one day. That image made him smile.

"Something smells wonderful," she said shyly.

Realizing he was staring, probably with his mouth open, Brad stood. "Kate sent over some lasagna yesterday. I had some last night. It's pretty good." He shifted in aggravated discomfort. "Sorry, but I don't have anything for salad. We can go to the store tomorrow and get something for you to eat."

She grimaced and followed him to the kitchen. "I can definitely live without salad tonight. Maybe for the rest of my life. You wouldn't believe how many bowls of green stuff I've eaten." She sauntered to a barstool and sat before a place setting he'd added earlier. "Thank you again for allowing me to stay here with you. I hate putting you out."

"You're not putting me out. That room's been empty for a while. It'll be nice to have some company. I hope you're more of a talker than Matt was." Now why the fuck had he said that? He hated the incessant chatter that some women were prone to deliver. *Please don't let her be one of them and ruin that perfect image I have of her. Her long legs, subtle curves, her beautiful hair fanned out on his bed, their conversation perfectly aligned. Perfect.*

That stopped him short. He liked the woman he dreamed about. Always had. Would being around her ruin that? She'd been his fantasy for so long, that he couldn't see straight. What if the real person burst that bubble of perfection he'd been building since they first met? Even their arguing hadn't wavered who he thought she would be. He'd understood her anger, but now…it appeared they'd put that scene out of their minds, and he was thankful for it.

"Brad," Madison prodded. "Are you all right?"

Shaking his head and feeling foolish, he gave her one of his charming smiles. He knew the smiles he gave, because when he'd been in college, he'd practiced them in the mirror until he had them down pat. Vain, maybe, but something he appreciated at times like this one when he wanted to put his best face forward. "Sure. What did you say?"

"I can't guarantee I'm more of a talker. I've lived alone, so I'm used to only talking to myself." Her smile brightened her face. The face free of cosmetics. Holy shit. She was even more beautiful. Smooth and shiny. He wanted to reach out and touch her.

Turning to check the lasagna instead, he also checked himself for control. He lost some of that control around her. His thoughts jumbled, and he could only focus on her. It had to be because he had so many fantasies he hadn't lived out with her. Maybe once he had, he'd be free of this madness that had overtaken his mind and body.

Reaching around with potholders, Brad set the hot pan down on a trivet on the bar. He'd decided earlier that eating at the bar was less intimate than eating at the dining table. He could be wrong since eating close to her could possibly be *too* close to her. He took away the potholders and said, "We also have dessert. A cheesecake of Kate's."

She bit her lip before she answered. "I don't know about that. That might be taking it too far."

He couldn't imagine a life where dessert was a dirty word. She'd missed so much in her world, and he wanted to give it back to her. Settled on the barstool beside her, he served her a generous portion of lasagna and one for himself. "When's the last time you ate dessert?"

A sigh escaped her. "I don't even know."

"Then you can have a bite or two of mine if you don't want a whole piece."

"I might take you up on that."

Her smile and bright eyes did something to his chest. He blurted before he could think straight, "I want

61

you back in my bed." He internally smacked himself on the forehead. Where the fuck had that come from?

The weight of his statement settled over them like a heavy blanket. Then, Madison stood. "Staying here was the wrong thing to do. I'll find someplace else tomorrow. Now, if you'll excuse me, I'll retire for the evening." With that stilted and formal goodnight, she turned and walked to Matt's bedroom, and Brad did nothing to stop her, too pissed at himself. Why had he been such an idiot?

He'd probably just ruined any chance of getting to know her better, and something inside him broke a little with that thought. There was more to Madison Maxwell than a vixen in his bed, and Brad wanted to find out who that person was.

No more was his thought on only having her naked in his bed. Spending the day with her had changed that. So had her need for protection. Yet it led to a challenge of wills.

He faced the one challenge he'd never had—how to get the woman—all of her.

Chapter Seven

Madison plastered on a smile, rolling a suitcase full of lingerie into her sister's home. She'd avoided Brad that morning at his house and snuck out like a thief in the night. Facing him wasn't something she could handle. Staying up most of the night thinking about him—again—had to stop. Her focus now was on the business. Nothing but the business. And finding herself somewhere safe to stay until she closed on her place.

After much thought, she considered him overreacting in the need to be by her side 24/7. Surely he exaggerated. She still shivered at the thought but figured the men hadn't threatened her, and they wouldn't do anything in broad daylight. Would they? She internally shook her head. Of course they wouldn't. Brad had exaggerated for whatever reason. Was he trying to get closer to her? Was that it, and he couldn't think of a better way to accomplish that feat?

No matter. If there were a threat—which she doubted—she'd be with her sister, who could kick ass and take names like it was nothing.

"Good morning," Rylee said as Madison wheeled the suitcase toward the open living room. "Would you like some coffee or a cappuccino?"

A pleased sigh escaped her at the thought of a decent coffee. "I'd love a latte." She halted by the couch and lowered the handle on her luggage. She slapped her hand on the hard-sided suitcase. "I brought the samples. We need to decide on a couple of pieces." Then she grimaced. "There's another suitcase in my trunk."

"I'll get it," a deep, male voice said behind them. Her heart jumped. Christ, Devon had snuck up on her. How the hell had he been so quiet on the hardwood floors? Surely one of them creaked. Didn't all old floors?

"Thanks." She smiled at her brother-in-law. "The trunk's open. Just close it after you get it out. It's the only thing—besides my emergency kit—in there." Her emergency kit wasn't just in case the car broke down. It was also in case she was stranded in the cold. She'd never understood how one of those tiny folded silver things they called emergency blankets worked—and she hoped to never find out—but she had two in her pack. Just in case.

As Devon breezed by his wife at the door, he softly kissed Rylee's lips. Madison sighed dreamily. Her sister and her brother-in-law were so much in love. She didn't wish her sister anything different, but she was jealous of the life Rylee had been able to create for herself. Rylee had it all together. Career. Man. Home. Family.

Family besides just her. A large family that Rylee loved. With a slightly sinking heart, she asked, "Where's Mitch?"

"Asleep. I expect he'll be awake in a few minutes. Devon has agreed to stay home and care for him so we can get this all together."

"You don't need to work today?"

Rylee shook her head. "No, but I do leave for

Belgium soon."

"Oh," Madison said, unsure what else to say. She knew it would be Rylee's first time leaving her son, and although she'd never experienced it, she heard it was an emotional time for mothers—especially first-time mothers.

"It'll be fine," Rylee asserted. "Really," she continued, as if trying to convince herself, "it'll be fine."

Madison bit her lip and watched sadness and loss sweep over Rylee's face. Would her sister be able to handle the separation? And Belgium. Geez, could she get further away where she couldn't rush home in an emergency? Maybe she'd become more involved in the boutique and less involved in HIS. Madison could hope, but it must be her sister's decision. And, it'd be a tough one because Rylee loved her job. From what she'd gathered when she'd been around the group in Vegas, her sister was damn good at it also.

"I've been thinking," Rylee started. "We should change the name. PYNK is a good name, but with a big name boutique having a line like that and the name being tied to a nightclub, it'd be better to start fresh."

Welcome air whooshed from Madison's lungs. *Thank you, Jesus.* Her sister had brought up the topic. Madison wanted the change but had hesitated to bring it up since the initial name had been Rylee's idea before they'd opened the club to women. "I think that's an excellent idea. Do you have any thoughts?"

"How about Naughtie Nighties?" Rylee laughed on her way to the kitchen. "I'm not sure our high-end clients will like that one, but I do."

Laughing felt good. Freeing her mind of the

confusion and fear she'd felt at being shot at and learning a man had been killed. As if all that had happened to her had passed. She hadn't even told her sister the story of her being shot at. Well, not shooting at her exactly, but she'd been there and could've been hit. Her legs weakened at the thought. Her sister would freak when she heard the whole story. If Brad told, Rylee might have already heard, but she hadn't said anything.

With a sigh, Madison followed her sister to the kitchen, where she waited while the coffee machine hissed and spat out her coffee. Then the steamer whirred the milk to a warm, frothy mess. When Madison had the finished product in her hand, she smiled. Brad had only had regular coffee—which she drank—but cafe lattes were her favorite, even though they contained fattening milk. No sugar, no extra flavor, just plain stoked her appetite.

After Rylee had picked up her drink, she turned to Madison. "What happened on the road?"

Shit. It sounded like she already knew what had happened. She'd heard Brad tell his brother on the phone. She should've guessed someone would tell her sister. She'd wanted to be the one to give her the story, but she just hadn't figured out how. Rylee had always been protective of her when they were growing up, even though she was only a year older than Madison. They'd met when Rylee had been eleven and Madison had been ten. Their parents—Rylee's mother and Madison's father—had fallen in love and married. Madison hadn't wanted a new momma, but she'd come to love Rylee's mother as if she'd been her own. The woman had a massive heart that her daughter seemed to have inherited.

Recently, Madison's father had passed away from a heart attack, leaving her with only distant cousins who preferred to live off the grid and didn't want anything to do with her since she was considered famous and would bring the public with her. She never considered herself famous. Popular, yes. Sure, she'd had her share of paparazzi, but not like movie stars.

"Maddie?" Rylee prompted.

Her pulse rate increased just thinking about the danger she'd been in yesterday, through no fault of her own. "Let's go sit down, and I'll tell you all about it."

They perched on the cream-colored sofa, and Madison wondered how her sister kept it so clean with a small child. That was also when she noticed the second suitcase. Devon must've settled it in the living room for them while they were in the kitchen making coffee on his way to take care of his and Rylee's son. Madison could hear him cooing to a giggling baby. Oh, to have a man like that. Would Brad ever—? No, she couldn't think that. It was stupid and irrational to feel like that. Even though he'd been a brute before, he was kind and caring with her, and no matter the situation, her heart fluttered.

Once settled, Madison walked her sister through the events that began with her witnessing the accident—which Rylee knew about since she'd been speaking with her on the phone—to the congresswoman's rescue, the dead driver, the shots, and Brad covering her. She left out how they'd both been turned on, even in the face of danger. It had disgusted her at how inappropriate it had been, yet her body had reacted to him at such a time. And, he'd definitely responded to her. She'd felt his reaction against her pelvis.

"I can't believe all that happened, and you didn't call me later that night. I called twice to check on you. Your cell phone went to voice mail. The Ivy wouldn't confirm if you'd arrived, which pissed me off, but then Devon heard the story from Jesse." Rylee sat her coffee cup on a wooden side table. "I had to hear about it from my husband. I almost stormed over to the hotel myself, but I didn't know what room you were staying in, and they surely wouldn't share it."

Madison winced. She hadn't wanted that to happen. She'd just wanted to cocoon herself that night in the safety of her room. No bullets. No Brad Hamilton. But then last night at Brad's…. "I'm sorry I didn't pick up your calls. I just needed time to decompress, and yesterday I was tied up with a realtor."

"You may be in danger," her sister stated matter-of-factly.

Had she heard of the potential buyers of the club visiting her? Christ, she couldn't keep anything secret with her sister. Or, she groused, when Brad Hamilton was involved. He must be the big mouth telling everything to his brothers and Rylee. "I can't see why I am. They were trying to kill the senator, not Brad or me. Besides, I think Brad overreacted about the potential buyers for the club."

Rylee's back straightened. "What happened exactly? I got the information thirdhand."

"They were at The Ivy yesterday"—a shudder raced through her—"wanting to speak with me about the offer. Brad showed up, and he said they were dangerous, and I needed to stay away. Anyhow, I stayed in his brother's old room at his house because he said the hotel wasn't safe." She set her empty cup on the coffee table with a barely noticeable tremble. "I think he was overreacting. I'm getting a new hotel today unless you think differently. If that's the case, I still want somewhere else to stay."

Jumping up, Rylee paced quietly. When she halted, she frowned. "Devon worried about me when I told him we would turn down the offer. He's pretty much stuck to Mitch and me like glue. I'm unsure if he's right, but I listen to his instincts. If Brad says the same, they probably know something we don't. And"—she shook her head, her auburn hair swishing around her shoulders—"I think Brad's right, and you should have protection."

"But—"

Plopping back down on the couch, Rylee cut her off. "No buts. Look, it may be nothing, but it can't hurt. So you have company for a while and stay at Brad's. Besides—" She grinned mischievously. "—I heard you *really* like Brad." She stressed the word like it meant something.

She gasped. Rylee knew. It had to have been Devon who'd told her, but how many others knew? These brothers seem to be one big grapevine of gossip—nothing got by them. "You know?" she whispered.

Nodding, her sister smiled. "Yep, and I'm upset you never told me about it. Well, not exactly about it, but the fact that you slept with my brother-in-law at my wedding. Second wedding," she corrected herself.

Second, considering Rylee hadn't remembered the first due to being drugged. Her husband, Devon, hadn't drugged her and had no idea she'd been in that state. He'd had his own memory issues, so they'd had a second wedding for not only themselves but family and friends. Because their life together had started in Vegas, they held the wedding there, where Madison had once again been with her sister's new family, which included Brad. Even though he had a twin, she'd picked him out right away and could somehow tell the difference in them. It was something about the old broken noses that set them apart.

"I'm not proud of it. It just happened."

With a laugh, Rylee picked up her cappuccino. "Of all my brothers-in-law I could see you with, Brad would be the last one. I'd have expected Trent."

Madison grimaced. "He did hit on me. I understand he's married now."

Rylee nodded. "Mm-hmm. To Kelly. She wasn't there," she added absently.

With a shift in her seat, Madison set her shoulders. "Well, it only happened once, and because of how he acted, I don't want to be around him."

Her sister stilled. "What do you mean how he acted? Did he hurt you? I heard he's into tying women up, but I was assured it wasn't worse than that. Wouldn't be the first time the brothers didn't tell me the entire truth 'for my sake.'"

Yes, he had tied her up in Vegas, and the thought of Brad tying her up again sent a shiver of excitement rippling through her body. Damn traitorous body. Of course, she wouldn't admit to that. Not even close. "No, he didn't hurt me."

"Then what happened?" Rylee asked over her cup before she took a sip and sighed.

"He—" Not sure how to put it, she started again. "He said something that I didn't want to hear. Something that threw everything into perspective and ruined it."

"What?"

She swallowed hard. Sharing this with Rylee wasn't as easy as everything they shared in life. And they shared pretty much everything. This wasn't very comfortable. "He said he could check sleeping with a supermodel off his bucket list."

Rylee gasped and rage immediately filled her features. She jumped up from the sofa. "I'm going to kick his motherfucking ass."

Without a doubt, she knew Rylee might do just that. She couldn't have it happen where her older sister took up for her. "I don't want you to get upset. First, I'm only sharing because you're my sister, and we've always been close. Second, Brad apologized and said he didn't mean to insult me, so I'd rather we keep this between us." Wincing, she asked, "Who knows we slept together?" *Please don't say the whole Hamilton clan.*

Rylee plopped back down on her seat. "As far as I know, just Devon and myself. I imagine Matt probably knows since he and Brad are super tight. Are you sure you don't want me to kick his ass? Or, I can hold him down while you cut off his balls."

She laughed at her sister's gross and disturbing thoughts of such violence. Then again, she was probably joking—at least for the second scenario. "Now you can see why I don't want to stay with him. If I need this protection the men are worried about, where else can I go?"

"Hmm. Let me think. With the sprouting of all the kids, most of the spare rooms in the brothers' homes have become nurseries. Our couch is available, but you're taller than it is long, so it probably wouldn't be comfortable." She grimaced. "The team heads out soon, which doesn't leave anyone but Brad, unless you want to go to Kentucky with Matt. Jesse might be staying behind, but you don't want to stay there. Talk about alpha and overprotective. And with no Kate as a buffer since I know she's leaving too...." She shivered.

A pang of disappointment settled in Madison's stomach. She couldn't set up the business hiding out in another state. "Kentucky is out." And, it sounded like Jesse might be out, but she'd keep that possibility in the back of her mind. And she would not be able to have a good night's sleep on her sister's couch.

She wanted to listen to the men about the danger to herself, but she just couldn't see how things were that bad. No one shot at her personally, so that event was out, and the men who wanted to buy the club hadn't even so much as threatened her. Yet, she trusted her sister like no one else. If staying with someone for the short term would put Rylee's mind at ease and keep herself safe, if that really was the case, she'd suck it up and do it even if it had to be with Brad. She could be an adult around him, even if it drove her insane. Okay, bad pun. "Okay, Brad it is." That nearly killed her to say that. A thought hit her. "Speaking of Brad, he and I were invited to dinner with the senator. I'm going to need a new dress. Are you up for shopping?"

"I'm always up for shopping. I'm not sure you should go if someone is trying to kill the senator though."

That was a good point, but she couldn't decline. It was a senator. Granted, she was registered to vote in New York, not Maryland, but you still didn't decline those types of invitations. "I've got Brad. Remember?" She hoped he didn't try to back out of the invitation. And getting back near the senator with the potential of bullets flying required Brad to be at her side for protection. "Besides, we're carrying some high-end merchandise, and what better place to begin to find that type of clientele? Politicians send someone to buy lingerie for whoever is warming their beds at the moment." She wiggled her eyebrows. "All I'll have to do is mention the boutique when someone asks me what I'll be doing now and *voilà*."

"That reminds me. We still need a name for the boutique. Devon says we should call it His Dreams." She shook her head. "He just wants promo for HIS."

Madison chuckled. "What about Her Dreams?"

"No. I think we need something different.

"How about La Belle? A friend recommended it, and I like it."

"I love it!" Rylee exclaimed.

"Good. La Belle it is." Madison smiled, pleased they agreed so quickly on a name. "Now, let's go through this lingerie and see what we will carry. You're going to love the Madison pieces Javier designed."

"Did someone say lingerie?" Devon walked into the living room with his son on his arm. "My wife could always use some." He winked at Rylee, who stood and kissed him and the baby.

That's what she wanted. Would she find it in Brad if she tried?

Chapter Eight

At HIS headquarters, where Brad and his brothers prepared the team for their mission to Belgium, Brad's thoughts kept reverting to Madison. He'd known when he'd woken that she'd been gone, and his gut had clenched with worry. Yet, when he'd found out she was at Devon and Rylee's—and they both were there—he settled, but made her promise to come straight back to his place when she was done for the day. For some reason, she hadn't been argumentative when he'd said it, so Rylee must've convinced her not to take things lightly.

Had his brothers had this problem trying to protect their now wives? Not that Madison would be his wife, but she was just as slippery, which drove him insane. He hoped he fared better than they did at the time.

More importantly on his mind was that damn dinner with the senator. He didn't want to go. After all this time, he still couldn't face the Secret Service brethren he'd cut ties with when he'd resigned. He harbored embarrassment and anger over the situation. He'd not been able to convince anyone that he'd been innocent. So, before he was potentially fired, he'd resigned. Even if they hadn't fired him, he couldn't have remained working in the agency. Trust. It had been lost, never to be regained.

When his phone rang, he excused himself from the

gathering of the Hamilton brothers who lived locally, saw who was calling and smiled. He'd expected this call at some point before the dinner. "Hi, Dad."

"What's this I hear you're going to a fundraising dinner at Senator Walden's?"

He'd assumed that was the type of dinner he and Madison had been invited to, but hadn't pursued the topic. If raising money was the goal, the two of them would be left alone for most of the evening. Thank the fuck for small favors.

"Yeah, well, Madison saved the senator's life, so she invited us to attend. It's not like we could say no." Even though he'd wanted to, he knew he couldn't, not with his father in politics. U.S. Senator Blake Hamilton's sons knew when to toe the line for their father's reputation in the political arena.

"Madison who? And, if she saved Sharon, why did you get invited? Are the two of you an item?"

Probably wishful thinking on his father's part. Brad was the lone remaining unmarried son. It'd been six months since they'd had a wedding in this family and people were getting antsy for him to tie the knot. He enjoyed his freedom too much to settle for one woman long-term. Short-term dating worked. Besides, he watched his brothers become pussies chasing around their wives. No, thank you.

He explained about the accident and how he'd come upon it. The saving of the senator. The shots. The invitation. His father had remained mum during his recitation. "Madison Maxwell is Rylee's sister. You met her in Vegas at the wedding." He sighed heavily. "And no, Dad, we're not an item."

"Oh. Pity. She's a looker, and if she's Rylee's

sister, she's bound to be a good person. Maybe you should take this opportunity to escort her to the dinner for something more. And, I'm not talking about just sex, son."

Brad groaned. He did not want to have this conversation with his father. Who wanted to discuss sex with their parent? He'd been given "the talk" at fifteen, which was one of the most embarrassing conversations they'd ever had. Even though his older brothers had already given him the lowdown, he'd had to sit through his father fumbling the topic. He had to get the conversation off this track of thinking. "What did you want, Dad?"

"First, I wanted to make sure I was right. Get your tux ready. It's formal. And, please leave any attitude at home. You're representing the family. Second, I'll be there with Elizabeth, so you'll have someone to speak to in the sea of strangers who'll want to talk nothing but politics and money." After a pause, he added, "There's going to be Secret Service there. Are you ready for that?"

As Brad's gut clenched at the thought, he wondered how he would react if it were someone who'd been part of the scandal who was working the event. Someone who could've potentially set him up. He'd just have to work through it if he planned to escort Madison so no perv went after her. "I'll be fine."

"Okay. How are things otherwise?"

Leave it to his father to cover what he needed first and save pleasantries for last. At least he'd added them. Elizabeth—Brad's stepmother—must be rubbing off on his father. "Things are good. The team will be leaving soon, and so will AJ and Jake." He hadn't been slated for the trip and was thankful since Madison needed him.

"Is this the Belgium detail?"

His father wasn't a part of HIS, but he kept his finger on the pulse and knew what his sons were doing—whether good or bad. "Yes. It'll be Rylee's first one back after Mitch was born."

"You're not going?"

"No, neither are Jesse, Devon, and Matt. We didn't need everyone for this one. The extra members of the team we hired are up and ready for the assignment, so we let them take it."

"Use the time to find a wife," his father said with a chuckle. "It's about time you did. I want more grandchildren."

Fuck that. "Come on. You've enough grandkids already on the way." His sister, Emily, was due to deliver any day. She was as big as a house. Caitlyn—Matt's wife—was pregnant with twins. Then, there was Kelly—Trent's wife. She was also pregnant. He was sure his brothers believed the philosophy of barefoot and pregnant since Brad had welcomed a slew of nieces and nephews in the past two years.

"I'm waiting on you. Try to be nice to Madison. Maybe you'll get lucky."

If only his father knew how lucky he'd already been. His libido felt the kick of recalling the memories of having her in his arms. He scanned his surroundings, ensuring no one from the agency was around and adjusted himself. *Damn, that woman can get me hard just at the thought of her naked.*

In response to his father, he knew not to argue that Madison might not be his type or that she might not like

77

him. His father was a master debater, and his sons always lost, so he just answered, "Of course."

"Good. Good. I'll see you at the dinner." His father disconnected the call before Brad could respond, not that there was anything left to say. At least his dad would be at the dinner.

With the dinner still implanted on his mind, he decided to talk it out with his twin. After a couple of taps on his phone screen, Matt answered on the second ring.

"Hey, what's up? Did we miss something on the conference call earlier?" Matt asked.

"No. It's not the conference call. We're all set in planning. Now it's just packing and any last-minute travel problems. It's about a dinner I have to attend. I'm stuck, and I'm not sure I can do it."

"Then don't. When have you not said 'fuck you' and done your own thing?"

Brad winced at how crass he sounded from his brother's mouth. Although it was true. He hadn't been such a big asshole before he'd left the Secret Service. What happened changed him, and not in a good way. "I have to go. Madison's going, and I can't leave her to those lechers in politics. Dad excluded," he tagged on the end.

"Madison? Rylee's sister? Have I missed something? You gave me the particulars about the rescue and shooting on the side of the road, but what does that have to do with this?"

He sighed wearily. He was tired of repeating everything. "The senator invited Madison and me to dinner. A fundraising dinner, Dad said. I'm going to protect her, but…."

His brother assumed the lead. "The Secret Service will be there."

Nodding, even though his brother couldn't see it, he responded, "Yeah. I'm not sure I'm ready to be around them. What if it's someone from that time? They'll know me, and we might get kicked out. That'd be an embarrassment for Madison and Dad."

"First off, they won't kick you out. The senator invited you, so they can't do anything unless you were a threat to her. You know that." He took a breath and continued. "Second, this is a prime opportunity to do something and find more information about that night finally. Maybe you'll learn enough to clear your name."

One night in Colombia, a Secret Service team that had been sent in advance of the president, screwed up and a big scandal ensued. Brad had been pulled into the mire whether wittingly or not.

It started with a prostitute who hadn't been paid and went to find someone who'd listen to her. Then, it snowballed into a nightmare of a story for the men and the public. Prostitutes were found in some of the rooms with Secret Service agents.

Brad was woken with a prostitute in his bed. However, he didn't remember picking her up. In fact, he'd never do that. Or so he thought. Two thoughts came to mind: that he'd been drugged and set up or that he'd gotten drunk and stupid. He'd fought for the drugged and set up possibility, but it'd gotten him nowhere with his superiors. Since they didn't believe him, they wouldn't test his blood, and he couldn't leave and get it tested himself because they had been restricted to the hotel pending a quick trip back to the States for disciplinary action.

Matt was the only brother to whom he'd told the entire truth, but he imagined his other brothers and his father had an idea. Thankfully, the Secret Service hadn't released his name when he'd resigned concerning the scandal.

Assuming he'd been drugged—which he thought was the only way it could've gone down—why was the question floating in his mind? Of course, who committed the act of drugging him was a necessary evil to find out the true story. And if he found out he'd actually been drunk and stupid? What then?

That thought was why he'd stopped pursuing the situation. But, he had to man up and be strong enough to deal with a embarrassing and infuriating reality. "They won't speak with me while they're working. But you're right, of course. I need to start asking questions." He loved telling his brother that. Brad could imagine Matt's head swelling already at the comment.

"Of course I am. You might want to get Dad to help."

"No. Absolutely not. I don't want him to know." At least not for sure.

"Listen to me, he can get you to where the Secret Service agents you need to speak with are working and can probably find out when they're off duty so you can corner them and ask questions since everyone was tight-lipped after the incident."

Matt made a valid point. He could reach out to those who were in Colombia, but cornering those who avoided him wasn't a bad idea. "I'll see what I can do."

"Good. Now, tell me again why you have to go with Madison to this shindig?"

"Well, I was invited. Besides, she'd be

unprotected, and we both know what kind of men attend these things. They seem so harmless on the outside, but inside they're disgusting sharks."

"Last I remember, she's a grown woman. Considering the fan base she's dealt with over the years, I bet she can handle herself."

Damn his brother's logical brain. He wouldn't tell him he was right again. Once in a conversation was enough. "I'm going. That's all there is to it. Besides, with Dad going and knowing I was invited, I can't back out."

Matt chuckled, and Brad wanted to reach through the phone and wring his neck.

Changing the subject, Brad asked, "What do you know about Richard Casden and Jeremy Rogers?"

"From the strip clubs?"

"Yeah."

A whistle came over the phone. "As far as I remember, they're bad news."

"That, my brother, is the other reason Madison isn't going anywhere alone. Casden and Rogers want to buy the club."

"I didn't realize Madison and Rylee were selling it."

"They're not. They're turning it into some store Madison calls a boutique. Whatever the hell that is."

Matt laughed. "Well, I don't think they'd harm her or Rylee."

"We think differently."

"We who?"

"Your brothers."

"Did you guys have a meeting without me?" Matt sounded was as if he were pouting, and Brad felt that pang of longing his brother must feel not being in the mix all the time.

"Are you pouting, oh brother of mine?"

"No," Matt grumbled.

"Sure." He chuckled. "It was a conversation in passing. The outcome was that I need to protect Madison from the two thugs."

"You, huh? Not HIS?

Brad sighed. "No. Not HIS. Besides, they're busy."

"Humph. I think you've got a crush."

"Fuck you." He disconnected the call, knowing his brother was right once again.

Chapter Nine

It'd been a long time since Brad had cared about how he dressed. He turned in the mirror to check his back before facing front again. The black button-down shirt and clean jeans were pressed and fit snugly but not tight. He wanted Madison to see what he had to offer—in case she'd forgotten—but he didn't need to offend her sister at dinner with too-tight pants that showed his every detail. His dark hair wasn't cooperating, and he ended up overapplying product, then had to rinse it out and reapply it with a lighter hand. He never realized he had a slight cowlick on the side of his head. A haircut was in order, and he wished he'd have done that earlier in the day.

Feeling ready to tackle his wayward emotions around Madison, he went into the living room, silently hoping she had returned. Devon had invited him to dinner and told him that Madison would be there, but he hadn't asked if she'd come to his home first or wait it out at Devon and Rylee's. Seeing that her suitcase was still in the guest room, he smiled, happy the hurdle of her staying with him had been won.

After a quick call to Devon to ensure Madison had remained in place, he took a deep breath, exited his home and climbed into his truck for the short drive to his brother's house. Except for Jesse, who lived well outside the city so he could have enough land for HIS, the brothers who lived in Baltimore were within about fifteen minutes of each other—traffic notwithstanding.

Parking at Devon's house, he noticed Madison's BMW and breathed a sigh of relief that she hadn't taken off to avoid him. With her missing from his side, he worried that she could be in trouble even though he'd known she'd been at Rylee's—courtesy of Devon, not her.

While waiting for someone to answer the door, he had the sudden urge to have flowers or something to give Rylee. He glanced around her yard to see if she had anything in bloom and was disappointed there weren't flowers he could pick to make a bouquet. Didn't dinner guests do shit like that? He'd never done that in the past, so that errant thought threw him for a loop. Since everyone took pity on the single guys in the family, he'd eaten dinner at all his brothers' houses—until recently with Matt as his wingman—but had never felt this off-kilter, like it was something more than just a delicious meal and enjoyable conversation.

Was he thinking of impressing Madison? That had to be it, and thoughts like that had to stop. She liked him as he was or not at all. And based on that kiss in the hotel room, she liked him plenty—whether she admitted it or not.

Holding Mitch on her hip, Rylee opened the door and welcomed him. In dark slacks and a flowery blouse, she'd dressed nicer than one of their casual dinners without her sister. Yep, that itch to have brought flowers hit him again. Fuck. This night was not starting off right.

For some unknown reason, every fiber in his being wanted to bolt away, but then he heard Madison's laughter from within the house, and his insides did something funny that he didn't want to think about or admit—even to himself.

"I owe you flowers," he said before kissing Rylee's cheek and the top of Mitch's baby-soft head. Without waiting for her, he strode through the house, passing the living room with a blanket and baby toys strewn about and entering the dining room where it appeared they'd been waiting on him. He glanced at his watch. Fuck. He was late. He'd spent too much goddamn time in front of the mirror like a teenager getting ready for a hot date and a chance for a piece of ass. Not that he wouldn't argue with the last part of that thought.

"I'm sorry I'm late," he offered to Devon and Madison.

"It's fine," his brother replied. "I was just listening to the plans for changing the club into a boutique. Did you know it's going to be lingerie?"

Stunned, his gaze swung to Madison's bright, shining one. "No. I didn't know." Now, all through dinner, he was going to imagine her in lingerie. Fucking great. He'd have wood all night.

Brad plopped down next to Madison and disappointment drove through him. She'd changed clothes and hadn't returned to his house, which meant she had more clothes in her car. That also meant that because she left a suitcase at his house, it didn't mean she was coming home with him like he and Devon had discussed. Worry for her and how she wasn't taking the possible threat seriously settled in his gut.

While Rylee strapped in Mitch, Devon brought out a casserole dish, and Brad caught the whiff of Italian food.

Uh-oh.

Madison leaned into him and whispered while she settled a napkin on her lap. "I didn't tell her you had lasagna last night. She worked hard on that—even making the noodles herself—so don't spoil it."

His eyes twinkled as they captured her gaze. "Deal. Does that make us co-conspirators?" He smiled broadly with warmth.

Her lips twitched up at the corners. "Sure."

He'd been ready to ask her to shake on it when dinner was served. "Is that lasagna?" he asked eagerly as Devon set down the pan in the center of their seating arrangement.

"I know it's your favorite," Rylee said with a smile.

His favorite was barbecued beef ribs. But once he'd overcomplimented Megan's lasagna—it'd been worth the praise—and AJ's wife must've told the other wives. Henceforth, they'd all made him lasagna when they sent over a dish, worrying he wasn't eating enough. Hell, he'd made it to thirty healthy and nourished without them. Yet, he never turned down a good meal or their efforts even though some were not great. As one of Rylee's guinea pigs, he'd eaten many of her new recipes and had seen her grow as a cook. However, some of her dishes were barely edible.

Brad flashed her a smile. "It is. I love it." For effect, he rubbed his hands together in anticipation while his stomach clenched in worry at whether this would be one of her less-than-fine recipes.

Everyone served themselves, and Brad wondered about the tiny piece that Madison had cut for herself. Truly she couldn't survive off that. Then, Rylee jumped up and returned with four salad bowls, yet Madison's was larger than everyone else's. Rabbit food. Hell. Not for the first time, he thought the woman could afford to put on a pound or two, but he'd be damned if he'd say that. He did know his limits, even though his mouth didn't always listen.

The salad he'd been given went untouched as he devoured the unexpectedly delicious lasagna and garlic bread. He wasn't kissing anyone later. Who cared if he had garlic breath? The only woman he'd like to kiss again was Madison, and she was eating it also, so there you go. The thought of their lips locked sent a firestorm of need raging through him. A storm he worked hard to control, but being beside Madison, listening to her laugh and enjoy herself with her family made him appreciate her more and more.

"Rylee," he said, "This is wonderful."

His sister-in-law blushed. "Thanks. I worked hard on it."

Remembering what Madison told him, he said, "These noodles are fantastic." And they were. She'd outdone herself.

"I made them from scratch. Devon bought me a noodle press not too long ago, and I used it."

"Well, whatever you did, it's superb."

"He's right," Madison added.

They quieted while digging into Rylee's creation until Devon cleared his throat. "Let's talk about Casden and Rogers."

Thank the fuck someone else had some sense in them. "Yeah," he said.

"I think they're fine," Madison said stubbornly.

"Same here," Rylee said before popping a piece of

garlic bread into her mouth.

Frustrated, Brad said, "Did you forget how they tried to intimidate you at the hotel? You don't understand. These are dangerous men." He wanted to knock the sisters' heads together. Did they not listen to the men who'd grown up here and knew what was happening?

"Devon thinks there's enough of a threat, so I'll carry, but I'm not going everywhere with a bodyguard when there's been no verbal threat," Rylee stated.

Brad pushed his empty plate forward. "They're dangerous."

"So are the men of HIS, but you don't see me protecting myself against them," Rylee quipped.

"Rylee, honey, you know these men are dangerous, but you're right in that they haven't made any threats or come back to push the offer. Just be extra vigilant when you're out and about, but I want to be with you when you take Mitch out. At least for the time being."

What. The. Fuck? Brad wanted to scream. Sure, the men hadn't made a threat, but they were dangerous men who'd dared to talk with some of their women. He'd think on the latter part of that statement another time. "Dev, come on."

Holding up his hand to forestall any argument, Devon said, "You know we're being overprotective. There is no definite threat against them."

What had changed his brother's mind? He'd agreed with him before. Damn Rylee and Madison and their nagging at his brother. He'd bet every penny on that being the reason.

Devon turned to Madison. "Are you comfortable protecting yourself?"

Madison nodded. "Yes. I've taken self-defense courses and carry Mace."

That wasn't nearly enough. She needed someone there to keep her safe. She was like a china doll that could be broken if touched. Although when he'd touched her, she'd come alive.

"Brad, I'll still stay at your house if it's all right, since Rylee and Devon don't have room. But I won't need you shadowing or following me."

He had one win—she was staying—and one loss—she didn't want him to protect her. Maybe Devon was right about the threat or lack thereof. He always reacted strongly when family was in danger, and Madison and Rylee were family now. They shouldn't be rubbing elbows with the Casdens and Rogers of the world.

Ignoring Madison, he focused on Rylee. "Did you officially decline that offer?"

"Yeah. Today in fact."

If trouble were coming down for them, it'd be soon. And he'd be there to protect Madison—no matter what she said.

"Staying at my house means you're out with either Rylee or me when you're out." He trusted Rylee with Madison's life. Trusted her to protect them both if that happened to be the case. Rylee was tough and smart, and she loved her sister.

Madison shook her head. "Not necessary. You just heard—"

He cut her off. "Nonnegotiable."

Narrowing her eyes at him, she then turned to her brother-in-law. "Devon?" she asked.

Devon, who had been studying Brad intently, shook his head. "His house. His rules."

Thank the fuck she didn't start with the whole hotel thing again. He'd had to watch for that.

Rylee stood to clear the table. Everyone also stood and took their plates to the kitchen, where Rylee directed them to be stacked.

Once they returned to the dining room, Rylee offered, "How about a game of Monopoly?"

Brad couldn't remember the last time he'd played the game, and agreed along with the others. Rylee did warn them that Madison was a ruthless trader of property. He planned to give her a run for her money.

However, her skill and luck of the dice put Madison in the lead early in the game, and no one could catch up to her before she bankrupted each of them.

Throughout the game, they laughed over family stories and quibbled over the game, and she let her guard down around him. His chest ached for the woman with no barriers in place to separate them. He felt comfortable with that side of her even though she tied him up in knots.

He had to admit it. Madison Maxwell was special to him. More than any other woman he'd ever met. That only reinforced his desire to get to know the woman better and discover how far their relationship would go.

Chapter Ten

On a bright, clear day, with Rylee—her approved bodyguard—riding shotgun, Madison drove to meet the contractor to discuss the build-out for La Belle. Happiness had infused her that the man came highly recommended, and he'd appeared as excited as she and Rylee were about the transformation discussed. The turnaround time was expected to be swift, which was unusual, and ripples of satisfaction ran through her at the prospect.

"Did you apply for the new business license? The retail trade one?" Madison asked. Rylee had been managing the initial transition plans, while Madison had finished up a couple of modeling gigs. She'd trusted her sister, but with a baby at home, Rylee sometimes forgot to do things they'd discussed. Once Rylee left, it was up to her to do everything and know that Rylee trusted her. Thankfully, she didn't have the distraction of a little one. *Just one big man that set her world afire,* her mind added.

"Yes." Rylee tapped the folder in her lap. "It's all set. New name and all. We should have it soon."

"You know," she began hesitantly, "I worry that we'll fail." Her stomach took a somersault. While spoken softly, her admission would never have been uttered to anyone but her sister. She could never admit that fear to anyone else. A fear ate at her day and night whenever she thought of what they were doing.

After a moment, Rylee said quietly, "Me too." Then she cleared her throat. "But I think our plan is sound, and we already know plenty of customers we'll have. I feel good about where we are. You should too."

She put on her turn signal and slowed. "I do feel good. We've got primo real estate. In the back of my mind, I just worry."

"You wouldn't be human if you didn't. We're going to be fine."

The two had put a large chunk of their savings into buying the building and turning it into a club for women. It had been a bar before they'd purchased it, so they'd just made the change and let it run independently. They'd had two good managers over that time, so the club had been successful. But neither she nor Rylee were happy with what they'd created. When the time had come for Madison to take her place at the business, she'd cringed at the thought of it. That's when the idea of a boutique had come into play. She'd pitched it to Rylee, and they'd both readily agreed.

Please don't let Rylee lose her investment because of my idea.

As they rounded a corner, the nightclub PYNK came into view, and Madison slammed on the brake, her body snapping against the seat belt, her mouth agape, and her heart plummeting into the pit of her stomach.

She swallowed against the large lump that had formed in her throat. Across the front of their red brick building, spray-painted in big, white poufy letters outlined in bright yellow was SLUTS OWN THIS PLACE. Her pulse raced. Worse, the front door appeared to be ajar. *Good God, why would someone do this?*

Putting the swirling emotions in her head in check, Madison drove to the parking lot where the two women sat for a moment in utter silence with tension radiating from both, taking in the ugly words in the graffiti and possible loss inside the club.

"I'm calling the police," Rylee said in a cold, stern voice. It was one that Madison expected she would use on the missions she talked about with HIS.

"Shouldn't we check out the damage inside first?"

Madison's sister vehemently shook her head. "No. We don't know if someone's in there. Under no circumstances will we check it out ourselves."

Conceding that Rylee was right, Madison sat helplessly as her blood boiled more and more until steam should've been seeping out the top of her head. Someone vandalized their building. Kids? Pissed off men whose women were members? Casden and Rogers?

That last thought brought her up short. With the stories Brad had tried to terrify her with, this sounded juvenile for the big, evil men she should be afraid of. But then again, she'd never understood the criminal mind. It just wasn't in her.

Within minutes, two patrol cars arrived, and the officers cleared the building, citing that no one was inside. They called Madison and Rylee inside to survey the damage before they completed a police report on the vandalism.

The place was destroyed. It was spray-painted if it couldn't be broken—like the bar. Devastation surrounded Madison—wooden barstools were broken, leather booths, and their stuffing removed. All the alcohol and liquor bottles behind the bar were shattered, and the large mirror that ran the length of the oak bar was smashed, with crude words spray-painted on bolted-down tables and the bar. Her stomach churned at the evilness of it all. She and Rylee had planned to sell all the equipment in the club as part of the startup inventory for the boutique. Madison could easily cover the cost herself—and she would now—but the sale wouldn't compensate Rylee's portion, which she insisted on contributing.

"Well," Rylee said, coming up behind her as she stared at the shattered mirror behind the bar, "I guess it's okay to close the club now instead of waiting until they can start on the transformation."

Madison forced a smile. True. Although she hated that Rylee wouldn't have the income during that extra time it took, she knew Rylee wasn't hurting for money. Maybe she didn't have the savings Madison did, but she would be fine. With Devon and HIS at Rylee's back, Madison felt it in her bones, and she didn't have that feeling very often.

"We can see if the contractor can start early." She'd offer him a bonus on the side if she needed to. "He probably also knows someone who can help us clean this place up quickly." She turned to her sister. "Unless you do."

Rylee smiled, and her face lit up. "I know a bunch of men who would help, but I don't know if any of their talents include removing the paint on the brick wall outside."

Without a doubt, Madison knew Rylee was talking about the men at HIS. What a family they appeared to be. She once again had a pang of jealousy for the life her sister had created. No. Envy. She envied her sister and how great her life had turned out.

Before the contractor arrived for their scheduled meeting, they searched for something they could sit on and came up with only one workable barstool. They should've upgraded to metal at some point, but they hadn't. Surely the vandals would've found a way to ruin them.

The contractor arrived as scheduled, and after a pleasant meeting, they found that, luckily, he could start early and would also take care of the current mess. While he could promise to begin early, he couldn't promise to finish early since he was only shifting another project. They didn't care. Relief flowed through her at the successful meeting and promise by the contractor. She and Rylee were ready for the transition, and the original date worked well for them. Heck, they'd even expected it to take longer, because didn't it always?

With the contractor's promise to send a cleanup crew the next day, they departed. On the drive back, Rylee asked, "How is it staying with Brad?"

It wouldn't be right to lie to her sister, but she couldn't tell her that she stayed away as long as she could to avoid him and the damnable attraction between them. "Fine. He's just still worried we're in danger, and that drives me nuts. I dread telling him about this. He'll go even more alpha than he already is. He actually confirmed with Devon that I'd be with you today and you'd be carrying before I could leave his house." Of course, she wouldn't admit his desire to see her protected warmed a place in her heart. It touched her like nothing she'd ever experienced.

Rylee laughed. "It's that alpha thing in them. Devon has it also, but Brad's one of the worst. Remember how he was when I'd been kidnapped? From your story, he'd turned into the biggest alpha there was. No, Jesse is the worst, but Kate keeps him in line."

"I met her at the wedding, didn't I?"

"Honey, you've met a lot of people since the entire family and team decided to show up. But, yes, you met her. Which reminds me, they're barbequing tomorrow. Want to come?"

Why did she suddenly get nervous about seeing all those people again? They'd been nothing but pleasant to her in Vegas. Brad. It was because she worried they knew about her and Brad. Then, something else hit her—a flash of disappointment maybe? Why hadn't Brad invited her to the cookout? Granted, he was under no obligation to do so. She was only his houseguest, and he felt she needed a bodyguard. But still. It would've been courteous.

With an internal humph, she realized he must not want her there. That confused her since he'd been adamant someone was always with her. As for being with her sister's new family, she really did want to get to know the group better. She'd just have to pray they didn't know her secret.

She'd been invited to parties to be shown off as a prize guest all her life. She had a feeling that at this cookout, she'd be nothing more than Rylee's sister. And that was all she wanted. To be normal and have fun without men panting after her. She couldn't guarantee they wouldn't, but she was safe based on how they acted in Vegas. Only Trent and Brad hit on her. Now that Trent was married, she didn't have to worry about him. That only left Brad. She thought too damn much about that man.

"I'd love to go. Just get me an address and time, and I'll be there." She couldn't think Brad would have a problem with her safety since the entire team would be there. It couldn't be safer.

"Just ride with Brad. He'll be coming. No brother misses one of Jesse's cookouts. It's probably a rule or something." She laughed at what must be an inside joke.

"Really?" she asked, perplexed.

"It's a joke. It's just when Jesse says to do something, they all do it without question."

"That must make the job easier, I'd think." Who'd want someone questioning or arguing when someone's life was at stake?

"It makes it fantastic. They're almost like their own little cult. Even the team follows Jesse without question."

She chuckled. "Even you?" she teased her sister.

"Well, not to the extent my husband does. That's for sure."

Thank goodness it wasn't Brad they followed. Surly and angry weren't traits a good leader had. Sure, he could be gentle and caring, but she'd only seen that once. Okay, maybe twice, but it was hidden deep down, and she didn't need a project. She had one called La Belle to deal with right now, and that project just got a little more complicated.

"Who do you think did the damage?" Madison finally asked. They'd avoided that topic since they'd seen the devastation.

"I don't know."

"You don't think," she started hesitantly, "that it's Casden and Rogers. Do you?"

Rylee bit her lip and thought for a moment. "I don't know. What I do know is that it'd take a whole lot more than that to get us to sell."

"They don't know that."

"True." Rylee groaned. "Devon is going to go apeshit and want to bubble wrap me and keep me under his thumb, worrying someone will come after me, even if they weren't responsible for the disaster."

Madison chuckled at the image. "I'm lucky I don't have an alpha husband to want to do that. From what I've learned about the two men, I don't see Casden and Rogers doing that juvenile style of damage to the club."

"Oh, but you have Brad."

Madison's pulse leaped, and she almost lost control of the car. "I don't—I don't have Brad."

"He's going to flip over this, especially since he didn't agree with Devon about protection. I'd say he'll be glued to your side more than he is now."

"I don't want him glued to my side any more than he already is." For some reason, that idea, while not wholly terrifying, began to appeal to her. "I can't step outside the house without him unless I'm going to see you."

"Why not have him?" Rylee sounded put out. "He's a great guy. A little rough around the edges…."

"Rough?" She almost snorted. "That's putting it nicely. I don't need Brad protecting me like he is. I'm grateful to have a place to stay because he is right about being safer than sorry, and I didn't like having those men approach me at my hotel. Regardless, I'm not his problem."

Rylee snickered. "I'm sure he'd want you to be his problem." A pause. "Again."

A shot of awareness ran up her spine. Rylee had said only two other people knew she'd slept with Brad. But what if he'd told people? And she would be facing those same people tomorrow. Her stomach twisted. She guessed she'd find out if her protector were trustworthy and honest when she was put on display among a lot of men and only a few women.

Chapter Eleven

Hearing about the club from Devon and not Madison almost sent Brad into a ballistic fit. Why had she hidden the truth about the vandalism? She had to have known he'd find out one way or another. Nothing was kept secret in this family for long.

Except his night with Madison.

Except for two people—Matt and, shit, probably three because Devon surely ran off his mouth to Rylee—no one knew, and he'd worked hard to keep it that way. If she'd not rushed out of the hotel room, not making sure the coast was clear, only Matt would've known because Brad had to speak with his brother about what a fool he'd been. *It'd been a fucking joke—an inappropriate one—that I wish I could take back.*

Now, to make matters worse, she'd balked when he told her he was protecting her from now on and that she should just get used to it. No way would he leave her vulnerable with a potential threat hanging over her head. Whether it was Casden or Rogers wasn't as important as someone *had* trashed her business. Someone had a grudge against her or Rylee. They'd have to go through him to get to her. Nonnegotiable.

He didn't question why he knew it had to be him protecting her or why he felt the threat was severe enough that he stuck to her. And after...?

Of course, he'd forgotten about Jesse's cookout,

and when he'd thought of it at breakfast and told her they were going, it'd been their first real fight. He didn't count when they'd discussed the club as she'd been freaked out enough over what had happened. And, he kicked himself for not being there with her as she surveyed the loss and destruction. It occurred to him that he'd wanted to be the arms she fell into for comfort, and that surprise told him a great deal about how much he had begun to care for her.

"You don't just tell me we're going. I'm tired of you *telling* me things instead of asking," she'd nearly screeched at him.

He hadn't seen the problem. They were going to Jesse's, so what was the point of asking so she could say no and then he'd have to haul her out over his shoulder—which appealed to him more than he cared to think.

"And another thing," she went on before he could respond, "why are you just telling me now? Am I only invited because you feel duty-bound to protect me— even though I'm not in any real danger?"

The cookout was today. How much notice did she need? It wasn't like he was hiding it; he'd truly forgotten. Of course, he'd opened his big mouth and made it worse. "How much notice do you need? Was I supposed to give you a shopping day first? Spa day to prepare? It's just a fucking cookout. And, you're invited because you're Rylee's family." Plus he was told to bring her by Jesse, and he didn't argue with his brother unless necessary. No one won against the eldest Hamilton brother.

He could almost see her blood boiling with tempered anger. Knowing that same look from Rylee, he shut his mouth. "That's not the point," she said. "I knew about this yesterday. Why did you wait? Do you not want me there? Is that it? But now you're stuck with me, so you're dragging me along?"

"If you knew yesterday, why the fuck didn't you say anything? I just fucking forgot. You"—he pointed a finger at her—"you hid that knowledge."

In his mind, the argument was over. Yet, while he knew he'd scored the point, he had a sneaky feeling he'd still lost the disagreement especially when she stomped off and slammed the bedroom door.

Conversation in his truck on the drive to Jesse's home had been nonexistent. While he enjoyed just being in her space, he didn't like the discomfort between them. So he'd probably been a bit of a bastard accusing her as he had. Okay, more than probably, but that was who he was. It felt unfortunate that he acted so ornery at a moment like this.

"Look, Maddie," he started, and then cleared his throat. The words stuck in his larynx. This was harder than he thought it would be. It was just two little words, but he rarely said them. He knew he needed to do so now. "I'm sorry. I was an ass, and you didn't deserve that." A massive pocket of air whooshed from his lungs in relief that he could get it out without crashing the truck.

When she didn't speak, he tensed. He'd fucking apologized for Christ's sake, and she was still giving him the silent treatment. Oh fuck no. Inside, something—probably the conscience he regularly ignored—told him to wait it out that she'd need time.

Instead of accepting his apology, she asked a question. "Why are you like you are? A great guy most of the time yet bitterness resides in you and comes out on occasion."

The question took him back. He was bitter because his career had been snatched out from under him. He wouldn't leave HIS and go back, but it was the principle of it all. Angry? He wasn't angry always, and it was more at himself than anything else, even though he took it out on the world. But to explain it to her? No, he may desire and want to be with her, but he wasn't opening his heart to her. He doubted he'd ever open it with a woman. He had too much pain inside to be angry with himself, which he knew wouldn't make great relationship material.

Putting on his best smile, he glanced at her before looking back at the road. He then tried to be jovial when he said, "What me? I'm never angry and bitter. You must have mistaken me with my twin."

She huffed out a breath that, by the sound of it, was chock full of frustration. "You're impossible."

He wanted to laugh, but he expected that would piss her off more, so instead, he agreed. Somewhat. "Possibly."

No other words were spoken until they arrived at Jesse's. His gaze landed on the abundance of cars, trucks, and SUVs just as Madison asked, "Are you sure it's okay that I'm here?"

He looked at her, noting the anxiety in her voice. His gut dipped when he realized she was nervous. He was so used to a confident, self-assured Madison that it took him a moment to respond. "Of course. Rylee invited you, and so did I." He reached for the door handle and offered her a reassuring smile. "Being Rylee's sister makes you family; this is a family cookout." Her eyes searched his. He only hoped she could read his sincerity. "So, let's go. We can go around the back and say hello."

To his relief, after another brief hesitation, she exited his truck but also made sure to keep a respectable distance from Brad, preventing him from placing his hand on her back as they walked into the crush of people. He felt the need to touch her...connect with her...but didn't want to push her. Not only was the Hamilton family there—wives, husbands, and kids included—but the team was in attendance, with only one unmarried.

When Madison spotted Rylee, she split off from him without a word. He shook his head. With a small smile, he watched her walk away, happy that she appeared more relaxed.

At the large grill, the Hamilton brothers huddled around as if it took all of them to cook for the group. Surprised at seeing his twin, he strode toward them, only stopping to pick up a beer from one of the coolers and twisting off the top.

When he arrived, he hugged his twin—close in for a second and a pat on the back. He enjoyed that his brother had chosen to surprise him with this trip. "Hey, bro. How's Kentucky? Where's Caitlyn?"

"She's at home, but we have great news. She's expanding and has chosen Baltimore for her next project so we can be close to the family."

Pleasure at the news swamped him. He'd missed his twin more than he realized. "That's awesome."

"We'll live outside of Baltimore where she can get the land and permits she needs, but it'll be closer than Jesse."

Thank goodness his twin would be closer. No offense to Jesse, but his elder brother lived between Baltimore and Silver Spring, where they grew up. It was a small haul to get here, but Brad also might be a bit lazy since he lived in town and almost everything was within walking distance—restaurants, bars, and shops.

"Hey," Jesse said. "You guys love this place, so don't even knock it."

"Oh," Brad started with a grin, "we love it. It's the drive we could do without." Giving Jesse shit about how far out he lived was commonplace with the group, and he never passed up the opportunity. Any of them would drive to the ends of the earth for each other.

"Tough shit. I'm not moving closer. This place is perfect for mine and HIS's needs."

"So, what's going on with Madison?" AJ asked. Hadn't he asked him that before? Nosy little shit.

Without a thought, Brad blurted, "She's in trouble and doesn't realize it." His stomach churned at the thought of the danger she might be in. No matter what, he'd do everything he could to protect her.

Frowns marred his brothers' faces, except Matt's. Good old Matt.

"That's why I'm here," his twin stated.

Confused, he could only ask, "What?"

"Jesse told me what was happening and that you had taken it upon yourself to protect Madison and thought you might need help. So, here I am. Rylee will be gone, so we only have Madison to protect."

Relief rushed through him. Even though Jesse hadn't agreed she needed protection, he'd called Matt to back up Brad. Had he planned to get Matt to talk some sense into him? No fucking chance of that. Maybe Matt could help him figure out how to remove the threat.

"Jesse?" Brad questioned. There was no need to say anything more than that. He knew what Brad was asking.

After turning over a rack of ribs, his eldest brother turned to him. "Look, I still think you might be overreacting, but if you're going to do this, you can't do it alone. You must sleep at some point, and that's when you're most vulnerable. I just mentioned it to Matt. With a pregnant wife at home, he packed up to have your back."

The love of his brothers almost misted his eyes. But, he was a fucking dude, and they didn't cry over sappy shit like that. He cleared his throat before he could respond. "Thanks, man. I hadn't thought past her being in danger."

"We'll work it out later. Right now, she's safe in this group."

The men looked toward the gaggle of women at the picnic tables, some holding young children in their arms or on their laps. The group quieted and stared at the men with curiosity. While smiles broke out between the women, who were presumably looking at their husbands, Madison's brow furrowed as if trying to figure out what the hell was going on.

Even though she'd dressed in jeans and a pink T-shirt with a big flower, she stood out among the women. Her beauty and poise were miles above the others. Following his brothers' suit, he just grinned at her, and she gave a small smile back that lit a warm glow in his chest. That meant she'd been looking at him instead of the group. Him. He'd call that progress from earlier and vowed to continue to move them forward.

With the clearing of throats, as if they'd been caught doing something wrong, the men turned back to the grill—their focus on ribs, burgers, and hot dogs that would get wolfed down by this crew.

Ken—who'd been tossing a football with the team—approached the group and asked when the food would be ready.

"Ken," Devon said, "we're just wondering how long Brad will last as a bachelor watching over Madison."

Rubbing his cleanly shaven chin, Ken looked over at Madison, then gave Brad a once-over before responding, "Oh, he's toast. I expect another wedding in the near future."

"That's what we were thinking," Jake, his brother-in-law, added.

Hackles rising in defense of his brothers' joking, Brad gave them his usual, "Fuck off."

"No, he's not going to survive this one," AJ taunted.

Once again, he came at them. "Fuck you, she doesn't even like me." Except maybe she did since they'd shared that hot kiss at The Ivy. "Besides, I'm not getting tied down. I thought we'd already established that."

"Yeah, well," Jesse all but drawled, "the right woman will change your mind." He glanced at his wife across the yard and smiled.

"Oh no," Matt said. "What the fuck have you done? And don't tell me nothing. I can tell you've already tried to sabotage any chance with her."

Wariness flooded his veins along with an acknowledgment that his brother, who knew him best, was right. But he didn't plan to admit that to the rest of the family. "I haven't done anything, and who says I want a chance with her? She's Rylee's sister after all, not some chick from a bar."

"Oh, come on," Matt said. "I've seen you gawk at her when Rylee would show us pictures of her modeling career."

"I do not...gawk," he practically shouted. Hands fisted at his sides, he took a deep breath. His brothers were trying to rile him. That was all. Only two knew he'd taken her to bed, and they wouldn't share that with his brothers unless he gave the go-ahead, and that shit wasn't happening.

Not wanting his confused feelings for Madison to show, he had to get the conversation away from himself. He turned to his twin. "When are you moving back?"

They all laughed. Laughed at him. He felt like a child and wanted to stomp off after flipping them all off. But he was a grown-ass adult and would be one, even with them.

"That's a valid question," he insisted. Okay, probably a bit childish.

"Okay," Jesse said. "We won't tease you anymore about Madison."

"Today," AJ added with a chuckle.

Fuckers.

"Seriously, if this thing with Madison becomes real"—Jesse held up a hand to stop him from saying anything—"this thing with Casden and Rogers—then Devon and I are also here to help. If it worsens, I'll figure out how to extricate some of the team from the mission."

A lump formed in his throat. Only Jesse could go from being an asshole to being supportive with the change of a single breath. It was a wonder Kate still dealt with him. "Thanks." He had an inkling the danger could be more because he didn't trust Casden and Rogers.

"Have you heard anything more about what happened with Senator Walden?" Jesse asked.

Brad shook his head. "No. But, I'm going to that dinner, so maybe I'll hear something. Since the hit had been on her driver, she's agreed to Secret Service protection." His old stomping grounds. "Maybe I'll find out something then."

"How's Madison holding up?" Matt asked.

He sighed. "She hasn't said anything, but occasionally, I catch her staring off into space, and I wonder what she's seeing or remembering." It had shaken her even though she'd tried to hide that fact from him. Her desire to be a strong, independent woman kept her showing as little emotion as possible. Once they became closer, he'd work on getting her to open up with him.

Reagan—Jesse's eight-year-old daughter—and Amber—Emily and Jake's five-year-old daughter—raced over to them. Reagan patted her father's arm. "Daddy, Uncle Trent is here."

"Yeah, and he brought Ashley," Amber added. "Yeah, and Mom says Aunt Kelly is pregnant again." "Yeah" apparently was her new word, but at least it beat the "Guess what?" question Reagan used when she was younger. It'd been cute and annoying.

Brad glanced over at Em—his very pregnant sister—who was having a girl she and Jake were naming Leslie in honor of Les—a HIS team member who'd given his life protecting Amber. He couldn't believe Jake was going on assignment with her due to deliver soon. Or at least it looked soon. She was as big as a house, but he'd be damned if he'd tell her that. He loved his sister too much to hurt her feelings. And she had a great right hook.

"Daddy, are the hot dogs ready yet? I'm hungry," Reagan said.

"Sure, honey. Let me get them off the grill now. Can you carry them?"

"Daddy"—her hand went on her hip, and she cocked her body like the women in the family did when they were frustrated and trying to make a point—"I'm not a child. I can carry plates without dropping them. Mom lets me do it all the time. Hurry. We're hungry."

Put in his place, Jesse smiled, dished up the hot dogs on the top rack of the grill, and handed the platter to his daughter with care. "Here you go. Take it to your mom, and she'll set you up to eat."

The two girls turned back toward the picnic tables, walking very slowly this time with Dottie—Kate's Dalmatian—and Angel—Devon and Rylee's dog—on their heels, probably waiting for something to drop.

A smile split Brad's face, and his heart expanded. He loved his nieces and nephews and was truly excited there'd be more, especially from Matt and Caitlyn. The kids offered hours of entertainment. Not so much fun when they were still crying all the time, but after they passed that stage, he tried to be the cool uncle.

Turning, he saw Trent—the lifelong friend they'd

later found out was actually their half-brother—approaching with Ashley, who must be about ten months old, sleeping with her thumb in her mouth on his shoulder. "Hey, guys. Thanks for inviting me." Careful shoulder slaps went around as everyone welcomed him and his daughter.

"You're always invited," Jesse said, turning more of the food on the grill, shifting the burgers to the top rack where the hot dogs had been. "How's the ranch?"

Brad loved the ranch in Montana for Trent but hated it for the men since Trent had been an integral part of their team. Brad knew he could speak for them all to say they missed having him around. But his life was with Kelly on the ranch. Too damn far away and too many responsibilities to work like Matt from afar.

"Yeah, riding those broncs?" AJ asked with a laugh, knowing Trent had been thrown more than once. Kelly had been good to her word and sent videos of his first time trying to break a horse. They'd laughed for hours.

"Giddyap." Trent reached up, pretending to tip back the rim of an imaginary cowboy hat.

They chuckled at the drawl Trent added, and before they could start a conversation, Jason—Jesse's fifteen-year-old son—raced up to them. "Dad, are the burgers ready yet? I'm starving."

Jesse rolled his eyes. "When aren't you starving?" Then addressing the group, Jesse said, "The boy is a bottomless pit." A few chuckles erupted and probably some remembrance of their endless hunger at that age. Jesse turned back to his son. "Five more minutes."

Jason took off and shouted, "Five minutes!" to the HIS team members he'd been tossing the football with.

Brad knew they'd all play a football game later, and he looked forward to it. It'd been a long time since they'd enjoyed themselves like that. Damn winter sucked all the fun away.

"What were you talking about when I came over?" Trent asked the group in general.

"Brad and Madison," AJ piped up. "Kissing in a tree…," he added in a singsong voice.

The men chuckled.

"Hell yeah," Trent said with a grin, as if he had the entire story.

On that note, Brad held his tongue, spun around, and marched over to join the men tossing the football, hoping to level the erratic beating of his heart. He didn't need his brothers' shit. There wasn't a "Brad and Madison" to worry about. Yet after watching his brothers and their wives, a small part of him wished there was, and that screwed up his insides. Sex? Yes. Anything more? Not a chance.

Chapter Twelve

Madison opened the door of the second boutique she, Rylee, Kate, Kelly, and Megan had entered that morning. Emily had wanted to come, but there'd been too much work for her to do at HIS to leave for the day. She talked about how she and Devon provided all the support the team needed to prepare to deploy. She also looked very uncomfortable with the size of her belly, so Madison imagined being dragged around town didn't appeal too much.

Although Madison really didn't need so many people to go with her to find a dress for the political dinner, she was having a good time with them. The women could be witty, and they had been honest in the first store. She needed that if they were going to find her the right outfit. She'd been so used to designers sending her outfits for events she attended, so that she could say their name when asked. So instead of just three or so to choose from, she had entire boutiques, and none were picked especially for her size and coloring as the designers tended to do. This was a more complex task than she'd expected, even with the assistance of her new friends.

"Thank you all for coming. I'm sorry to drag you from place to place." A pang hit her: Jacques would be disappointed she didn't hit him up for something to wear. She couldn't always rely upon him to clothe her for special events, even though he'd probably do it. He had new models to worry with now. But maybe if she couldn't find anything, she'd call him. He'd make her look fabulous, and she wanted Brad to think her fabulous.

Kate waved a hand. "It's nothing. We've done this before. Typically with wedding dress shopping, but it doesn't matter. We enjoy it."

"Especially how they gush over you," Megan, AJ's wife, added.

Madison sighed. "They want me to say I bought the dress from their shop to increase traffic. But I really wonder if it works."

"It's been like that since she was on the most beautiful people list," Rylee added proudly.

"Unfortunately, it was before that, but it got worse after. But only if people followed fashion." Madison looked around the shop. It was small, and she worried they wouldn't find anything. She had to remember she'd also need to make connections. Dress shops were a perfect referral point to a lingerie shop, and maybe she and Rylee could do something to reward them for sending clients their way once they opened La Belle.

A short, heavy-set woman bustled over with a tape measure draped around her neck. "I'm finishing up with someone now. I'll be with you in a jiffy."

Madison looked over her head and saw the seating area facing a slightly raised platform. Three full-length mirrors angled so the person trying on the gown could get the best view of the fit. The flowered couch and two green armchairs were full of young women with champagne glasses, gushing over the red cocktail dress the woman on the pedestal was spinning around to show off.

"Feel free to look around, and I'll be right with you." She turned and bustled off again. No recognition of who Madison was in the fashion industry. Cosmetics and perfume industries, too. She hadn't accumulated her millions by doing only runway.

Her insides settled, and a calm came over her. This was the shop she wanted to buy from—assuming the lady didn't screw up when she was trying on the dresses.

Excited now, she turned to the women who considered her family. "Let's look around."

"Are you sure you want to wait?" Rylee asked. And, in a lower voice, she added, "She didn't even recognize you."

"And that's why we're going to shop here and hope I find the right dress."

With that said, the group headed for the racks to see if they could find something suitable.

While they searched, Kate started the conversation they'd tried to have with her at the last boutique. "So, what's going on with you and Brad? He wouldn't let you out of sight today until I assured him I'd watch over you and Rylee."

Struggling to keep her aggravation at bay—not at Kate, but for the spectacle Brad had made earlier when she'd told him she'd be dress shopping. She understood his need to protect her. The need was ingrained in his DNA, but it was not the reason. Not completely anyway. He had her scared plenty, but she had Kate and Rylee with her who were just as trained as he was in all that protection crap. Yet, he'd still balked because Rylee herself could be in danger. If she didn't know better, she'd think he wanted her locked up in his home 24/7, which wasn't going to happen. It was already tense there; she couldn't imagine them being together for that long in close quarters. Yes, she could, she admitted to herself. They'd end up back in bed. It was a sure bet.

"He's just overreacting." Madison pulled out a deep blue dress and looked at it. "I'm back and forth on it. Whether I need protection or not. I think he's crazy about my being in danger when the men only offered on the property." Yet, she'd known fear when they'd crowded her in the hotel lobby. "Then, I think of the vandalism and all the stories he's told me of the men, and I'm glad he's there." She hung the dress back on the rack. Too shiny. She turned to Kate. "But I'm glad you're here. Just in case."

Kate patted her black leather purse. "Here's our just in case." She winked.

Aghast, Kelly whispered, "Are you carrying a...a gun?"

Looking taken aback, Kate responded, "Of course."

"I am too," Rylee added, patting her blue shoulder bag.

Megan rolled her eyes and sighed. "Of course they are. They're part of the team. Always ready for danger."

"Well, I hope it doesn't find us here." Madison certainly hoped that, but if it did, any threat would have a lot to contend with the HIS women.

After nearly five minutes, Madison's heart sank. Nothing. They'd found nothing she wanted to wear to the dinner.

"I'm sorry that took so long. I'm Margaret. How

may I help you?" the saleslady asked.

Madison turned to her and smiled. "I'm looking for a dress but didn't find anything that would work."

"What's the occasion?"

"Formal dinner. Political dinner," Madison told her.

Margaret scanned Madison's body and smiled. "Wait right here."

She hustled off toward the back before anyone could say a word. She knew boutiques usually had stuff in the back, but the styles she'd seen just weren't her thing. Of course, she'd worn plenty of styles that weren't her thing on the runway. She never said it aloud, but some designers' outfits were hideous. Thank goodness she'd never had to wear one that would've made her ashamed to show her face after the event.

Rushing back in the room—Madison smiled at how fast the woman bustled around, reminding her of the Energizer Bunny—Margaret held a sapphire blue gown folded over her arm.

"Now, I know it's not one of Jacques or Valentino's, but I think Roberto Cavalli's gown will look spectacular on you."

Taken back, it took Madison a moment to get her breath. "You know who I am?"

"Of course, Miss Maxwell, and I'm honored that you not only came in but waited." She held up the gown. "I think it's perfect for you."

Madison instantly fell in love with the floor-length gown and wanted to snatch it from Margaret's hands and rush to the changing room. "Are you sure it'll fit?" Was she drooling? It sure felt like it.

"I think so. Follow me and we'll see." She turned

toward where Madison assumed was the changing room. Madison could do nothing but obediently follow.

Ensconced in a good-sized dressing room with mirrors covering the walls, she fingered the dress. Delicate lace insets were mingled in the silk on each side of her waist. The plunging V neckline made the dress. God, she wanted to look good, and this dress was perfect.

As she slipped on the dress, she caught the bias-cut silhouette and loved the embellishments on the lace sleeves. Sleeves were important since they were just coming out of winter and it was still cold in the evenings, but lace was better this time of the year because you had no idea how warm or cool a room would be.

When she zipped it in the back—a feat in itself—she finally appraised herself in the mirror. It was perfect. Not too flashy, not too dreadful. She wouldn't stand out, but she wouldn't be dismissed either.

What would Brad think? He'd think her neckline was too low, and it was lower than what she'd hoped, but it wasn't unseemly. Dammit. She shouldn't worry about what Brad thought. Those types of thoughts needed to stay out of her head.

He may have apologized, but she hadn't forgotten the hurtful words. His words had been too crude. Joking or not. But that was sex. At least in her experience. She'd had her share of men who acted as if they cared, treating her like a cherished woman, only to take her to bed for bragging rights. It also left her with too many one-night stands as she didn't invite those vile men back to her bed. She shifted at the embarrassment of it all. The effects of being used so made her trust in men shaky. That included Brad, even though he didn't take her to bed to tell all his friends.

Yet, something about him moved her, and she could deal with him out of bed. The rest wasn't that bad. He was a rough and tough guy, but deep down, she knew there had to be softness. Tenderness.

After several twirls and falling more in love with the dress as she did, she stepped out of the room for the moment of truth. Would her friends and critics like it?

Unexpected nerves assailed her, and she tried to shake them off, as there was no reason for them. Although she'd stepped on many runways and platforms before, this was nothing in comparison.

But she loved the dress and didn't want them not to like it.

Kate, Megan, Kelly, and Rylee sat on a couch and two chairs, some sipping champagne and all giggling.

Here goes. She stepped on the platform and waited. The room went quiet, and a slight tremble tried to take hold of her body. She did a slow turn so they could see even the lace inlay around the entire waist.

"That is—" Kate started.

"Perfect," Rylee finished for her.

The group readily agreed. No dissension. No comments except how perfect it was. Relief swamped her limbs, and she relaxed the tight shoulders she hadn't realized she'd held in tension. Pleasure stole though her at their agreement on the dress.

After some chitchat and allowing the saleslady to fuss over the fit, making sure it didn't need alterations, she left the platform to go change. Before she closed the door to the dressing room, she heard, "Brad's going to love that dress."

"Love it, he's going to go ballistic and try to make her wear a wrap."

Madison smiled. Just let him try it.

Chapter Thirteen

Brad's frustration rose as his twin made more and more sense. Why couldn't he toss logic out the window and agree with Brad?

"You need to tell her something. She's going to be on your arm. If you get the unexpected chance to ask questions, she will notice. Do you really want her asking why at dinner?"

"It's nothing she needs to be concerned with," Brad firmly stated.

Matt shook his head. "Come on. Just tell her something. She doesn't need to know everything, just what you might be doing so she doesn't interrupt out of curiosity."

Brad had shared with his twin that, should the opportunity arise at dinner to question any Secret Service agent who might know something about what happened to him, he would find a way to approach them. Of course, he knew he couldn't just walk up and talk to an on-duty agent. He could, but they would likely avoid him to do their job. Matt knew the truth about Brad leaving the Secret Service. He also believed Brad when he claimed he must have been set up. Again, that nagging doubt that he might have messed up crept into his mind, but he vanquished it.

Yet keeping Madison close presented a small problem. She'd listen, maybe even interrupting him as he talked to his old colleagues. That wouldn't do.

Heck, he may not know an agent there. The agency was large, and people were spread out. He'd been presidential detail. There were only an elite few who had climbed to that level.

His brother sighed. "Look, she'll be a help or a hindrance. That's for you to decide right now. The dinner is tonight."

He'd spent another day with Madison, taking off without him protecting her. He'd not fought her but made sure someone was with her. Spending her day with Rylee while working at their bar worked fine because he knew Rylee carried a concealed weapon. He'd have preferred it to be him, but at least she was protected.

"Help or hindrance for what?" Madison appeared at the door to his small office. He'd invite her in, but there was barely enough room for him, the desk, a bookshelf, and the other chair Matt was sitting upon.

Both men stood and faced her. Her jeans fit snugly, and her T-shirt accentuated her luscious chest. She and Rylee had gone to the spa after the club so that Madison could get all that girl stuff done before the dinner. Her hair hung in waves ending in large curls. It looked so silky that he wanted to run his fingers through it and wrap it around his hand as he pulled her into a deep kiss. He might have had been drooling while she waited for a response.

"Nothing," he finally said.

She raised an eyebrow and looked to Matt, who put his hands up in surrender. "This is him." He stepped forward as if to leave, but Madison didn't move from her space in the doorway.

"Brad?" she questioned.

Fuck. Matt was right, but he couldn't tell her he'd woken up with a prostitute, and the fallout was why he'd left the Secret Service. He'd never have a chance with her again. That stopped him short. What kind of chance did he want? Sex? More? He internally shook his head. Sex. That was it. No, it was more. He just had a difficult time acknowledging it.

"I can give you two privacy," Matt offered. The chickenshit was leaving him to deal with this alone. After it was his idea? So much for brotherly love.

"That's fine," he managed, still unsure what to say. But he knew to watch his words because too often he said the first thing that came to mind, and that was usually the wrong thing with her.

Madison stepped away while Matt exited with a backward glance that could've been "don't fuck this up" to "you're screwed now." Both seemed appropriate.

Once she was sitting opposite his desk, he sat, perched on the edge of his chair because for some strange reason, nervousness rose within him and he felt the need to bolt—no real way to do that in this room.

Brad cleared his throat before he began what he hoped sounded normal. "At the dinner, I'd like you to stay with me if possible."

"I won't know anyone else, so that's okay, but why?"

"Lechers," he stated.

"Lechers?"

"That room will be filled with men looking to grab onto their next mistress, and you will be a prime candidate once you enter the room. Don't get me wrong," Brad said, "they'll still try, even with you on my arm. It just won't be so blatantly."

"Oh." She thought for a minute. "This is supposed to be a small dinner, though."

Brad shook his head. "Doesn't matter. Trust me. The only safe man in there is my dad."

"Your dad will be there? Good. I will know someone, even though I've only met him the once—at the wedding. Do you think he'll remember me?"

Was she fucking kidding? Remember her? Who could forget her? She brightened any room she entered and made everyone feel special with her smile and friendly demeanor. She was impossible to forget, which had nothing to do with her being a model. She left an impression that kept a man—or woman—smiling for days. Remember her? What a stupid question. "Yeah. I'm pretty sure he'll remember you."

"Okay. That doesn't make sense with what you two were talking about, though. How could I be a hindrance?"

He sucked in a deep breath and held it. Hell, he'd just have to give her basics—like Matt suggested—and hope she didn't dig deeper. "I might be asking some questions of the Secret Service agents and didn't want you to be caught off guard and say something you shouldn't." *Or ask the wrong question in public.*

"Why?"

Yeah. He knew that question would come. Here's where skirting the truth came into play. "Something happened while I was an active agent, and I'm trying to solve the puzzle. It's been bugging me since I left."

"What happened?"

Of course she'd ask more. "That's not important right now. What is important is finding anyone who knows about what happened in Colombia some years back."

With a happy smile, Madison rubbed her hands together. "Ooh. I get to be Nancy Drew. I've always wanted to be her."

What. The. Fuck? Nancy Drew my ass, he barely kept himself from saying out loud. She couldn't be asking questions in case there really was something fishy. He'd only wanted her to behave, not be involved. What gave her the impression she could play his game? Well, he'd put an immediate halt to that thought process.

"No fucking Nancy Drew. You aren't doing anything but smiling on my arm and ignoring it when I start to ask questions. If I even get the chance."

Her eyes narrowed so fast, he felt the heat from her gaze to his bones. "Maybe I can help. Did you think of that? Men like to share their secrets with beautiful women. I'm not vain, but I do know I fall into that category, or else I wouldn't have made a living with my face."

"You can't help. You can only hinder if you try to get involved," he stated.

"So, I'm supposed to act like an airy woman clutched to your arm like I can't think for myself?" Her voice rose as she spoke.

Good God, this wasn't going as he'd planned. Actually, he hadn't planned it. Matt had just convinced him. This would've been easier if he'd had time to think it out.

Wearily, he wiped his hand down his face. "That's not what I'm saying." He sighed and spoke softly, hoping to fend off another fight with her. They'd had far too many already. "Madison, I'm just asking you not to interfere when I'm asking questions. I can't have you questioning what's going on in public."

"What's this incident in Colombia you're so interested in?"

"Nothing."

"The only thing I know of with the Secret Service and Colombia is—"

Fuck and double fuck. Everyone knew of the incident. While the memory faded in some, most could draw the facts from the back of their mind in a minute. "Yeah" was all he said to that.

"Were you…were you involved in that?"

Fucking Matt. "Talk to her. Just tell her the basics," he said. Look where that fucking got him. He could not bear his soul to someone he didn't even have a relationship with. They may live in the same house, but they only saw each other rarely and hadn't formed a bond that would open his heart.

Avoiding her question, he said, "I think there was some foul play and want to check it out."

"Foul play?"

"That's not important right now. What's important is that you agree not to interfere when I question someone."

She watched him, and those questioning eyes burned bright and tore at his heart. She looked like she was trying to trust him but wasn't certain. Well, he couldn't do anything about that. It was her choice whether she trusted him or not. If she'd quit avoiding him, she'd see he was trustworthy. He wanted to slap himself mentally. Wrong. He needed to earn her trust, not sit back and wait for her to decide he was worthy.

Yet reaching out was daunting as he'd never worked to gain someone's trust before. He'd never cared enough.

"Okay," she finally said, and stood. "I'll behave. No Nancy Drew." She offered him a small smile that shot hope to his heart.

When she turned and walked out the door, he had the unnerving urge to reach for her, tell her everything, and then hold her until he felt whole again.

Now wasn't that some shit for the confirmed bachelor of the family to want that? Next, he'd be asking her to go steady.

Chapter Fourteen

Madison had attended many events in her profession, and usually with confidence, but she had nervous butterflies in her stomach for this dinner. She'd never dined with just politicians before. She and Brad didn't belong at this dinner, and it would show. Thank goodness his father would be there. Would his father see it as a date? Did Brad? He'd been speechless about her dress, and it had taken him a minute to say how beautiful she looked. She'd have sworn she'd blushed if she hadn't known better. To her, it might not be a date, but it was the next best thing to it, and it was with Brad.

On the drive, Brad—dressed handsomely in a tuxedo—must've sensed her nervousness because he kept up a steady stream of questions about what she and Rylee planned to do with La Belle and how they proposed to make it happen.

"Devon said you're selling lingerie. If you need someone to preview each item—preferably on a model—then I'm your man," Brad offered.

Madison shook her head and chuckled. "You're such a dog, Brad Hamilton," she teased.

"Dog is it? I've been called worse." He glanced at her in the waning evening sun. "Will you be my model?"

She wanted to reach out and mock-slap him while they were in this playful mood that built on the connection they were creating. But he was driving, and it probably wouldn't be a good idea. Not to mention, she wouldn't make a dent in his hard muscles. She'd probably hurt her hand. And she'd never slap him across his beautiful face, even though he deserved it more than once.

But as she entered the senator's residence on his arm, she didn't care about his immaturity concerning sex and all things related to it. He exuded confidence that made her feel comfortable and safe. Seeing the senator brought back the last time she'd been around their hostess—Madison had been shot at. How could she have easily put it back in her mind? Thankfully Brad had been there to protect her before, and he was here to protect her now should she need it. Hopefully, she wouldn't.

A man in a black tuxedo opened the heavy oak door inlaid with stained glass and welcomed them. He escorted them to a large room where people mingled, mostly in small groups. Servers in black tuxedos— skirts for the women—walked around with trays of champagne and bite-sized appetizers, while a man served mixed drinks from behind a portable bar.

Social hour. She could do that. Yet the nerves returned. Maybe it was because she didn't have the support she usually had at functions. No Jacques there to keep her company. Instead, she had Brad, who might be asking questions of the protection detail she'd witnessed outside and standing on the fringes of the party. He'd said he couldn't just walk up to them, so she hadn't figured out how he planned to speak with any of the men.

"There's my dad," Brad said, nodding in the

direction of Senator Hamilton. "Let's go say hi."

Still holding onto his arm, they made their way, declining the appetizers and champagne. With her nerves, she didn't think her stomach could handle anything at the moment. Hopefully, she'd be more relaxed by dinner.

Madison checked out the crowd and saw several senators she knew from television and print but had never met. She also saw many men and women she had no idea who they were. She guessed they were donors since Senator Walden was running for president.

"Miss Maxwell," Brad's father, dressed smartly in a black tuxedo of better quality and cut than Brad's elegant one, began. "It's great to see you again." He took her hand in his and squeezed it softly before releasing it. He put his arm around the woman standing beside him in a gorgeous cream gown. "This is my wife, Elizabeth."

She recalled Rylee telling her that he had married, but she'd completely forgotten that. "Hello, I'm Madison," she said, holding out her hand to shake.

Elizabeth took it. "It's a pleasure to meet you, Madison. I'm a big fan."

Embarrassing heat rose up her neck. She'd never gotten used to someone saying that. "Thank you."

"Brad," his father said with a nod.

"Hey, Dad. Elizabeth." He smiled at Elizabeth when he addressed her. So Brad liked his stepmother. That was a good trait in a son and a man.

"I love your dress," Elizabeth told her.

"Thank you. I love yours." The cream silk gown was lovely, with its fitted bodice and flowing skirt. It was created for an older woman in mind, and it set off the air of sophistication with Elizabeth. As for conversation, Madison hoped it would progress from the little pleasantries.

"Your first political dinner?"

Madison smiled. "Does it show?"

With a slight shake of her head, Elizabeth answered, "No, but I figured you hadn't moved in this circle with your career, even though you may know many politicians."

"You'd be right," she said, noticing Brad and his father had stepped apart from them, their heads close and talking low. Brad's body language changed. He appeared to be agitated. Curiosity opened within her, but she couldn't blow off Elizabeth and eavesdrop. Damn.

Of course, it was none of her business she had to remind herself.

She and Elizabeth chatted, with Elizabeth pointing out people in the room and giving Madison some background and a keen knowledge of who not to be alone with—ever.

When dinner was announced for the group of about twenty-six—*small dinner my ass,* she thought—Brad took her elbow and guided her along with the mass into an elegant dining room with the largest table Madison had ever seen. She'd expected they'd sit at smaller tables in groups or something, not all on this one long table. On the white tablecloth, there were groups of lavender and white flowers staggered down the center, intermingled with candles in silver candelabras that were lit; stemware was set at each place—probably crystal—silverware, and a white cloth napkin shaped like a bird. It looked magnificent.

Thankfully, there wasn't a seating chart or cards at each setting. Brad and Senator Hamilton sat so that she and Elizabeth were in between them, saving the two from unwelcome attention and conversation.

It wasn't until after she'd been served a stuffed chicken breast with roasted asparagus that she remembered Brad had a mission for the evening. She leaned toward him. "How are you going to ask your questions?"

He smiled. That smile melted her tough veneer. "Don't sweat it. There'll still be time after dinner. And since the agents have been rotating out here to check me out, I might have some luck."

She still wanted to help him in this quest, even though she knew he wasn't telling her everything. While curious, she wouldn't push into his personal life. It wasn't hers to invade. "Would it be easier if I weren't with you? Maybe they'd open up more?"

He hesitated, and that gave her the answer she'd expected. Disappointing but probably true. "Maybe. But I don't want to leave you alone."

"You won't. I'll stay with Elizabeth and your dad after dinner while you see what you can do."

"They'll be making the rounds, introducing you to many people. You'll have to stick close to Dad for protection from those lechers I told you about."

She'd already caught the eyes of two men she had a feeling were the lechers Brad referred to in reference to needing protection. Her skin crawled at their looks upon her. "I can do that."

Relief crossed his face. "If you're sure."

"I am. Do your thing. I think they'll keep me safe from," she lowered her voice even more, "lechers."

Then she smiled and picked up her silverware. Something inside her wanted to do anything she could for Brad. It confused the hell out of her, considering how he was with her. Usually, tonight had been another exception. Actually, if she was honest, there weren't exceptions any longer. They enjoyed each other's company.

After dinner, as promised, she stayed with Senator Hamilton and his wife, meeting person after person and listening to more politics than she ever wanted to in her lifetime. It told her that a politician was out of the running when she settled down. Of course, the only man she cared about now was the one speaking in hushed tones to a Secret Service agent who looked mighty uncomfortable.

She secretly smiled. Brad could do that to a person. She only hoped he was getting the information he sought in order to ease his mind.

Chapter Fifteen

Quickly rethinking having Madison on his arm and then discarding the idea, Brad spotted his old boss—Jacob Little—and after catching a questioning look on Brad's face, the agent said something into his microphone, and soon another agent replaced him. He nodded to Brad to follow him, informing Brad that he had a couple of minutes available.

In no uncertain terms, he told Brad to leave the past alone. That had only pricked Brad's interest more. He couldn't tell whether the man was angry at Brad's inquisition or the man's removal from the presidential detail following the event in Colombia. Although guarding a strong potential for president—Senator Walden—wasn't all that bad. Unless you didn't want her to win, which many people didn't, and he imagined that included some of the Secret Service agents. But they'd put their lives on the line regardless of their feelings for the person they were assigned to protect.

"It's water under the bridge," Jacob had said. "Because of your dad, you got out unscathed." The bitterness in the man's voice hadn't been hard to miss. Brad had wondered why his name had been kept out of things, and he'd had an inkling it had been because of his dad. Now he knew. Which meant his father knew what had happened. Curiosity as to what his father believed *actually* happened filled him. Deep inside, he knew his father would believe and support him. His mind slipped to Madison. Would she?

"Did you find out anything helpful?" Madison asked as they drove home in the dark. Home. He liked the sound of that where she was concerned. Wow. He had to stop thoughts like that. His plan was not to create a cozy family with the world's most beautiful woman. She might have only won that contest one year, but she belonged to that class all the time.

Without taking his eyes off the road, he shook his head. "Not really. Only two people were there who'd been in Colombia, and I could only speak with one since he was in charge and could step off for a few minutes. Unfortunately, he didn't have anything helpful to say."

"What are you going to do now?"

He wasn't going to let it go. His old boss had been insistent that he do just that. Too insistent. To Brad's way of thinking, the man doth protest too much. Something was there. He just had to find a way to get hold of that information.

Since he hadn't admitted to being involved in the scandal, he wasn't ready to accept it now. "I'll keep asking questions since I can't remember anything."

"Why can't you remember anything?"

He shifted in the seat. "Well, the reports say I drank too much, but I think I was drugged. I never drink to excess."

"Why would someone drug you?" she asked with concern lacing her tone.

Boy, she was full of questions. Maybe he should've let her play Nancy Drew. "That, I don't know. If I did, this would be over."

Out of habit, he always watched his rearview mirror. When a car came up fast behind him, he tightened his grip on the wheel. The worry that some drunk driver would be out at this hour bothered him. On the deserted road, he slowed so the vehicle—by the shape and height of the headlights, it was a truck—could pass him. They were about to hit an area where passing wasn't possible and having someone ride his ass on the two-lane highway wasn't his preference.

The truck didn't pass. Instead, he rode close to them, and Brad tensed, his nerves on edge. Ahead, a long stretch of lake with guardrails keeping vehicles from plunging off the side hugged the roadway.

As soon as he passed the beginning of the guardrail signaling they were officially over an incline of some kind, the truck rammed him, and his heart pounded in part fear and part anger. Madison gasped, and a soft noise escaped her at the impact, and he felt his stomach drop out of him at the thought of her getting hurt. Holding tight to the steering wheel to keep his truck straight, Brad cursed the situation and asked if she was okay. Hearing her say she was fine, he sped up, and the vehicle behind him did the same. The errant driver acted to pass Brad, but Brad was leery of the move and focused on the truck's maneuver.

"Hang on," he told Madison in a firm voice. He wanted to look at her and reassure her it was all right, but with his heart pounding, he couldn't take his eyes off the road or the rearview mirror. His mind whirled. He had to do what it took to get her to safety. Although it was his job to protect her, he hadn't realized how much his heart beat for her safety and his. In all the jobs he'd completed, he'd never felt the need to protect so profoundly.

Although he'd increased his speed more—hell, they were doing eighty miles an hour—he couldn't outrun the man trying to run them off the road. With the truck's headlights blinding him in his driver-side mirror, the vehicle tapped them on the left bumper.

Brad's pulse skyrocketed as he let off the gas and tapped his brakes, when his truck began to spin as he fought for control. Before Brad could right his vehicle, they hit and broke through the guardrail—the impact deploying the airbags—and the truck teetered over the edge of about a forty-foot drop-off to the water below. The back wheels must've caught on something to stop them from ultimately plunging over the side.

As soon as he could catch his breath, he was calling for her. "Maddie," he said into the airbag that was shrinking down by the second. "Maddie," he said again, more clearly.

No answer. A sick feeling hit his gut, and it got worse after the white material didn't impede his vision. If they moved, they could send Brad's truck over the edge. Fuck. Scared shitless didn't begin to describe his feelings. Well, there was pissed off at the driver, but right now he had to get Madison to safety, and he didn't know how he was going to do it.

Looking her way, he saw her leaning forward as much as her seat belt would allow. Her head lolled down to her chest. A pit formed in his stomach, and a strange ache started in his chest. He couldn't even reach over and check on her without shifting the vehicle. *Shit. Shit. Shit.*

Ever so gently, he removed his cell phone from his pocket to call 911. On one hand, he hoped Madison would not wake up and start moving, putting them in more danger, and on the other hand, he hoped she would wake up and tell him she was okay.

With emergency services on the way, all they could do was wait. An unwelcome thought hit him, and his blood froze and his pulse sped up to nearly racing. What if whoever had tried to run them off the road came back and finished whatever job he'd been trying to do—scare them or worse—he gulped past a painful lump in his throat—kill them? Sweat broke out on his brow, and his gut clenched. He couldn't protect Madison because he couldn't shift to grab the weapon he kept in his truck. That sinking feeling that he'd failed her assailed him, and he swallowed against that potential. While afraid—yes, he'd admit he was worried at the moment since they were basically immobile and defenseless—he wouldn't give up protecting her to his last breath.

This had Casden and Rogers written all over it. He knew there'd be trouble with them. His blood boiled at the fact they'd tried to kill Madison for not selling her club to them. Since this accident hadn't worked, what was next? He was sticking to her like glue no matter what she said about needing protection.

While still thinking of ways to get back at the two men, the state police arrived. After much shouting from the roadway to Brad's truck, a trooper—ensuring they were safe first, as safe as they could be—notified him a tow truck was on the way and to sit tight. His stomach revolted at his wonder of how long they'd need to sit tight—before the tow truck arrived or his vehicle slipped down the incline. He couldn't remember the last time he prayed—really prayed—but he took a moment to say a silent prayer for their safety and Madison's health.

Concern swamped him because of the abundance of vehicles that arrived with sirens blaring and the jolting of the truck as they pulled it back onto the road. Madison didn't wake. Christ, his heart dropped to his stomach in panic. Had he killed her? That ugly thought played around in his mind and turned his insides out.

As soon as the truck settled on even ground, he removed his seat belt and slid to Madison, his fingers on her neck, checking for a pulse. An EMT opened the door and told him not to move her. Feeling a strong pulse, he dropped his head and released his breath. Thank God she was alive.

Reluctantly, he exited the vehicle and stepped aside so the EMTs could work on her. His gut clenched when they put a C-collar on her. He knew it was just in case, but anger at the man who'd done this stormed him and scared him with the fact that she might actually need it. Removing her from the truck, the EMTs treated her like she was precious cargo—the way she should be treated.

When Brad tried to go with her, he was stopped by the state police to make his statement and get his truck towed off. The trooper assured him he'd take him to the hospital as soon as they finished. Brad wanted to fight him, but knew the man was only doing his job. Okay, for now, since he couldn't do anything for Madison, he'd best be there by the time she woke up. His heart couldn't take anything less than that. That told him more than he'd known how he felt for her.

She wasn't aware, but things were going to change for them. His heart was involved now, and he wanted her to be a part of his future. A future they could build together. He knew winning her wouldn't be easy, but he wouldn't give up. That heart of his knew that they were destined to be together.

****

Madison woke confused…and scared. She was on her back and looking at many bright lights as she passed them. It was like an amusement park ride where you had no control over where the ride took you, and it turned her stomach, just as those rides did.

Noises. People talking, and then someone wearing a frog-covered scrub top leaned over her. "Oh, you're awake. The doctor will be happy to hear that." Yet, the frog-covered scrub top lady didn't stop moving Madison.

Panic hit her hard when she realized she was in a hospital. As her pulse pounded through her veins, she tried to think of what had happened to get her here. Madison attempted to turn her head to the lady who'd spoken to her but couldn't move her neck. Her panic escalated. Was she paralyzed? A sudden whoosh of despair railed through her at the thought. No. She refused to accept it. She couldn't be.

It didn't register right away that when her hands were reaching for her neck, she couldn't be paralyzed if she could move her arms.

"Hold still," the same woman said. "It's just a C-collar. It's a precaution. We're on our way to X-ray now. After the doctor says it's safe, we'll get it off you."

Relief surged through her, but worry still crowded her as she searched her mind for what had happened.

The dinner. A vehicle rammed them. Brad.

They'd been driving, and then they'd been hit by

another car. Oh God, was he okay? She tried to sit up, but a hand on her shoulder guided her back down. "Settle down. We're almost there."

"Brad," she said.

"Who?" the woman answered.

She wet her dry lips. "He was in the truck with me."

The nurse shook her head. "You were the only one brought in from the accident."

No. No. No. Was he dead? Did he not get brought in because he'd died, and they waited for something other than an ambulance to remove his body? Her insides churned at the thought of Brad dead. She couldn't accept it any more than she'd received that she might be paralyzed. But, he wasn't here. Her heart was crushed, and she wasn't sure it could be repaired. *No. Not Brad.*

Her brain righted, and she thought maybe—just maybe—he was okay and hadn't needed to go to the hospital. But, why wasn't he here with her now? She bit her bottom lip with worry.

After X-rays and the doctor agreeing she was okay, they removed the collar from her stiff neck muscles. She rubbed it, happy to have the uncomfortable reminder that she'd been hurt away from her body.

"You hit your head on the side window pretty hard. You'll probably feel some pain in your entire body from the impact of the two vehicles. I'll prescribe you something for it," the doctor said, tapping the tablet screen. He looked up at her. "I'm worried about your concussion. Unless you have someone who can wake you and check on you all night, I will admit you."

"She's got someone," Brad said, slipping inside the

tiny room and taking up all the available space with his presence. Her heart jumped at seeing him with his jacket and bowtie off and the sleeves of his white dress shirt rolled up. She wondered if his coat was like her dress and had white powder from the airbag. Either way, he looked rough and sexy, dressed how he was in the exam room.

The doctor's head swiveled back to her from Brad. "Okay." Then he went into what Brad should do, expect, and look out for because she'd been knocked unconscious. That almost sent her over the edge, and her anger flared. She'd been run off the road and injured. Someone had deliberately hurt her. Her stomach tightened at the thought, but it didn't stop her from wanting revenge.

Once the doctor released her and they left the exam room, Madison wondered how they were getting home. Had his truck been salvageable?

"Were you hurt?" she asked him now that the focus wasn't on her.

"Nah. Maybe a bruise from the seat belt, but nothing I can't live with."

"How's your truck?"

He grimaced, and her heart went out to him. She knew he loved his truck by the way he cared for it. "It's going to need some work."

"Then how are we getting home?"

Reaching over, he clasped their hands together, and she let him. It felt good. Right. "Matt's on his way. He should be here shortly. Let's sit in the waiting room until he shows."

Dressed in her formal dress, they sat in the waiting room with open stares at them. Brad didn't seem to care as he tossed one arm over her shoulder and his other captured her hand. As if in unison, both thumbs rubbed gentle circles on the back of her hand and collarbone. His touch settled her, and the unconscious caresses warmed her. Her heart fluttered.

Thankfully, Matt arrived quickly, and they left. Instead of escorting her to the front seat, he opened the back door, and after she slid into her seat, he gently buckled her in before moving around the SUV to the other side and slipping into his seat.

"Thanks, bro," Brad told Matt, who didn't seem perplexed that no one sat in the front seat beside him.

"Anytime." Matt drove his SUV, which she'd learned he'd driven from Kentucky, out of the parking lot and to the highway back to Baltimore.

The SUV was eerily quiet, and she could sense the agitation shooting off Brad in waves.

"Casden and Rogers," he said.

Matt nodded but didn't turn back to them. Keeping his eyes on the road, he said, "Maybe."

"No maybe about it," Brad stated. "It had to be them."

"Hmm," Matt murmured before clearing his throat. "What happened tonight? At the dinner?"

Madison felt the question was meant for Brad, so she remained quiet, watching the conversation and the men. Matt appeared calm, as if there wasn't a threat to Madison.

"What do you mean? We ate and mingled. Saw Dad and Elizabeth."

"Did you ask questions like you'd planned?"

Brad tensed. "Shit."

They quieted again, and Madison didn't understand

what had happened. Did they have some twin thing going on to communicate? Not able to stand the thick fog of tension in the SUV, she asked, "What does that matter?"

Reaching over, Brad clasped her hand, and she didn't pull it back. No longer wishing to question her feelings—their feelings—she decided to relax into the touch and let it settle over them. Deciding that, she took in the strength and warmth he held in his hand. Their connection did funny things in her stomach. This hand-holding was the start to something great.

"That means," he began and then squeezed her hand, "that if there's something to hide, someone wouldn't want me digging around in it."

"I still don't see how—" It hit her what he meant. "Do you mean they could've been after you instead of me?" Her stomach clenched at the thought. Whether it was because he put her in danger or whether he'd been in danger, she didn't know what bothered her most.

"Right. It could've been me they were trying to silence. I'm sorry."

The first apology he'd given her was necessary. The second one really wasn't, even though she'd been glad to hear it. Neither was this one required. It wasn't his fault, even if they were after him. She squeezed his hand. "Don't be sorry."

"What are you going to do?" Matt asked with a quick turn to look back at his brother.

"I'm not sure now," Brad admitted. "When I thought it was Casden and Rogers, I thought to stick to her." He looked at Madison, and even in the dark SUV, she could see the intensity in his eyes. It burned down to her soul. "But if it's from my past, that could be dangerous to Madison."

What did she want? She wanted Brad by her side if it had been Casden and Rogers. She wouldn't be afraid to admit she was wrong, and since they'd escalated, she wanted full protection. But if it was from him…. She wanted to help him find out what he was seeking. She couldn't help it—she cared about what happened to him.

Matt spoke up before she could voice her choice, "I guess it's a good thing I'm here then."

Madison swallowed. She should be happy someone would be there as a barrier to doing something stupid with Brad. What would be stupid, though? Now that she had these feelings for him swirling inside her, she wasn't sure what the limit would be. She chewed on her lip, trying to decide whether her libido appreciated his brother being there or not.

"How's Dad?" Matt asked. "I haven't seen him in a long time."

"Same as always. He asked about you, and I expect you'll see him while you're here. Elizabeth too."

As the men talked about family, Madison leaned back and listened.

Chapter Sixteen

"Jesse, I know I'm not wrong," Brad insisted, frustrated with his eldest brother. They'd been discussing what had happened and the theories behind it. After much thought, Brad concluded that Madison had to be the intended target. After all, there'd be no reason for the Secret Service to try and kill him because he asked about a taboo subject. The idea was ludicrous. They'd been his brethren after all. Besides, they wouldn't have had time to stage it.

"You need to quit being so damn hardheaded and be open to the possibility at least." It wasn't the first time he'd been called that, and it surely wouldn't be the last.

Could it have happened as Matt and Jesse said? The Secret Service going after him? Anything was fucking possible. It just wasn't probable. Casden and Rogers were more likely suspects. They'd been slighted when she and Rylee had turned down their offer to buy the club. He conceded because he didn't wish to argue anymore with Madison asleep in the next room. "Okay, I'll give you that, but it's not the least bit likely. It's got to be those two fuckers. We both knew they wouldn't take this lying down." If the club hadn't been in such a prime location, this wouldn't be happening. It would give Casden and Rogers a more upscale clientele and provide them with another outlet to sell drugs.

"True. I need you to rethink this. If you're the target, taking on her protection jeopardizes her." He paused, probably for a dramatic effect since that's what he did. "However, if she's the target, she needs you. Rylee will be out of the country soon, and Devon has her protected until then."

"If that's the case, I really could use some help," he admitted, almost with his tail between his legs. It shouldn't be hard to ask, but it automatically said he couldn't do it alone. He couldn't protect her enough.

"Well, you've got Matt. I'm staying in town, so you've got me when needed." He heard the rasping of Jesse's hand on his scruffy morning beard. He couldn't expect his brother to be cleanly shaven at three o'clock in the morning. Hell, he'd been lucky his brother wasn't reaming him out for calling at this hour. But, after the accident...and Madison being injured...it couldn't wait.

While Madison slept in Matt's old room, his brother prowled outside to alert them of any threats. He'd been fuming that they'd agreed it was okay for Brad to take her to the dinner alone since they'd be so much security already in place.

"I'll tell you what. I'll keep Ken behind. Rob can lead the team. Also, Sam wasn't going anyway, so you've got our best sharpshooter should you need it." Then, as an afterthought, he added, "Although, given the location of your house to the park, there's no good place for her to set up regularly."

Relief whooshed through Brad at the extra help he needed to keep Madison safe from harm. He'd love an entire team but take two more hands. "I pray we don't need her in that capacity, but extra eyes on the neighborhood wouldn't be unwelcome."

He only hoped that he was right and Madison was in danger, not that he was bringing danger to her. In no way would he let things go on his investigation. Especially now that he has gotten the pushback from his old boss. Someone who should want the truth to be out there.

Unless it was the truth, crept into his mind, and while he couldn't ultimately push the true fear away, he banished it so he could think clearly. He didn't do it.

"Ken will be there tomorrow. Hell, today. Just don't give him shit. Let him do his job. I recommend you put him and Sam on days and Matt on nights. Seeing Matt and thinking they saw you 24/7 could surprise someone."

Without thinking that Jesse couldn't see him, he nodded in agreement. The element of surprise was a good weapon. "Okay." Had it not been Madison he was thinking of, he'd have argued on principle of his brother telling him what to do. He was the one with the best protection background. That was his job 100 percent of the time, unlike his brother, who did it when necessary or none before they joined HIS.

"Go wake up Madison and see that she's okay. A concussion is nothing to play with."

Brad gritted his teeth at Jesse continuing to tell him what to do. What pissed Brad off was that he was right. It was time to wake Madison and check on her.

"It'll be okay, brother," Jesse said. "Devon and I will track down Casden and Rogers and see if we can agree. You just protect Madison, but watch your back."

After ending the call, Brad took a moment to himself and his swirling thoughts. Was he responsible for Madison being injured in the accident? His stomach lurched at the thought. A tinge of unease flowed through him at the thought that maybe—just maybe—he should push her off on the few men from HIS and fight his own battle—alone. Just in case he was wrong.

Although he didn't have an entire team, he had two men he'd trust with his life, an unknown woman he had to trust, and Madison. Whether he was the target or not, they'd keep her safe, with their lives if necessary. He hoped it didn't get to that point, but knowing the team's devotion to his case almost overwhelmed him.

The fact that he could've lost Madison tonight made his heart ache and his gut revolt. They could've both lost their lives. Whoever hit them must've hoped for that. They'd waited until the right location and hit the truck at the opportune spot to spin it toward the guardrail. The fear that had filled him when he'd spied Madison unconscious and stuck in her seat belt had him silently praying, and he couldn't remember the last time he'd done that.

He'd endured the sucker punch to his gut when he'd realized she meant something to him.

The truth was that Madison had so many excellent attributes that he couldn't count them all. All he knew was that everything about her called to him. And their attraction most of all.

The world between them was magnetic, and they'd fought it long enough. Their night together and that kiss told him more than they had been willing to admit. He wanted more of his princess. He needed to show her that he cared for her. He didn't plan to seduce her even though he wanted her back in his bed, but he planned to woo the hell out of her with his kindness—yes, he had some—and his caring. If that wasn't enough, he might just remind her—with a kiss—how good they were together.

With a shake of his head to ward off the thoughts, he walked into Madison's room. It'd been two hours, so it was time to check her.

Before he could bring himself to wake her, he watched her sleep. Her chest's slight rise and fall reassured him that she was okay. She'd survived.

Lying on her back, her long, dark hair was swept across the pillows, giving her an angelic glow. Her oval face, pale and free of makeup, added to the effect. Unable to resist, he touched her cheek with his hand. When she didn't rouse, he had a moment of panic that grabbed hold of him and twisted his insides.

He felt a strong need to make sure she was all right, so he touched her shoulder and called her name until her beautiful, dark eyes fluttered open and took a moment to focus.

"Brad, why did you wake me?" Her voice, rough from sleep, touched him deep down to his soul.

"Because the doctor said. What's your name?"

She sighed and pulled the cover up her chest, covering her luscious breasts encased in an overly large T-shirt that he remembered almost fell to her knees. "Not this again. Madison Maxwell. I'm guessing by now it's a new day, so it's March 31st, and it's Saturday."

He chuckled at her spunk. "Lucky guesses."

"Not at all. Can I go back to sleep now?" She yawned and closed her eyes.

Satisfied she was okay, he agreed, albeit reluctantly. "Sure, princess." After watching her a moment more, he turned to leave, even though everything called to him to crawl up in bed beside her and hold her until she was well.

"Brad," she said sleepily.

He stopped and turned back to the bed, hoping his naked desire didn't show on his face. "Yeah."

"Would you—would you hold me until I go back to sleep?"

Had she been reading his mind? He had a moment of panic that she'd somehow known what he was thinking. Ridiculous, but it still hit him.

At his stunned expression, she continued. "Just don't be an ass this time. I need the comfort that I know you can give. It's holding. Nothing more."

Shocked beyond belief at her request, he quickly processed all the things that could go wrong with that scenario then tossed them aside and gave his dick a quick, silent lecture. Then he remembered her hitched breath and saw the blush across her cheeks. He'd happily hold her and nothing more. No way would he take advantage of her. "Scoot over." He moved back to the bed and kicked off his shoes. After sliding under the covers, he turned on his side, maneuvered her so her back was to his front, and wrapped his arm around her. "Sleep, princess."

Lord, help him. His dick hadn't listened and was already talking to him. He gritted his teeth. Holding her seemed so right, and he wouldn't deny her anything even if it could be the worst decision he ever made.

"I'm not sleepy now," she told him.

Great. Now she would notice his arousal. He scooted his hips back a smidgeon. "I'm not singing a lullaby."

She chuckled. "No. I'd rather you didn't. Tell me a

story. I bet you've got tons."

What the hell kind of stories would he have? None that would be exciting to his princess. "What do you want to hear?" he found himself asking.

"How did you break your nose?"

"Which time?" He chuckled.

"Hmm. Let's go with the first one."

Remembering back, he chuckled at his stupidity. "I was sixteen. There was this girl—"

She interrupted. "Maybe I don't want to hear this."

"It's okay. You might find it humorous. Most people do. In fact, I even do now."

"Okay. Keep going."

"As I was saying, there was this girl—Rachel Jeffreys—prettiest girl in high school. She had long, flowing hair like you," he added.

"Did she sock you for saying something inappropriate?"

Her dig hurt, but he deserved it. "No, she didn't hit me at all. She kissed me."

"Then her boyfriend hit you?"

"Are you going to allow me to tell this story?" he asked jokingly.

"Sorry. Go ahead."

"Well, she kissed me one night after a football game behind the bleachers. She told me I was the best kisser she'd ever had. Little did I know she'd done the same with my twin earlier in the evening."

"Uh-oh," she said softly.

"Uh-oh is right. After she let it be known she'd kissed both of us, we had it out. It never occurred to us, as we sat there each with broken noses trying to explain it to our father, that she'd toyed with us."

He'd so wanted to pay her back, but his father had made them promise not to retaliate, as a gentleman never does. At sixteen, he hadn't wanted to be a gentleman; he'd wanted to be a man bent on revenge. But he couldn't think of a good payback, so he followed his father's dictate.

"Who did she choose? I'm assuming you made her choose."

"We didn't have anything to do with her after that."

"So," she said, her fingers mindlessly running across his hand splayed on her belly, "you and your brother broke each other's noses over a girl that neither of you ended up with?" He could hear the smile in her voice.

"Yeah." He sighed. He'd been an idiot as a kid, but he guessed most kids were at some point. As for Rachel, eventually, someone taught her a lesson on playing with people's feelings. He'd watched her public humiliation and said nothing. He had no idea how she fared now and didn't care.

"That is a good story. Now tell me about the second time you broke your nose."

Shit. She didn't need to hear about violence. It had been a fucked mission of retrieving a little girl. They'd saved the girl, but a couple of the team, including himself, hadn't fared all that great in the end. "Maybe something else," he coaxed. "Or maybe you want to go back to sleep." He didn't want to stop holding her and knew he would need to after she went to sleep so she didn't wake up in his arms—which would be fantastic—since she'd only asked him to hold her until she fell asleep.

Madison yawned. "I might be sleepy now."

"Go to sleep. I've got you." Watching her even breathing, he considered his next step—bringing them together. Not just sex but a relationship that might just last.

Chapter Seventeen

Before Dawn, Brad had slipped from Madison's bed for several reasons. One, she might have felt differently about him being in her bed when she was wide awake. And, two, he didn't want Matt to see him leaving her bed. Sure, his brother knew the two had slept together already, but he didn't need to think it now, especially after the shit Brad had given each of his brothers for getting involved with the woman they were protecting. To admit the truth to himself, he'd been a real dick about it.

Now here he was, wanting the woman he was protecting, knowing it would fuck with his concentration, which could be deadly. Yet he wouldn't step back from it.

True to Jesse's word, Ken and Sam showed up first thing in the morning. Brad worried a bit that Ken might be upset about missing the Belgium trip, but he seemed focused on Sam, and since she hadn't been going with the team in the first place, it might've worked out for the best. Although Brad had never seen Ken so focused on a teammate and whether he or she could hold their own. Hell, Sam had been SWAT. Of course she could hold her own.

Riding in the back seat of Ken's SUV, he and Madison were on their way to Devon and Rylee's for dinner. If it hadn't been for Devon telling Brad that he and Rylee needed to talk with him, he wouldn't have been leaving his house. And since he did leave his house, so had Madison, who looked forward to seeing her sister and not hearing him check on her constantly.

Whatever the hell Devon had to share had best be worth putting them at risk by being out and about. If not, he might kill his brother for being so stupid. What could he do with a former CIA agent, though? Devon was more intelligent than the team gave him credit for. He may not like the action—preferring his computer— but he could hold his own, as he'd demonstrated when Rylee had been in danger.

"We'll stay outside," Ken told them as they parked in the driveway. "Rylee said she'd pack the leftovers for us to eat later."

Good of Rylee to think of that. Shit like that always slipped his mind. He hadn't prepared to feed three extra people at his house. He'd best remedy that right away. He wondered how Madison would enjoy a grocery-shopping trip with him and a tail.

She'd seemed fine with the extra people around, treating them like she'd known them all her life. Earlier in the day, she'd explained that many times on shoots they might have some security, so it was like a walk in the park for her. Yet, she'd never expected trouble before. Her trembling lip when she'd said that had him almost rushing to her and pulling her tight, then kissing that lip until she had her calm back. But, he wouldn't make it all physical with them.

The front door opened before he could knock, and Rylee hugged her sister. "I was so worried about you."

Without separating them, Madison responded, "I'm fine. Just a small bump on the side of my head where I hit the passenger-side window."

Thank God for seat belts and airbags, or it could've been the windshield. He shuddered at the image of a severely injured Madison. A stone sank in his stomach at the thought that she could've gone through the windshield to the unknown rocks and water below, where his truck had ended up leaning over the edge.

The women broke apart. "Come in. Dinner's ready."

"What's on the menu?" Madison asked as she entered the house.

Please don't let it be lasagna, Brad hoped.

"Chicken enchiladas. I got the recipe from Kate."

Brad smiled. "Sounds yummy."

"Don't worry, I have plenty of salad for you," Rylee told her sister.

Rubbing her belly, Madison said, "Believe it or not, I'm more interested in the enchiladas than rabbit food. Besides, I don't have to starve myself any longer. Moderation. As long as I can still fit in my clothes, I'm good."

Hallelujah, Brad wanted to shout. She needed to transition into being a regular person, not someone always on display.

Devon walked into the room with Mitch leaning against his shoulder. "We're going to have an extra for dinner. He's not the least bit sleepy." Walking away, Devon stopped at the highchair at the table and strapped in the little boy.

"Sit. I'll get the food," Rylee instructed.

Once again, he sat beside Madison but felt awkward this time. She hadn't said anything about her request the night before, nor had he. It hung over them like a heavy blanket.

Settled at the table, Devon dished up the food, and Brad took his first bite with trepidation. It wasn't that Rylee couldn't cook; she just had a limited recipe book. She'd been expanding out, making him and Devon guinea pigs, for a while. Madison had also become a guinea pig.

He swallowed in surprise, which wasn't fair to his sister-in-law, but it was what it was. "Excellent. Tastes just like Kate's."

"This is delicious," Madison added.

"Where's Matt?" Rylee asked.

"Probably asleep at his hotel. He's taking over later. He's going to be pissed he missed this though."

Rylee waved her hand as if to wave off the problem. "I'm sending plenty home for him and the others. I didn't figure you had something ready to feed the extra mouths."

"You're right there." He took a bite, chewed, and swallowed. "I was just thinking of that on the way over."

"I'll help with a casserole or two for you before I leave," Rylee offered.

He wouldn't turn down help to feed the extras at his house. Her food lately had been all edible, so he'd just keep his fingers crossed it remained that way. "I appreciate it. Thanks, Rylee."

Devon fed Mitch a spoonful of something that looked like vomit. It was a good thing babies couldn't compare because Mitch seemed to be enjoying whatever it was.

"How's the cleanup going?" Madison asked Rylee. She'd been pissed Brad had made her rest all day and not get involved in her business. It had been a controlled anger, but she'd obeyed, which meant she hadn't been feeling as well as she'd said.

"Almost done." Rylee smiled at her son and husband. "The contractor can start taking out the bar since he'd had to leave it until he had more of his workers."

Madison set her glass of iced tea down on the shiny wood table. "That's good. I'm ready also."

"Well, it'll be all you, day after tomorrow."

A silence settled on the table. Brad knew Devon didn't like for Rylee to put her life on the line, but he'd settled into that was who she was. He dealt with it but wasn't happy about that fact.

Clearing his throat, Brad tried to bring the conversation back on track. "What did you want to talk to me about?" Time to get down to brass tacks. The conversation and food had been pleasant, but there'd been a purpose for this, and he wanted to know what it was.

"Let's clean this up, and I'll bring in dessert. I baked a pie."

"A pie? Great." Uh-oh. The last pie he'd eaten of Rylee's hadn't been entirely edible. It had been one of her first "from scratch" efforts.

"I'll help clean this up." Madison stood and took both plates to the kitchen before he could stand, leaving him lost as to what to do. So, he watched Devon play with his son, probably hoping the little tyke would go to sleep.

He smiled at his sister-in-law with a slice of apple pie and coffee in front of him. "Looks great." The crust actually did look fluffy this time and hopefully had some flavor. He hesitantly took a bite and smiled in satisfaction. The crust had a light, airy taste, the apples were cooked to perfection, and the sauce with the hint of cinnamon made his mouth water. Rylee had outdone herself. "Exceptional," he complimented.

"Really?" Rylee looked like a small child waiting for her parents' approval.

He nodded. "Really. In fact, feel free to send the rest of it home with us." He winked, and they laughed.

By this time, Mitch was nodding off, fighting each fall into slumber. "Let us put him to bed, and we'll talk." Rylee and Devon left him and Madison sitting at the table, drinking coffee, which he prayed was decaf because he needed some sleep after staying up to check on Madison the night before.

"What's going on? What do they want to talk to you about?" Madison asked.

He fidgeted. He didn't like not having an answer to a question. "Don't know."

They sat in silence, and his mind drifted back to earlier in the day when she'd woken and shyly come into the living room where he'd been dozing. She'd said nothing about his being in her bed, but she'd been friendly and something else he couldn't describe. But he enjoyed that side of her. They'd talked about nonsensical things and had long moments of silence where it had been comfortable.

When she'd first come out in that long T-shirt, he'd had to hold himself back to keep from dragging her back to bed and removing it from her. She mustn't have had any idea the pink around her nipples had shown through the fabric or that the giraffe design that ended below her pelvic bone did nothing to hide his imagination of what lay beneath it.

Although they'd done nothing during the day so she could recuperate, they hadn't fought. That made the day perfect. She hadn't treated him like he was a pariah either. He'd take that win.

When Devon and Rylee returned from putting their son to sleep, Rylee held a brochure in her hand. After they had sat down, Devon cleared his throat. "As you know, Rylee and I had memory problems when we first met."

Brad nodded. Hell, everyone knew that. Well, after they found out the two had married.

"We were talking about your memory problem from back when." He looked covertly at Madison, not knowing what he'd shared with her.

Brad's gut clenched. They'd talked about him? About his stupidity or failure, however you looked at it. "She has an idea of what happened." Of course, he hadn't come completely clean with her, but she was an intelligent woman. She'd eventually figure it out. Something inside him told him he'd best tell her before that happened. He'd seen how his brothers suffered while waiting to spill their guts.

"Well"—Devon linked his hand with Rylee's on the table—"we tried to decide if we really wanted to know what happened, so we checked out our options. We'd heard of hypnotherapy and considered it, although there was no guarantee our memories would surface."

Brad swallowed at the thought. To remember. To be able to figure out how things happened and why. Then again, that niggling feeling that he might not like what he found tried to encroach into the possibility of bringing his life back into balance. That's how he'd felt since coming home with his tail tucked between his legs as a failure. "And?"

"We're still considering it. We kind of like the mystery of exactly what brought us together. But we thought this might be something for you. If there's something hinky about what happened to you, this could be your chance to find out truly. Your missing memory might be the key."

Sitting frozen, Brad didn't know what to think. He didn't want to get his hopes up. What if he went to the trouble only to find they couldn't retrieve his memory? Or worse. But even the slightest chance had him wanting to rush off and make an appointment.

Rylee thrust the brochure forward. "I have a brochure for the place we'd recommend, should you decide to do it."

After a moment of hesitation, he stood and reached for the brochure. "Thank you." He glanced down at a wide-eyed Madison. "I think it's time to get Madison home and back to bed." A bed without him.

But, he was leaving with the possibility of clearing his name. That put a bit of pep in his step.

Chapter Eighteen

Madison remained quiet on the drive home in an SUV that smelled like a restaurant from all the leftovers. Brad seemed to be lost in his own world, and Ken and Sam must've had an inkling something was wrong with him because they also remained silent. It made for a long drive home with Brad gripping the brochure like it was a lifeline. Her heart went out to him and the turmoil he seemed struggling to handle.

For her, doing the hypnotherapy would be a no-brainer, but Brad didn't seem so sure. She couldn't understand the problem. He wanted to know. That was why he'd asked those questions at dinner, right?

Either way, she'd found sitting next to him at mealtime a challenge. She hated how much she was drawn to him, but loved it all the same. The heat that flowed between them was hard to deny. And she was tired of doing just that.

Last night, she'd wanted more from him than to hold her, but she'd been so distraught over the attack and then drowsy that she couldn't ask for more. Tonight though…maybe she could get up the nerve.

She'd tossed over the idea of having more with Brad in her mind many times. Maybe he only wanted to be with her because she'd been a supermodel and maybe not. His tenderness last night belied one of those possibilities. Either way, she'd never felt so precious as she had in his arms. And when he'd called her princess, butterflies fluttered in her tummy.

She couldn't remember when he'd started calling her that, but she liked it from him. It was the way he said it, not as a slight for some spoiled child, but with care and respect. It seemed silly, but she wouldn't stop him from giving her a pet name.

Inside his home, they kicked off their shoes and stood awkwardly. Inspiration hit her. She would do something to lighten the mood and help bring him out of the funk he lived in. "You look like you could use a nightcap." She began walking to the kitchen. "Let me get you something. Have a seat."

She took the leftovers to the kitchen. Ken and Sam had taken a portion home with them, and Matt had already eaten, so they were entirely alone.

With two bottles of ice-cold beer in her hand, Madison returned to the living room and sat beside Brad on the couch. If he thought anything of her sitting there instead of a chair, he didn't say a word to that effect. He just stared at the brochure.

Wanting to break the tension, Madison started to say something polite, but instead blurted, "Why don't we play cards or something?" When he looked at her, dazed, she grew bold. "Strip poker." That was one way to get him back into her bed.

It took him a moment to react with a questioning look. "What?"

She swallowed hard. She decided not to back down since she'd already thrown it out there. "Let's liven up the evening and play strip poker."

His gaze ravished her face, searching for something, and her body heated. Heck, they weren't even touching yet and desire burned inside her. "I do believe I have a set of cards." He launched himself from the couch, dropped the brochure on the oval coffee table and went to a side table, pulling out a drawer and rummaging through it. She smiled at how quickly he'd dropped the brochure and how this step was getting his mind off all that was worrying him. Her heart warmed when he turned back to her. With a large smile, he produced a pack of red-backed playing cards. "Are you ready to lose your shirt?" His smile grew. "Pun intended."

His smile was infectious, and happiness bubbled up inside her. She liked this playful side of Brad. "I think it'll be you who loses your shirt…and pants."

They made their way to the table with their beers and discussed some ground rules. Five card stud. She had to lose her socks since she had on one more piece of clothing than he did. His socks were one set of clothing. The winner chooses the garment the loser must remove. Ties result in each player losing a garment. Easy enough, she thought. Then, she decided to play with him more.

"Can you write down for me what beats what? I always forget," she asked, with as much inexperience as she could summon.

Something akin to lust and greed flashed in his eyes. He was seeing this as an easy win. Her emotions swelled at the change in his mood—how uplifting it had become. She hoped his humor remained when he realized she'd set him up. She secretly smiled at the thought of beating the pants off him.

Brad grabbed a notepad and pen beside the phone and wrote down the sequence of hands for the win. She didn't know why he'd even write royal flush since it was doubtful either would have one.

"How about we tell a story during each hand before we show them? It'll help us get to know each other better?" she asked. She'd love to find out more from him. He was a hard man to get to know. Maybe this would help.

He nodded. "Okay. But, we trade off stories."

"Agreed. You don't cheat, do you?"

With a mock affronted look, he said, "Who me?"

She giggled and enjoyed hearing the fun in his voice.

"I'll deal first, and I get to ask you the first question," Brad said.

She stiffened for a second. "How about we ask each other one question, then go with stories we'd like to share—a funny time?"

He studied her, probably thinking she was too scared to answer questions, and part of her was because there was no telling what he'd ask. "Okay." After shuffling the deck, he dealt the first cards and set the remainder of the stack between them.

She shuffled her hand to make more of it. In the end, she discarded three and inwardly smiled at what she'd picked up. "What's your question?" she asked and took a drink of her beer.

He grinned mischievously. "When did you lose your virginity?"

Madison almost spewed the drink out of her nose. Instead, she was reduced to a hacking cough. "Wow. That's a question."

He shrugged, and his grin shined bright. "I only get one, so I wanted to make it a good one. Are you too afraid to answer?" he goaded.

Back stiffening, she narrowed her eyes at him. "No. I lost my virginity when I was eighteen at the senior prom."

"Why wait until you were eighteen? Don't most girls start losing their virginity around sixteen?"

"I don't know about that, but my dad had me so afraid I'd get pregnant if I had sex that I couldn't bring myself to do it. Until then."

"What changed?" he asked.

"I had started the pill when I turned eighteen, and my father didn't know about it."

"I see. Was it good?"

"You were only allotted one question. But I'll answer. No. It was short-lived."

Brad shuffled his cards and snorted. "Teenage boys."

"Yep."

"Are you ready to remove some clothing?" he asked.

"Show me what you've got."

"Two pair. Tens and fours."

She tried to look at the sheet he'd given her, so it appeared she didn't know what she was doing. "Well," she said, looking up with a smile, "it appears my three jacks beat that."

He looked stunned and then smiled. "Beginners luck. What should I remove?"

"We'll start with your socks." She wasn't sure she could sit there and stare at his bare chest the entire game, but at some point, she'd have to.

"Okay." He tossed his remaining card down and leaned over, making a production of removing his socks and throwing them across the room.

"My deal." She collected the cards and shuffled them. As she dealt, she asked her question, "Tell me about your tattoo."

He chuckled. "That's an easy one." He tossed two cards to the center of the table. "I'll take two."

She checked her hand and almost fell on the floor in excitement. She already had two pairs and the hope of a full house. "I'll take one."

Cards dealt with, he began his story. "The night before I was leaving for the navy, my brother and I, drunk as skunks, went to a tattoo parlor to get something to remember each other by, to brand us as twins forever. Now that I'm sober, it seemed a stupid reason, but we did it anyway."

"Who chose the design?"

"Well now"—he grinned playfully—"that sounds like two questions. But, since you answered mine, I'll answer yours. One of the women we had with us. Now show me your hand."

"Two pair, queens and sixes." She hadn't pulled the full house, so she hoped this was enough.

"Fuck. Pair of aces. What now?"

Trying to look as if she'd given it deep thought, she tapped her finger on her chin and looked at him. "Let's go with pants."

He tossed the rest of his cards, and with mischief dancing on his lips, he stood to remove his jeans. The man drew down the zipper slowly, playing with her. What she could tell once his pants were removed was that he'd already been thinking about getting her naked.

"Give me the damn cards," he said with a grin, utterly unashamed of the tenting of his underwear.

She laughed at his frustration. She should tell him that she wasn't a novice card player. She'd learned a great deal while on a long shoot in Vegas. Although it really was a lot of luck of the cards sometimes.

He dealt and slapped down the remaining deck. "Your turn to share a story."

Looking at her cards, her heart sank. Not a thing worth keeping except the ace. She had to take four cards, and that meant she could still end up with a crap hand. "Four."

He looked at her, startled, and then his grin grew mischievous as he also took four cards. "Story. Make it a childhood one."

She thought for a moment and brought forth a memory. "After my dad married Rylee's mom, they moved in with us. Rylee brought a dog with her, and my cat, Puddles, a yellow, short-haired cat didn't like the dog. Rylee and I constantly tended to the dog from scratches from Puddles. The first time they fought, I thought to separate them. I mean Puddles was swatting the hell out of Champ—Rylee's dog. He wasn't fighting back. So I grabbed Puddles, picking her up."

"Uh-oh," he said. "I see where this is going."

"Yeah, there are times I can still see the scars of her scratches on me."

"Let me see."

She pushed up her sleeves and showed him her arm, tracing the barely noticeable lines inside her forearm. "But Rylee and I bonded real well after that. First, she tended my wounds, then we worked together, and it took us about six months for the dog and cat to cuddle together."

He shook his head. "Why don't you have a cat

now?"

"Too much travel before. Maybe I'll get one once I settle down with the boutique and moving. Okay, what do you have?" She was keeping her fingers crossed on this one.

"Nothing but ace high."

Relief flowed through her. "A pair of twos."

"Fuck," he said again at his loss. "This is not happening. How come I'm half-naked, and you're fully dressed?"

"Luck of the cards," she offered as an excuse. "Shirt," she added. Now she'd have to stare at it, but it was that or underwear, which definitely had to be last. "You're not new to this, are you?"

Without further comment—or ogling his fine chest—she took the cards to deal. "Your turn. A story from your childhood."

"Okay. Let me think." He fanned out his cards and grimaced at his hand. "I'll take three."

She also took three, and what a three she pulled. The game was in the bag. Or at least she hoped. His chances of beating it were slim.

"Okay, when I was about twelve or thirteen, my brothers and I had a bonfire to see Jesse off to college. While we were there, AJ brought up that we should all work together to protect people, and we joked about it. It didn't stick then, but I think when Jesse left the FBI, that thought came back to him because he started HIS for all of us to join. Me, I joined about a year after it was established." He nodded and smiled, and she could see his joy radiating. "Best decision I ever made. Working with my brothers is fantastic, and I love what we do."

"You've got a great family," she offered.

Their eyes connected, and she put the happiness for him and his family in her gaze. His eyes widened briefly and then softened. Electricity shot between them like in the old romance novels she'd read while hanging around on modeling shoots. They sat there, frozen, just staring at each other with hunger in their eyes.

Brad cleared his throat and broke the moment. "Thanks. Let me see your hand."

She turned over a flush, genuinely expecting to take the hand.

"Not so fast, princess." He turned over a full house, eights over fours.

Shit. She'd hoped to run the table. Oh well, she could manage one more hand. "What do you want me to remove?"

"Your shirt."

She sighed. At least she had a bra on. A sexy, lacy one, but at least it was one. Many times for comfort, she'd go braless when she wasn't going anywhere. She took off her shirt, folded it and set it on the table's edge. Then she thought better of it, picked it up, and tossed it across the room like Brad had been doing with his clothes. She laughed as it landed on the chair. Freeing her tight control, she was lost in the moment...the game...the possibility of what would occur when a champion was crowned.

"Okay. Your deal."

His eyes stayed on her chest as he shuffled the cards and dealt. "Your turn for a story. Anyone, but the more embarrassing, the better."

She laughed at that. "Let me think." She fanned out her cards and stopped. Could she win with the hand?

She'd thought so last time, but he'd still beat her. The odds were that this would be her hand for the win.

When she didn't take any cards, he raised an eyebrow, and she could've sworn she saw sweat on his brow.

"Okay, my first time going down the runway. I was so nervous that I threw up right before it was my turn for my first walk. I had three outfits I'd be modeling. What's worse, I hadn't eaten, so it was mostly the dry heaves. I missed my first two walks but finally made it for the third on shaky legs."

"Wow, what did the designer say?"

"Jacques laughed about it and took me under his wing. We're great friends now."

He cocked his head. "Do you keep in contact with him?"

"I haven't, but we promised to."

Brad nodded. "Then you should if he's so important to you. Don't let too long go by." He winked, changing the subject. "Okay, let's show our hands simultaneously since this may be the game-ender."

She nodded.

"One, two, three."

They both laid down their hands, face up, and Brad cursed. Her flush beat his straight.

"How the hell did you pull that again? Were you cheating?" he accused.

"How could I be cheating when you dealt?"

He stood and took off his underwear, his excitement in full swing. "Go to your room. I'll be there in a minute," he dictated as he stood.

A shudder raced through her at his voice. It wasn't how she'd expected the conversation to go after the game, but he was coming to her room. Her heartbeat pounded, and her pulse rate accelerated, and he hadn't even touched her. Heat began to infuse her body. Without questioning him, she bounded up from her chair, leaving their drinks and cards behind, and entered the room where she'd been staying. With her thoughts tangled around her feelings for Brad, she paced. Should she finish undressing and wait for him under the covers or would he undress her? Both ideas sent her a shiver of delight, and she hoped he'd hurry.

Since he didn't show right away, nervousness ate at her. Deciding to give herself the best chance of him coming to her bed, she quickly stripped off her jeans and undergarments, tossed her clothing in a pile, and climbed under the covers. If they were naked, the quicker they could have sex.

As she settled, Brad knocked softly then walked into the room—naked—holding a box of condoms and a red scarf. Delicious thoughts tingled through her. He'd surprised her the first time when he'd tied her wrists, so she should've expected he'd do it again. A man was serious about it if he took his scarf on a trip to Vegas—Sin City. And it had been an experience she'd not forgotten and somewhat craved. Thankfully, he wasn't all BDSM—or so he said. She wasn't ready for that lifestyle in the bedroom—even if it was Brad. He had explained that he liked to be in control and tying a woman's hands helped him achieve that feeling. Since he'd loved her body like crazy, she wasn't arguing, but she did miss rubbing her hands all over him during sex.

Seductively, she lowered the covers to below her chest, exposing her bare breasts to him. Brad's eyes didn't leave the mounds for a few minutes—at least, it seemed that long.

He looked away from her only long enough to deposit the box on the side table. Then, he pulled back the covers, baring her entire body, and whistled. "Even better than I remember."

The man did not have a way with words, but she knew he didn't mean it as a backhanded comment on her beauty. It was a compliment for both before and now.

Her breath caught when he ran a finger outlining a circle around her breast. "Heavenly." Her nipple puckered at the thought of what he might do to her.

When he leaned down, she thought he was going to kiss a nipple, but she was pleasantly surprised when his lips stopped just short of hers. "Are you sure?" he asked quietly.

Her heart melted. He was such a different man in the bedroom, and she wished…and hoped this man would appear more often. "Yes," she breathed, craving his kiss and touch.

And then, ever so softly, his lips touched hers, and something near an electrical shock reverberated around inside her and settled down low in her belly. As his lips moved over hers, it didn't take long before he became more aggressive, more dominant, taking control of the kiss with a fervor of desire and fire.

There was no denying that the man knew how to kiss.

His tongue slipped between the slight parting of her lips, and she sighed in pleasure. As their tongues met, he reached for her hand and pulled it above her head. He broke the kiss long enough to say, "Keep it there." Then his lips were devouring hers, exciting her body and tossing kindling on the fire burning within.

He tasted of beer, apple pie, and all male if that were a taste. Still, it's what she imagined when their tongues intertwined in a loving dance.

While he kissed her, he pulled her other arm above her head and held both wrists in one large hand. A delightful shiver ran through her knowing what he planned to do next. She never thought she'd enjoy this, but the want and need for him were too strong.

Breaking the kiss, he lifted his head and smiled before leaning over her and binding her wrists together, then tying them to the headboard. Not too tight. Nothing that would leave marks or cause her pain. "Are you okay?" he asked.

She nodded against the pillow. "I'm fine."

Brad's face morphed, and he looked like the kid about to grab a cookie from the cookie jar on the sly. Eager would be an easy word for his expression.

Climbing on the bed, Brad hovered over Madison, propped on his forearms. "I've wanted to be back here for a long time."

So had she if she were honest. It'd been nearly a year and a half. Okay, less than that, but not by much. Still, she remembered their night together like it was yesterday. Apparently, so had he.

Without giving her a chance to respond, Brad took her mouth in a heated kiss that curled her toes. This time, his tongue was all about domination and control. He didn't want her to forget he had it. He just didn't realize she eagerly allowed him to have that control. When something clicked in the bedroom and washed away the memory of every other sexual encounter she'd had in her life, she couldn't deny that she craved it.

Him.

When he broke the kiss, she moaned, but her pulse rate jumped as he kissed his way down her neck toward her breasts. She'd always had super-sensitive breasts, and having Brad love them nearly drove her insane.

Anticipation rode her, and she wished she could reach down and push his head close instead of him staring at a breast and breathing heavily on it. He shifted his weight to one side, and his hand captured her breast, massaging it.

Looking up at her, he gave her a lopsided, sexy grin. "You like this, don't you?"

Madison whimpered as he put his mouth on her breast. His touch—while grand—wasn't enough. "I don't like you teasing me," she responded with a slow smile.

He chuckled. "Princess, teasing is my middle name."

With that quip, he lowered his head and swiped his tongue across her taut nipple.

Madison instinctively arched her back to be closer to his mouth. "What's your real middle name?"

Another chuckle, and then he took her nipple into his mouth, sucked on it and then tugged it between his teeth while his hand squeezed her breast tightly.

Instant ecstasy.

"Lee. Bradley Lee," he breathed against her breast. Then, as if she hadn't had enough, he went to her other breast and gave it the same attention, and, once again, she almost jumped out of her skin in excited pleasure. She pulled against her bonds before remembering they were there. Relaxing her arms, she settled into allowing him to love her body without her interference.

"One day, I'll make you come by loving on your breasts alone," he stated.

Her body quivered at the thought. Anticipation flooded her veins. She liked that he planned to be with her again. She wasn't sure when she'd let her guard down—maybe it was when he'd cared for her after the accident, or maybe it was watching him all lost while looking at that brochure—but one thing was for sure, she was the one lost now. She wanted all of him. Wanted him to be the man she knew he could be and not the grump she'd seen, although he wasn't always that way with her.

"I need you, Brad," she heard herself saying. "Please."

Stroking his hand down her belly, he slid it between her thighs. When he reached her burning core, he exclaimed, "Damn, princess."

"Please, no more waiting," she begged, needing him to fill her.

With a lick of his fingers, he said, "Okay, this time. But before the night is through, my head will be between your thighs."

Another soft whimper escaped her at the promise of such exquisite pleasure.

Leaning across her, he reached for a condom, tore open the package with his teeth, and rolled it onto his magnificent length.

Her hands ached to touch and feel him sliding up and down, but she'd have to wait for that, too.

Brad positioned himself at her entrance and leaned back over her whole body. With one swift thrust, he nearly filled her. With a groan, he slid back out and pushed back in until he was fully seated, and she was ready to explode in orgasm.

"Good God, you feel so good. I'm not sure how long I can hold on," Brad admitted.

"I'm the same," she said through an erratic breath. With her heart beating fast, she moved her hips to savor the feel of him inside her.

"Christ," he exclaimed and started moving, stroking in and out of her in a steady rhythm, the friction rubbing her just right.

What began as slow, loving strokes became frantic and needy. For someone who needed control, Brad was rapidly losing it. And she didn't care.

Madison would die a happy woman with Brad inside her.

Reaching down, his thumb brushed across her nub and rubbed it, teasing her, taunting her with what she knew was to come. He suckled on her breast. Then, she was rapidly climbing that cliff, nearly ready to jump off into erotic satisfaction. "I'm going to come, Brad."

He lifted his mouth and looked at her through hooded eyes. "Go, princess."

Stars burst in front of her eyes, and she fell into the abyss of ecstasy. She cried out as every limb felt weighted and then free to float. The ripple of pleasure came in waves, and she refused to fight it. For what seemed an interminable amount of time, she came back to herself, sated in bliss and feeling Brad throb inside her as he came with a loud groan before he then collapsed on top of her.

Another drawback of having her hands tied was that she couldn't run her fingers through his hair or up and down his back at this moment.

With a groan, Brad lifted his head and smiled

before sliding out of her and leaving her empty. He leveraged himself off the bed and quickly untied her hands before going to the bathroom and disposing of the condom.

Although they didn't hurt, Madison rubbed her now free wrists and wondered if he'd ever let her touch him during lovemaking.

Walking back into the room with a hand towel, Brad smiled. "This is the point of the evening where I say something stupid, and you walk out on me."

Madison went instantly on alert. Was he trying to ruin a good time? Hell, she wasn't asking for anything beyond sex—at least not out loud—and she hadn't even asked for more than tonight. She swallowed at the lump in her throat. "What do you want to say this time?"

He reached down and gently cleansed her. Why did the man have to be so contradictory? "Only, thank you." He tossed the towel toward the bathroom door and told her to scoot over. When she did, he climbed into the bed and pulled her close. "Besides," he said, "I've still got plenty of time to put my foot in my mouth tonight."

Although he chuckled, she didn't find it very funny. He must've realized that when she stiffened in his arms.

"I'm just joking." He sighed wearily. "I'm sorry if I sometimes come across wrong. I don't always end up saying what I mean. I would never say anything purposefully to hurt you."

She didn't know him well enough to know if that were true, and her most significant remembrance was the bucket list comment. Not a shining moment for him. She really had to stop holding that against him. It had just hurt, whether he'd meant it or not. Like other men, he'd taken Madison, the model, to bed before. She thought this time might be different, but history had given her a slanted probability. She wanted to rely on him, but could she?

Chapter Nineteen

Watching Madison in her tight jeans and white blouse eating breakfast at his table, Brad's gut clenched in an unyielding knot. For the first time, he wasn't sure how to act after sleeping with a woman. In the past, it'd always been casual, where he might or might not see the woman again, depending on the sex and how she reacted. Clingy he didn't do. Madison acted calm, like he'd want her to react if he'd just picked her up or had that type of easy relationship with her, but deep down, he didn't want her to act like it meant nothing.

Because it had meant a hell of a lot to him, and even though he'd resolved Madison would be his, he'd never expected the power that came between them in bed, and that scared the fuck out of him. No woman had twisted his insides like she had.

Although he was a bit offset, he had a nervous excitement about him. He thought about exploring all that Madison was and all that could be between them, of becoming a couple. Just doing the little things, like holding her hand in public as they walked down the street, appealed to him, and he didn't feel like a pansy for it. Doing anything—and everything—with Madison appealed to him.

Putting her fork down on the now empty plate, which had held bacon and eggs, Madison sighed and drew his attention back to her in person, not in thought.

"That was good. I'd forgotten how tasty food can be. I will be as huge as a house if I don't watch myself."

He set down the coffee cup and winked at her. "Never. You're beautiful."

Their eyes met and burned from the heat searing between them. He could so easily pick her up and carry her back off to bed, but he wanted more than the bedroom between them. So, he held back his urge to reach out to her. "What's your plan for today?"

"Remember? I'm meeting with the contractor at the club, but not until later this morning."

"Do you want to just hang out until then?"

She shrugged. "That's fine." She paused nervously. "I'm wondering…."

"Yeah," he asked, not sure he wanted to hear what she'd been wondering. Her mind was a dangerous thing at least to his psyche.

"It's about the hypnosis. I guess I don't understand why you aren't jumping on it. Don't you want your memory restored?"

Ah, hell. He'd rather have his eyelids cut off than deal with this. "It's complicated."

"Then, uncomplicate it for me."

Wearily, he replied, "Let's just say I might not like what I find." That was an understatement if what he'd been told happened had been true.

She worried her bottom lip briefly, as if deep in thought, before she spoke again. "But you have an idea already, don't you?"

Brad shifted in his high-back chair, which had always been so comfortable, but now felt like he sat on hot coals. "Yeah."

Madison reached across the table and covered his

hand with hers, and heat shot straight through his body to somewhere down south. Damn the effect she had on him. "Tell me. I won't judge."

Fuck. People said that all the time, but they did judge, at least in their minds. But he should be honest about the situation if he wanted any chance at that relationship with her. That was easier said than done. He couldn't stand her censure on the matter.

"Talk to me, Brad," she requested softly.

A heavy burden weighed on him, and he wanted it lifted. He knew that wouldn't happen until he cleared his name—if possible. But maybe, sharing it with her— with Madison—would help ease it. That was if she didn't judge him as she'd promised. Fuck. He'd never even told all his brothers the truth. Only his twin. How was it he wanted to—*yes, wanted* to—share his embarrassment and disgrace with her?

It had been his long-held secret. One he probably should've done something about before now, but that feeling that he might've been wrong always sat in the way. He wasn't sure if he could hate himself more if that was the truth, and he hadn't wanted to find out. But he'd changed his mind and needed to find out the truth, no matter what it was. Could he share it with her and expect her to stand by him? Everything was so new and uncertain between them; he didn't want to scare her off before giving them a chance. She already meant so much to him. She always had, and it wasn't because of who she was in the public eye but because of who she was in private. Strong. Loving. A woman worth risking everything for.

"Come on," she coaxed. "Let's sit in the living room where it's more comfortable, and you can explain." She preceded him into the living room and sat on the brown leather sofa. When she patted the space next to her, he sat obediently.

Brad took a deep breath and held it momentarily while considering where to start. There was so much he didn't know. So much speculation. She pulled his hand into hers, covered it with the other, and settled them on her thigh. That jolt of touch shot a bolt of longing through him. The fact that she could do something so tender melted his heart. Looking at their intertwined hands bolstered his courage. She wouldn't judge. She wasn't that type of woman. He just knew it in his heart.

After Brad cleared his throat, he began, "When I was in the Secret Service, I was part of an advance team to prepare for the president's visit to Colombia."

She nodded. "You explained that before. You also explained you lost a day in your memory."

He swallowed hard. "Yeah, well, I didn't explain what happened after my brain cleared. After I woke up." His first memory had been a confused and frightful one.

Madison tilted her head. "Go on," she prodded.

Blowing out a breath, he went for it, laying it all on the line. "I woke up with a prostitute in my bed." He heard his heart pounding in his eardrums beating a staccato rhythm.

He watched her blink several times, but she said nothing, so he rushed on. "I have no idea how she got there, and I don't believe anything happened, even though she said it did. The prostitutes there were notorious for setting up Americans on business and running to their bosses to get paid. The bosses generally paid up to keep things quiet. The Secret Service isn't like that. They don't pay people off." His thumb rubbed the back of her hand. "Unfortunately, they do believe them without evidence."

She hadn't moved, nor had her expression changed. "Okay."

Without her saying more, he had no feel for what was twisting around in her mind. Yet she hadn't separated their joined hands. He took it as a small win.

"I think someone drugged me and that the prostitute was a setup."

It took her a moment to reply. She eventually asked, "But why?"

He heaved a weary breath and leaned back on the couch. "That, I don't know."

"So, you think someone drugged you and you lost all of that time and woke up with a…a prostitute?"

"Yes."

"Well, if that's the case, why are you worried about doing the hypnosis? Maybe you'll remember why someone did this to you."

His shoulders slumped, and he admitted his worst fear. "Because, what if I find out I really got drunk and hired that prostitute?"

After hesitating, she leaned back and pressed her arm on his shoulder. Damn, she felt nice and warm all next to him. He separated their hands and slid his arm behind her. Pulling her tightly against him, he reveled in the feel of her so close, the smell of the fruity scent of her shampoo and the sexy smell of her perfume.

"Somehow I doubt that's true. You don't seem like the type of man to do that. Even intoxicated."

He chuckled at that. "How do you know what kind of man I am?"

When her soft hand touched his chest, he almost jumped out of his skin with need.

"I know you're an honorable man. A bit ornery from what I've experienced and heard, but honorable nonetheless. Besides." she smiled, "you wouldn't have needed to hire someone for your bed."

Her unwavering faith in him shook him to the core. This woman barely knew him but believed in him...believed in his innocence. "Maddie," he started, "I want more than just the bedroom." Wow, he'd actually said it. And right after he'd dropped his bombshell on her. He might be the biggest idiot around.

She sat up, and his heart fell. Already she pulled away. Maybe he just should've settled for the bedroom.

"What do you mean?" she asked softly, her eyes large chocolate pools.

"Like date," he said with a swallow. He'd not asked a girl to date since high school. It had seemed hard then, but it was ten times worse now especially if she said no because he still would be protecting her, which would make it damn uncomfortable.

"Like a boyfriend?" she teased. "Do I get a promise ring and everything?"

He had a momentary thought of turning her over his knee and spanking that sweet ass of hers for her smartass mouth. Instead, he pulled her to him, where she belonged—beside him. "No, smarty-pants. No ring, just dating. A..." He swallowed against the words coming forth. "...a relationship."

Of all things to do, she giggled. That smacking her backside looked more and more promising. However, she might like it since she liked to be tied up. He'd have to explore that option. He'd never spanked a woman.

He guessed it could be fun and erotic, but he didn't see it. He didn't hurt women, and it had to hurt, right?

"That word seemed painful."

He chuckled. "It wasn't so bad since I was thinking of you. So, Madison Maxwell, do you want to date me?" *Out of your league* flashed through his brain, but he shoved it aside.

"That depends," she said.

He closed his eyes. He could suffer through anything if she agreed to be his. "Depends upon what?"

"Do you want to date Madison the supermodel, who was on your bucket list, or Madison, your sister-in-law's sister?"

What kind of fucking question was that? Shit. He was joking the first time they'd been together. His mouth seemed to catch up to him more and more often these days. He tilted her chin up to gaze into each other's eyes. "You, Maddie. It's always been just you."

When her eyes watered, he thought he'd said something wrong. Then she kissed him. A light, flirty kiss, something that had him craving much more. When she pulled back, she smiled. "Okay, let's try it. I'll be your girlfriend."

Elation filled him, but worry about her safety crowded it from his mind. "I'm still your bodyguard, though, and I must be vigilant when we're together." She had to know that no matter how much he wanted to, he couldn't give her all his attention when they were out.

"I understand," she said. "How about when you've got two people watching? Like now?"

The teasing tone of her voice sent a shudder racing through him, and all he saw was her lips as the words passed through them. Liking her line of thinking, Brad smiled while his pulse thudded. "Well, as long as we're inside, I guess we're okay."

She sat up and tossed him a sexy smile. "Bedroom."

Her smile shot straight to his gut. Damn the woman got to him, and he loved every minute of it.

Jumping up and sprinting to the bedroom, she was gone before he had a chance even to swat her sweet bottom. This Madison was the one he wanted—fun and loving.

He stood, already sporting wood. She was a loving partner, and his body heated thinking about what would come. With a fast pace, he crossed the living room and caught up with her in the bedroom before he remembered he needed a condom. "My bedroom," he dictated before she could finish undressing. He'd never brought a woman home to his bed. He always went to theirs. It was only right that she was the first one there because she might be the last.

Chapter Twenty

Madison Maxwell was Brad Hamilton's girlfriend. She almost snickered out loud. Girlfriend? What was she, twelve? But she couldn't think of another term to describe their new relationship right off the cuff. A flurry of nerves skittered through her at the thought of not only being in a relationship, but being in one with a supposedly volatile Brad Hamilton. She'd overlooked or dismissed something when she'd made the decision because she'd never seen that side of him. One she began to doubt existed.

He hadn't been bad to her. Not really. But she'd heard from Rylee all about him and his "attitude," as Rylee put it, and Brad had admitted to not being "sociable" all the time. She hadn't explored with him exactly what that meant. She guessed if she saw that side of him, she'd deal with it when it happened. Until then, she wasn't going to second-guess her decision. She liked Brad, even though she needed to learn to read him more. He held an excellent poker face she'd seen when he dealt with his brothers and men.

The drive to La Belle met with a tense silence as if anything said would break the new ground they were building. She'd wracked her brain the entire ride to think of something to say that didn't lead their thoughts to the bedroom.

A tiny sliver of worry broke into her thoughts that

maybe they only had the bedroom. But, it couldn't be. He'd shared something very personal with her.

The two of them took the rented SUV he'd received while his truck was in the shop, with Ken and Sam following in Ken's SUV. She didn't care that this might be overkill. After the truck accident, she didn't care to chance things. When they arrived at the club, Brad held her back in the SUV until Ken and Sam cleared the place. It took a while, and she wondered if they were questioning every worker. With a shudder at thinking of what had happened, she thanked them.

Finally released, but told to stay close, Madison entered the bar and was stunned at the transformation. The tables, chairs, and booths were gone. The place looked so enormous without most of the furniture. She spied Jeff Benzine, the contractor, and made her way to him. He and three men were studying the base of the long, mahogany bar.

Approaching the group, she addressed the contractor. "Hello." She smiled curiously. "How are you going to get it out?" She gestured to the bar. It would be a shame if the beautiful piece of furniture couldn't be sold to another bar owner like the other furniture—the furniture that had been salvageable anyway.

Jeff straightened. "It was brought in pieces, and that's how we'll take it out. It's just bolted to the floor, but don't worry, my guys will take care of it easy enough," he said with pride. He'd apologized for not getting to it sooner, but a regularly booked job had taken his attention as he was squeezing them in early.

She'd love to stay and watch this feat, but she'd promised Brad she wouldn't wait too long. "You wanted to talk with me about the change we requested?"

Nodding, Jeff turned and picked up large, rolled pieces of paper with the construction plans printed on them. "Yes."

They spent the next fifteen minutes discussing the change she and Rylee wanted in the dressing rooms. They found they had to give a little elsewhere to make it happen. No matter, it all still worked for what they wanted. Rylee would be happy they'd been able to make it happen. Most customers wanted more room when they tried on clothing. They'd survive with a little less storage room, but the place was still huge.

After thanking Jeff, Madison felt Brad suddenly close to her side, holding her elbow. "Where's the back door?"

His firm, authoritative tone stopped her, and her heart beat fast. What the hell was the problem?

Instead of answering his question, she asked, "What's wrong?" It hadn't slipped her mind that she'd agreed to do whatever he said, when he said it, or the fact that she didn't give him the chance to direct.

"We've got company. Ken and Sam can't legally detain them."

"Them?" A sick feeling settled in her stomach at the thought of running into Casden and Rogers again after the accident.

"Ah, hell. Why can't you just do as you're told?"

"I'll do it, but you must tell me what to do first."

"We're leaving via the back door."

"Okay, this way," she said, and turned them toward the rear exit without delay.

Before they could leave, Casden and Rogers

walked into the club with Ken tight on their heels, a pinched look on his face.

"Miss Maxwell," Casden said as he approached her.

Brad stepped before her, shoving her behind him when she tried to step aside. "Get out. You're not welcome here." His voice rang loud and authoritative.

Casden narrowed his eyes at Brad. "Ah, it's a Hamilton mutt. How many of you are running loose about the town?"

Brad stiffened but didn't take the bait. "I said, get out." His voice was strong and threatening. It'd make her think twice about staying.

At this point, Madison was confused at the contradiction she'd been hearing about the men. Casden and Rogers acted harmlessly at the moment, and Brad was taking over, taking away her ability to decide on whether she spoke with them. Her ire rose at him more than the two men bothering her—the two men who may have had them run off the road. A shiver slipped up her spine, and goose bumps skittered across her skin.

Speaking over Brad, Rogers's smooth voice said, "We're here about our offer."

"She turned you down," Brad spat out before she could speak.

"Yes, she did," Casden said, as if it were a bad taste in his mouth. "We're here with another offer."

"She doesn't want it," Brad once again spoke for her before she could say anything. She wanted to slap him in the back of the head, but didn't want to make a scene in front of the two unwelcome visitors, which was also why she didn't contradict his word either, no matter how much she wanted to jump in front of him and tell the two men off herself.

"She hasn't even heard it yet." Casden reached inside a leather messenger bag, and Ken and Brad's hands went to the weapons holstered on their hips. Casden stopped and put his hands up. "Easy, man. I'm just getting the offer." He slowly reached into the bag with one hand and withdrew a few sheets of paper.

"I said," Brad said, "she doesn't want it."

Ignoring Brad, Casden spoke directly to her, even though she could only see a sliver of him from behind Brad. "We've heard you have power of attorney for the place from your sister while she's out of the country."

She stiffened, and panic seized her. How had they found that out? It had been put in place since Rylee would be out on assignment, and a lot needed to be done in the meantime. But it wasn't a public knowledge thing as far as she knew. How did they even know about Rylee leaving the country? Fear laced her veins. Brad hadn't lied about their reach.

"If you look at our new offer, you'll find it more than fair. We'll even take the place as is."

"Are you deaf?" Brad started. "She's not interested. Now leave."

Not finding her voice, Madison stood there, still reeling from them knowing she had a power of attorney and that Rylee was leaving the country. It was bad, so very bad, in her mind.

"Well, I'll just leave this here for you." Casden slid the papers on the bar, and the two men left quietly with Ken hot on their heels.

When Brad turned to her, it all erupted from her. "What the hell is wrong with you? You don't speak for me!" Blood was pumping fast, and she couldn't stop herself now. "And hiding me? Treating me like I don't have a brain in my head to make my own decisions? If this indicates how you'll be treating me, we need to break things off now. I won't tolerate it."

Chest heaving from her outburst, she swallowed hard to calm herself. She appreciated his protecting her, but at the same time, she wanted to rip his head off.

"I didn't hear you say anything."

"You never gave me a chance. You spoke for me. And something tells me if I had spoken, you'd have cut me off since it had to be your show," she seethed and couldn't stop the anger racing through her bloodstream.

"Look, I knew what I was doing, and you didn't need to talk with those men."

"That's my decision to make," she insisted.

Brad rolled his eyes. "God, woman. You blow hot and cold."

That shot her blood pressure sky-high. "Oh no you don't," she said firmly. "You were a big, overprotective alpha male who acted like he had a damsel in distress who was useless. Protecting me is one thing, but I won't tolerate that treatment."

He reached out to touch his hand to her face, and she flinched away. "No, Brad. What you did was wrong."

"How? I protected you."

Frustration filled her. "Yes, you did, but I didn't need that type of protection. They were just here to give me an offer, not knock me off."

His nostrils flared. "How do you know? Are you trained to read criminals?"

"Well, no, but I had you and Ken here. That was enough. What you did was overboard." He didn't see it, and she wasn't sure he ever would. Her heart sank. She couldn't be with someone who treated her thus anytime he perceived a threat.

"Look, it's how things will be until you're safe."

"Then we have a problem, Brad, because I won't date a man who treats me like that."

"What the fuck?" he protested loudly, and looked like he wanted to kick a nonexistent chair.

She folded her arms over her aching chest. "It was a mistake to think we could have a relationship outside the bedroom." And she wasn't sure she'd allow him back into her bedroom.

Ignoring his astonished face, she turned from him toward the door. "I'm done here." She walked toward the exit, not caring if he followed or walked in front of her. She just had to leave, and knowing she had to get into the close confines of the SUV with him didn't help her relax.

She'd been in this relationship less than one day. That had to be a record for her, and her previous relationships had been short-lived.

Things were about to be tense between them, but she'd persevere. Maybe she could convince Matt to take his place instead of working at night. Then, it'd be like seeing Brad every time she glanced at him. That wouldn't work either. She was just fucked until they figured out this threat against her. Maybe she could help them bring Casden and Rogers down. That's what she needed to do. Now, to get Brad to agree.

Chapter Twenty-One

Brad's temper still soared as they pulled up at Devon and Rylee's home. Madison had wanted to visit her sister again before Rylee's trip began the next day. They'd stopped for lunch, and nothing had been said between them. That'd been the hardest burger to swallow.

Ken, being a witness to what had happened—minus Madison's blow up—seemed to understand the tension in the air and kept Sam quiet as they all had dined together instead of Ken and Sam at another table like normal. He'd wanted them closer to Madison just in case those two thugs decided to follow them. Madison may not worry about them, but he did. Someone had tried to kill them, and he didn't trust Casden and Rogers.

She hadn't said anything about everyone eating together, but her body language told him she didn't agree or didn't understand. She'd never be so rude as to ask to eat separately, but it must've added to her ire.

Slamming the SUV door like a petulant child, Brad followed Madison inside the brick home to a screaming child, who was teething, and two tired-looking parents.

A good reason not to have kids, he decided. He liked his eardrums intact and his sleep only interrupted by a beautiful woman reaching for him.

After settling Mitch to sleep, Devon invited Brad to

run with him. Brad knew it was a ruse to speak with him privately, especially when his brother had said they'd only be running a mile so they wouldn't be gone long. With Ken and Sam there to protect Madison, he agreed. He trusted Rylee could take care of herself. Plus, he needed to get away from Madison for a bit.

They headed out after changing into shorts from a small duffel bag in the SUV that held his workout clothing. About a quarter mile from the house, Devon said, "Spill it."

Acting as if he had no idea what his brother spoke about, he responded, "I don't know what you're talking about." Matt was the one he talked to about things, like what was happening in his life, and he wasn't sure he'd even speak to him about a woman. Yet he'd told Matt about his first night with Madison. Not the particulars, but that he'd slept with her at the wedding reception.

"Madison looks pissed off, which means you did something."

They turned right down another road, following the sidewalk. The suburban neighborhood had similar style A-frame houses with trim-cut, medium-sized yards, most sporting swing sets in the back of their fenced yards.

He may as well tell his brother. Madison would most likely tell Rylee. Then her sister would tell Devon, and who knew how much the story would have morphed by then, and he'd be the bad guy all around. Besides, his brother would understand and be on his side. Madison just didn't get it.

Brad cleared his throat and said, "Yeah, I pissed off Madison, but she's wrong."

Devon laughed. "When are you going to learn

women are never wrong?"

He did a double take with his brother. "The fuck they aren't."

"Wait until you find that one woman and marry her. Believe me, no matter what, she's never wrong. Even when she technically is."

That made no fucking sense to him, so he left it. "Well, we were at the club and the fuckers Casden and Rogers showed up."

"Fuck."

"Yeah," Brad said. "Anyhow, I put her behind me and wouldn't let them near her. She didn't like it."

"That doesn't sound bad," Devon said, not even sounding winded. "If that's all, she is wrong, but you still don't tell her. You two talk and compromise if you have to until you can live with it and she's happy."

"There's more."

"Uh-oh. Something tells me this is why she's angry."

He took a deep breath and then spoke. "Well, I also wouldn't let them speak to her. I spoke for her and told them to leave. I also told them she wasn't interested in the deal they brought her."

"Are you some kind of idiot?" Then, "Turn left here."

Being on the left, he led the way. "What do you mean? She needed to be as far away from that scum as possible, and if they'd started talking with her, she wouldn't have been able to stop when it was necessary. She's all heart and wouldn't be rude."

"Like you?" Devon chuckled.

He didn't take it as a slight since it was true. "Yeah, like me. Anyway, she said she refused to have a relationship with anyone who would act like an overprotective alpha on her." Didn't all women want an alpha? He fully admitted he was. There was no reason to act or react differently. That wouldn't change about him. And he was protective of those he cared about. She could call it overprotective if she wanted. It had needed to be done.

It took him a moment to realize Devon had stopped. He walked back to his brother, and before he could ask if he was okay, Devon asked, "Relationship?"

Shit. He hadn't meant to share that part. Well, fuck. Madison would probably tell Rylee that part, too, so he'd best set the record straight. "Yeah. This morning, we started dating each other." It sounded odd to say those words, yet concerning Madison, they just felt right.

Devon looked at him as if he'd lost his mind. "What the fuck are you doing, Brad? This is not some woman to fuck around with. This is my sister-in-law."

Standing in the middle of the empty sidewalk, they had this conversation. One he had hoped to have with no one, not even his twin. "I like her. This morning I asked her, and she said yes."

"Are you just fucking around? I mean, I haven't known you to admit to dating anyone, but is this for real?" Devon asked, his jaw clenched.

He thought momentarily, knowing what Devon's "for real" meant. Was he serious about Madison? They barely knew each other, even though he felt he knew everything about her. He wanted to be near her, share his day with her, talk about the intimate things couples do, and be in her arms and bed.

"I'm not in love with her, if that's what you're

asking. We're just getting to know each other."

"Look, I know you slept together in Vegas." At Brad's sharp look, he added, "I saw Madison leave your room. She didn't look happy then, and she doesn't look happy today after you claim you two came to an understanding. You can't treat her like every other woman you've met. Not if you care for her."

He did care for her—more than he'd admit, even to himself. "I don't see why. Either she likes me as I am or she doesn't."

Devon gave him a frustrated look. "Let's finish this run."

They set a comfortable pace, and it was about one-tenth of a mile before Devon broke the silence. "You're not who you were before you left the Secret Service. That man might not appeal to someone like Madison, but the old Brad would be great with her."

What. The. Fuck?

"You need to drop the anger, and doing that hypnotherapy might be just the thing to help you."

He chewed on that, unsure how to respond. Had he really been that different? He'd known he held a great deal inside him, and his temper was shorter than it used to be before the incident in Colombia.

"No matter what you find, I think it'll help you. You've been holding this anger at the world, and it's the not knowing what happened that's the real issue. Go. Find out."

"You and Rylee didn't do it," he shot back, trying to steer the conversation away from himself.

"We decided we didn't need it. Our lives came together in the Colorado mountains, and that's how we want to remember it."

"You're just going to let it go?"

"We are. It's not holding us back like it's holding you back. We don't need it to figure out our lives. We fell in love and got married twice. Once is all that matters to us."

They went straight past the point they'd initially turned right and continued, nearing the house. "Madison said I should try it," Brad added.

Devon stumbled and righted himself. "You discussed the particulars of the situation with her?"

He had. He'd opened up to her. A little offset at how light that revelation made him feel, he just grunted his response.

"Is there a reason you don't want to try it?" Devon asked when the home came into sight.

"None I want to discuss," Brad said gruffly.

"Fair enough. I'm always here if you decide you want to discuss it or anything."

Brad rolled his eyes. "Thanks, big bro."

Devon chuckled. "Usually, it's Jesse who's called that."

"Well, you've been acting like him."

"Okay. Then I will be my big brother and give you some advice. You go in there and apologize to Madison for being a jerk."

"But it was necessary," Brad sputtered, like a child losing an argument.

"Necessary or not, you apologize if you want her back."

This relationship crap was more complicated than he'd figured. Why should he apologize when he wasn't wrong? She just didn't understand. If she did, she'd have thanked him.

"Most importantly—you don't do it again."

They stopped in the front yard and stretched. He couldn't promise he wouldn't do it again. Her protection was first and foremost in everything he did.

After confirming with Ken that all was well, they entered the house, and Brad received a cold shoulder from Madison as Devon kissed Rylee. Hell, he'd have to apologize even though he wasn't wrong. Would she see it? No time like the present.

"Maddie, can I speak with you in the kitchen for a minute?"

She nodded once and led the way to the kitchen, where she spun around to him but didn't say a word.

God, she was beautiful, even when she was obviously angry.

"Look"—he rubbed his hand up and down his sweaty neck—"I'm sorry." There, he'd said it. Now it would be over, and she'd be back in his arms.

"Sorry for what?"

Fuck. He didn't expect questions about this. She should've just accepted his apology and been done with it.

"Um...whatever I did to upset you."

When her face reddened and her jaw tightened, he realized he'd said the wrong thing. But how was that possible?

"What exactly was it you did?"

Son of a bitch. He was going to kill Devon for this. He'd made it sound so simple. This was far from simple. He felt like he was digging himself a hole, and it was getting deeper with each word he spoke.

"For what I did at the club."

"You mean the hiding me and speaking for me?"

He winced. "Yeah."

She licked her lips, and his gaze fastened there. She hadn't done it to be sensual, but it was all the same. If only he could kiss her. They were good together like that.

"Are you really sorry?" she asked, crossing her arms over her chest.

Shit. He couldn't keep this up. Devon was wrong. Had to be. He couldn't lie to Madison about how he felt. He didn't feel one bit sorry for how things had gone down at the club. "No," he said softly. "I'm not."

"Then why did you apologize?"

"Devon said I should if I wanted to keep the peace between us."

The corner of her mouth ticked up. "He did. And do you always do what your brothers tell you?"

"Hell no. Except when we're working. But I've never been in a relationship before and had no idea how to handle our situation."

"Let me set you straight. With me, only apologize when you mean it."

Okay, he was definitely going to kick Devon's ass for that relationship advice. "Gotcha. Are we okay?" he prodded, hoping they were because he couldn't deal with all this bullshit of figuring out a woman's mind.

"No."

Stunned, his heart sank. He thought his bit of honesty would've broken through the anger she held.

"You still treated me terribly. I'm not ready to get over it. Probably not until you realize what you did was too much. Protecting me is one thing. Not letting me speak and treating me like you did was another."

Well, fuck. They were at a standstill because he wouldn't be sorry, and he'd do it again—in a heartbeat.

Chapter Twenty-Two

Damn, she held her anger for a long time. Couldn't she just get over it like men did? Why did women hang onto asinine things for so long? That was part of the reason he'd never allowed himself to get too entangled with a woman. Emotions and drama. He worked better with lust being the only emotion flowing between him and a woman. Yet something about Madison flowed within him, and while he'd yet to identify it, he couldn't dismiss it.

Winding the spaghetti they'd added as a side to their chicken parmesan around his fork, he bit the bullet and asked the one question that could possibly make her angrier. He probably would start World War III, but he had to get this over with before he went insane himself. He wanted her in his bed that night. And many nights after. So he opened his mouth and asked, "Are you still mad?"

Her fork paused halfway to her mouth with a piece of breaded chicken breast on it. "Are you sorry for what you did?"

He squirmed as if he'd been put under a bright spotlight. Hell no, he wasn't sorry. Why couldn't she understand he did it to protect her? However, the more he thought about it, the more he saw her point of speaking for her even though she would've had trouble getting rid of them like he had. "I think I was wrong speaking for you."

"Think?"

Ignoring that, he hurriedly added, "But I'm not sorry for protecting you from them." He shoved the spaghetti, dripping with marinara sauce, into his mouth to keep him from saying something else that would screw him worse than he already was.

Madison put her fork on her plate and gave him her full attention. He saw the bright flashing sign that said he was fucked.

"You think you were wrong or you know?"

Ah hell. No man liked to admit he was wrong. Part of him still didn't believe he'd been wrong, but if it bothered her so severely, he'd done something wrong. Keeping her happy should be what he was about. Safe and happy.

"I guess"—he toyed with the spaghetti on his plate—"that I could've allowed you to talk with them. Only," Brad added quickly, "I worried you'd be too nice and we'd end up sitting down with them. I couldn't allow that to happen."

"Why not?"

He looked up at her. "Have you forgotten the car accident so quickly?"

"No, I haven't. But I don't see what those men could've done in broad daylight with you and Ken protecting me. Plus, there were workers in the club."

He dropped his fork and rubbed the back of his neck in agitation. Leave it to her to make sense of the situation. "You've got a point there."

With one eyebrow cocked, she probed, "Have I?"

Shifting in his seat again, he grimaced. This apology thing was damn hard. "Okay, I was wrong.

But," Brad pointed out, "only for speaking for you."

Madison smiled brightly as if she'd just won a prize. "I can accept that."

A whoosh of air released from his lungs in relief. "Does this mean you aren't mad any longer?"

"Oh, I'm still a bit upset about the whole alpha-male thing, but I know you did it in my best interest. But no, I'm no longer mad about the incident as far as it matters."

"Thank God. Does this mean you'll be back in my bed tonight?"

"About that—"

Fuck. Fuck. Fuck. Could he not catch a break? "About that what?"

"I have a request. No, a demand."

What the hell? Women didn't make demands of him. In the bedroom, he was in charge. But he was curious about whatever it was she wanted. "Go on."

Her face went pink, and she had difficulty holding his gaze. "I want to—to tie you up this time."

He might've stopped breathing for a moment at the audacity of the question. Tie him up? That was an easy answer. *Hell no.* Even his twin—the gentler of the two—wouldn't become submissive in bed. Hamilton men didn't do it as far as he knew. "No," he said firmly, thinking that cursing with it might worsen the matter.

Crossing her arms over her chest, she seemed to have regained her pluck. "Well then, I won't be in your bed."

He wanted to bang his head against the table, dinner plates and all. *Women.* How the hell did his brothers live with them? Did they always get their way by holding back their favors? If he ever had a wife, he wouldn't tolerate that behavior. And, if he lived in a cave, that attitude would be okay. Since he didn't, he had to be realistic and keep his inner caveman hidden.

Brad tried to remember when he'd first tied a woman's hands. It had been in high school with Peggy Bell, where she wouldn't keep her hands off him and almost made him come before they got completely naked together. Plus, she'd left awful marks on his back that had scabbed and been a running joke in the locker room.

Yeah, it was after that he began tying his lover's hands to keep them at bay, and he'd found he liked the control and hadn't stopped. That'd been for what, thirteen or fourteen years? And she wanted him just to change. To give up control? She'd lost her fucking mind.

But he needed her in his bed. Needed her by his side. Always. That thought set him back a mile. Always was it? No. That must be his loneliness talking because he'd never thought that of anyone before. He couldn't love her, could he? No. *Definitely not.* But he did like the hell out of her.

Her firm setting told him she wouldn't budge on this issue. So, if he wanted her in his bed, he needed to bend. Hell, couldn't he just buy her flowers, chocolate, or some shit? Wasn't that how you made up to a woman?

They weren't even going to have makeup sex after their first big—albeit not the first—argument. What the fuck was wrong with this picture? She must not care for him at all if she puts a demand that she knows will keep them from being in bed together.

That was it. She was doing it on purpose. Pushing

him. Knowing he'd say no, she'd be free to stay out of bed. Well, he'd see about that. A woman would not win a battle of wills with him. No way in hell would he allow that to happen.

"Okay," he heard himself saying before fully realizing he was calling her bluff and possibly putting himself in a sticky situation.

Madison's eyes widened and darkened around the rims. "Really?" she asked, bewildered.

Oh fuck. She wasn't calling his bluff. What the hell had he just agreed to? "What I meant to say was—"

She cut him off before he could change his mind. "No, you already said yes." Something like glee entered her features. Was that how he looked every time he was ready to tie up a woman?

Tied up. Losing control. He hoped she realized how much she meant to him for him to allow this change in their sexual life. He hoped he could handle it. He wasn't a sixteen-year-old boy who could barely keep it back when a girl touched him, but with the way he wanted Madison, she would only have to touch him and he'd explode. That would be seriously embarrassing. Football stats, he thought, as he reached down and adjusted his bulging erection. He'd keep the numbers going through his mind when she touched him, and he'd last.

Eager to be inside her and get this over with, he stood. "I'm done eating. You?" He picked up his plate and reached for hers, not caring if she was finished. She'd asked for sex, and he wasn't going to disappoint her.

They emptied the contents of their dishes into the trash and loaded the dishwasher without a word between them, except "thank you" when an item was passed for either rinsing or loading.

Sensing her nervousness, he clasped one of her hands and pulled her close. "Are you looking forward to having me at your mercy?"

For a moment, she stood stock-still. Then her body relaxed, and she smiled. "Yes."

Where he thought he'd have to drag her to the bedroom, he was surprised when, with their joined hand, she tugged him to his door. Inside the room, he pulled her back to him, this time so close he could feel her pebbled nipples on his chest. The words "I love you" almost spilled out, and he freaked momentarily. Where had that garbage come from?

Instead, he said, "While you may have the lead in bed—tonight—I have the lead in undressing you, and I'm going to enjoy every moment of it."

She shivered, and he stood taller at her reaction. Knowing he affected her as much as she did him left him with a heady feeling.

To prove his point, he kissed her hard and demanding, setting the tone for the evening. His tongue slipped past her soft lips and into her mouth where their tongues played the tune of lovers. Kissing her was intoxicating. Something he might never tire of doing. He'd kiss her every day of her life if she'd let him.

He pulled back at that thought. Why did it keep coming back? The prospect of being tied down had impeded the thoughts in his mind.

"What's wrong?" she asked coyly, sliding her free hand up and down his chest. He couldn't wait until his shirt was off and she was touching his bare skin. The one drawback of tying women up was that he didn't get more than the cursory pre-sex touches. He also didn't get the scratches on his back that left scars. *Would she do that?*

With a shake of his head, he smiled. "Nothing." Then he slanted his lips over hers and retook her mouth, warm and loving, letting his feelings flow for him through his kiss. The things he couldn't say—was not ready to say—seeped from him.

Releasing her hand, he rubbed his palms up and down her back, sliding over her buttocks but not grabbing hold. Not yet, anyway. He slipped his fingers under the edge of her blouse and slowly tugged it up, breaking contact with her to pull it over her head. Then he saw her wearing the color red.

A red lace bra that took his breath away. She would have a winning business if she was selling stuff like that in her boutique. "You look gorgeous." He leaned down to kiss her neck after pushing her hair back over her shoulder. No, attack it was more like it. He wanted to taste her and touch her all over. So, he did both with his tongue on her silky throat and his hand on her beautiful breast.

She moaned, and his pulse rate accelerated. "You feel good too," he added as an afterthought. Actually without much thought at all. He could only think of loving her sweet body and making her his repeatedly.

He made his way down her throat to a bra-covered breast. He kissed the mound and reached around her body to unfasten the piece of lace. After slipping the straps over her shoulders, her perfect breasts sprang free of their confines, and the rosy peaks of her nipples stood at attention, begging for his mouth and tongue. So, he answered the request. Taking her nipple in his mouth, he suckled and flicked it with his tongue, doing all the things he remembered she liked from the times they'd shared a bed.

Making love to her breast, he reached down for the button on her jeans, undid it, and slid the zipper down. He felt he'd be seeing more red and was psyched about it.

"Will you sell the red lacy bra in your boutique?" Brad asked as he dropped to his knees.

Breathlessly, she answered, "No, but something like it."

Satisfied with the answer, knowing there'd be more lacy stuff to come, he trailed kisses down her belly while she made mewing noises and ran her fingers through his hair. He slid her jeans down and discovered the red strips of lace that barely covered her pussy.

She touched his shoulders when he helped her step out of her jeans. After he had her back at his mercy, he kissed her mound through the scrap of red lace. He wanted to pull them down and taste her. It'd been a long time since he had. Their first time together was the only one, and now he wanted to remedy that. But he'd promised to let her tie him up and be in control. If he wanted to build that trust with her, he wouldn't take over any more than he already had.

Reluctantly, he stood and smiled at the look of lust on her face.

"Are you done yet?" she asked with a coy smile.

"No. But I promised I'd only take control when we were undressing."

"I'm not completely undressed," she said, referring to her too-small underwear.

"Well, if I touch that, I won't be able to give you

the control you need tonight." At least he was honest about it all.

"I see." She put her arms around his neck. "Kiss me again."

Who was he to deny the lady what she wanted? He kissed her softly, gently, but before long, their kiss turned hungry. Her hands were no longer around his neck; they were jerking his T-shirt from his jeans and ripping it over his head, breaking their kiss. Hell, she had almost pulled off his ears, but he didn't tell her that. Sometimes, he did know when to keep his mouth shut.

After they managed to get him out of his pants and underwear, she looked at him questioningly. "Where?" was all she said.

Understanding her intention, he approached the bedside table and opened the drawer. He had no idea why a scarf was kept there, as he didn't bring women home, but he was glad he had it since it was what Madison wanted. Fingering the scarf, he pulled out the silky fabric from the drawer, turned, and handed it to her.

At first, she didn't seem to know what to do, so he decided to lead. If he was going to do this, maybe he could keep some control without her realizing it. He crawled on the bed and put his arms above his head.

She still looked at the scarf, lost.

"What's wrong?" Had she changed her mind? If so, he might not tie her up so that he could have her soft hands on his body.

"I don't know how to tie any solid knots. Now it won't do for you to break free, will it?"

He smiled at the thought. Okay. Knots. He sat up and extended his arms. "Here, I'll walk you through a knot that won't hurt and will be easy to open but not come apart."

Once they had his hands tied in a knot loose enough, all he'd have to do was pull; he lay back down to allow her to tie him to the headboard. He'd remember not to pull on his restraints while they made love. He looked forward to her on top of him, riding him to satisfaction.

After she finished, she stood by the bed and smiled. "I've dreamed of this," she murmured, but he caught her words. Had she? Go figure. Women's minds….

Madison removed her panties and climbed on the bed, straddling him, and his dick moved, trying to seek her warmth. She leaned forward and kissed him, tentative at first, then with a passion that fueled the fire burning within him. Their lips moved over each other's, and their tongues explored and then played a game of domination. He may have agreed to being tied up but wouldn't allow her to win that battle of tongues.

When her mouth left his, she trailed kisses down his chest, her fingers circling each nipple that shot slivers of ecstasy through his body. Knowing where her mouth was headed, he groaned in expected pleasure. Anticipation rode him like a wild buffalo. He almost pulled against the restraints to help guide her. He'd had blow jobs from women, he'd just tied them up before he fucked them.

She reached his engorged length and hesitated.

Blood thrummed through his veins. He wanted to scream for her to take him deeply into her warm mouth, but he held back. She had to want to do it. He'd have it no other way.

Grasping his erection in her hand, she proceeded to

lick it from base to tip. He bolted upward with the intense sensation of fire that shot through him. His desire for her just quadrupled.

After an excruciating minute or two, she took him in her mouth—warm, wet, welcome. He could've come right then. Football stats, he reminded himself, but he couldn't do more than watch her slide her luscious mouth up and down his shaft, bringing him closer and closer to the edge with each stroke of her mouth and hand. When she cupped and massaged his balls, and he felt that tingle at the base of his spine, he had to call a halt to things.

"Princess, that's enough. I can't take it anymore. You'd best quit if you want to continue this together."

She looked up and winked then took his cock out of her mouth, but not before she swirled her tongue on the head. He almost broke the bonds to pull her up his body so he could drive deep inside her.

Pulling a condom from the bedside table drawer, she opened it and slid it over his erection, driving him insane with the soft touch. As if to please him, she straddled him again and wasted no time sliding down his length.

He tossed his head back and groaned. This might be the quickest sex he'd ever had.

With playtime over, she rode him with gusto. Her breasts bounced with her movements up and down. He wanted to reach up and grab them, hold them in his palms, and love them, but he was stuck. Did the women feel this way with him? There was nothing for them to grab onto when he was making love to them, so it couldn't be the same. Still, he wondered....

When that tingle at the base of his spine made itself

known again, he informed her, "I'm getting close. How about you?" He didn't want to come without her coming too. He wasn't a selfish bastard.

"I'm ready."

"Then fly, princess," he said. God, she looked so good with her slick skin over him, making love to him with their bodies connected.

"I'm coming," she said and bore down on him. Her body flushed as her breaths came out in huffy puffs. When she arched her back and called out in pleasure, he didn't think he'd seen any woman as beautiful in the throes of passion.

In a flurry of sensations, he let himself go and came with her for what he hoped was the first of many times that way.

As she collapsed onto his chest, he knew he had to hold her, so he jerked on the bonds and freed himself. She didn't say a word when he wrapped his arms around her, holding her tight. This woman meant too much to him. Hell, he'd allowed himself to be tied up for her. He had to admit she meant that much to him and figure out how to move forward because heaven knew he'd never been in love with a woman.

"You could've done that anytime, couldn't you?" she murmured against his chest.

No sense in lying. "Yes."

She chuckled. "Well, at least you lived up to your word. How does it feel being tied?"

He wouldn't lie to her but knew where this would lead. "I prefer my hands on your sweet body."

"Then how do you think I feel?" He'd made it clear from their first time that to sleep with him, she had to be tied up. He'd been too set in his ways. Still was, but this little exercise made him reconsider.

"How do you feel?"

She propped her head on her hand that lay on his chest. "Like I want to touch you and hate that I can't."

This might be one of those times when Devon was right about compromise. At least, he hoped so. "So, we don't tie you up. Unless you want it."

Madison's lips twitched. "There's hope for you yet, Brad Hamilton."

Chapter Twenty-Three

Nerves assailed Brad as he passed through the doorway of Healing Therapies, which Ken held open. What exactly would he find out? Would it be bad? He had to push that aside because he wanted to know…had to understand what had happened to him, even if he were at fault. He didn't know how Devon and Rylee could let their memories remain suppressed when he chomped at the bit to know.

Instead of leaving Madison with Ken and Sam at home, he'd brought her, much to her insistence that she come. After ensuring there were no concurring appointments so the waiting room would be empty, he'd finally agreed—provided she stayed with Sam and Ken and did everything they said. He'd expected her to push to be in the room with him, and he'd have allowed it, but the therapist had not been in favor of it. She'd asked him if he wanted her to know everything, no matter what he said. With that thought, he'd nixed the idea. If it was terrible, he wanted time to process it and find the best way to tell Madison.

If the receptionist thought it odd that in a large waiting room with ten roomy chairs, they all sat close to each other on the back wall instead of spreading out, she didn't say anything. She just kept covertly looking at Madison, probably trying to figure out who she was or remembering her from her ad campaigns.

Paula Dixon, with a lot of initials behind her name, was a psychospiritual and transpersonal clinician, and would spend the next ninety minutes helping him try to recover his memory. She'd warned him that they might be unable to get to where he wanted in the first session. In fact, it was rare that it happened that quickly, but she said if he was willing and could throw aside all roadblocks, like his not wanting to know in case he'd done something wrong, they stood a chance.

He was the epitome of willing. The entire situation had festered for too long in his mind. It had eaten at his soul and made him into an asshole of epic proportions. Or so he'd been told.

When his name was called, he gave Madison a quick kiss on the lips and told her he'd be back as soon as possible. Then he nodded at Ken, who scooted into the seat beside Madison, where he'd just vacated. Following a short, blonde-haired woman back to the therapy room, they passed through the outer office, and he marveled at how clean the desk was. He couldn't marvel long until he was faced with the couch where it would all spill out.

Brad took a deep breath and sat down. "Are you sure you can help me?"

"As we discussed on the phone, it depends. Using hypnotherapy, we can recover memories as far back as birth. You just have to have had your consciousness present on some level. Consciousness does not mean conscious like you or I are right now. It's how people can recover memories from accidents, for example, where they've had head trauma. Like if they were dissociative. Now, if you were unconscious, like in a coma state, it would be harder to recover that memory.

If at all."

"I did pass out at some point, I imagine. Something had to have happened for me to just wake up with a monster of a hangover and a prostitute in my room." He still shuddered at the thought that he might've had something to do with the woman.

"I want to make sure you understand what will happen. There is a difference between hypnosis and hypnotherapy. Hypnosis is putting you into a relaxed state. We go in and out of our conscious state for about eighty percent of our day. So you're looking at the difference between your conscious mind and going into your subconscious mind. Your conscious mind is only really about ten percent of your mind. It's where your short-term memory is. It's what you and I are using right now. The subconscious and unconscious is the other ninety percent of our brain and of our mind, which is where our emotions and our habits are. Long-term memory is stored there. All the meat of who we are in our subconscious and unconscious minds.

"So, hypnosis will be the first part of your hypnotherapy session. Getting you into that relaxed state. You'll put yourself into hypnosis. I will just guide you."

He must've looked bewildered because she rushed to explain. "It's like when you're driving down a long road, and you stare straight ahead and zone out a little bit, then you suddenly realize you're at a point where you don't remember driving the last few miles. But, if you tracked back through, you could. And you're conscious enough that you're not running red lights. But you're working in your unconscious mind thinking things like 'Oh my God, I forgot to turn off the coffeepot.'"

With a nod, he smiled. "Yeah, I'm guilty of that. Maybe not the coffeepot, but something."

"We are all guilty of it. You've taken your brain waves from a beta state, which is where they're at when you're conscious—super fast—down into alpha, delta, and theta. Delta and theta are when we're sleeping. So when you slow down your brain waves, you can actually access and use your memory better. So, the point of hypnotherapy is to use the hypnotic state to heal. Meaning we're going into the part of the mind where everything lives anyway."

At this point, Brad was ready to move on and get this over with. He didn't really care about all of this explanation. A simple "We're going to put you in a hypnotic state so we can access your memory" was all he needed. But he listened because he found himself relaxing with each word that assured him this was the right path.

"I want to reiterate, so you're not disappointed, that we'll do regressive therapy, but you might not regress to the actual event today. It may take a few sessions."

Before she could move on, he said, "But I'm more than willing to find the memory, no matter the cost to my ego."

She smiled. "We'll see how today goes. As adults, though, we have hundreds of defense mechanisms, like fear, that prevent us from exploring the depths of our wounds. What if I remember something I don't want to or don't like?"

Yes, he had that fear, but he'd keep it aside. Willingness, he reminded himself. "I'm sure I have some defense mechanisms, but I want it more than I don't."

"Also, the more desperate you are, the harder it will be to retrieve the memory. Look at it like this: you lose your car keys in your house and begin a frantic search but can't find them. When you slow down and focus, relaxing your mind into it, releasing that fear of not finding them, then"—she snapped her fingers—"you'll remember that you had them in the kitchen, and you'll find them there."

He almost snorted out loud at that. He'd lost his keys a time or two. Sunglasses too. But the being desperate worried him because he was a little bit desperate to know. He had to lose that emotion somehow to make this successful. *But how?* Yet he didn't ask it out loud. He'd ditch it and make this work.

"Remember, you'll know you're in the room, but you'll be working dual consciousness. In this state, you won't do or say anything you normally wouldn't do. Those stage-show hypnotist acts are a sham when they have someone act like a chicken. Unless the person craves that attention and acts like it on their own."

He chuckled at that, having seen one such show while in Vegas, and the person had acted like a chicken.

"Well, let's get you into a deep state—a trance," Paula said. "The moment you close your eyes, your brain waves slow. The depth of your trance depends upon your willingness. Since you are so willing, let's begin. Lie down on the couch and get comfortable."

Putting his shoes on the couch felt awkward, but he thought it might be more awkward if he took them off. So, he lay on his back, his hands resting on his belly. Lying out like this, he felt like a fool and was anxious for this to work the first time.

He didn't fear being shamed or judged because that had already happened to him. He'd lost everything, and everyone involved believed he had truly done the deed with the prostitute and then refused to pay her. So that worry was unnecessary, and the potential barrier Paula had spoken of was not going to impact today's session.

"Okay then, let's start with eye fixation. Stare straight ahead at the ceiling and focus." She paused for a minute or two, allowing him to fixate. "Then take some deep breaths and close your eyes."

He did and instantly felt his mind slow as she'd said.

"Next, we'll do induction. I'm going to bring you down. Imagine yourself walking down some stairs or a hillside. Something that takes you down. I will count down from ten, and I want you to imagine you are taking that step. Ten," she said, in a calm, hypnotic voice. "See yourself taking that step. Nine. Feel your body begin to relax. Eight—"

As a visual person, Brad could see himself walking down a green hillside, and his body felt heavier, as if he were walking. By the time she'd counted to one, Brad had sighed, a deep relaxing breath, and had settled completely, feeling like he was in another world that was so calm and therapeutic.

"Go to your favorite place. A safe place."

Immediately, his mind went to being in bed with Madison. Maybe he was supposed to think of the beach or mountains, but his favorite place involved being with her.

"Really let all your senses be there. Notice temperature, the colors, the texture."

Visualizing the scene, he felt his arms wrap around

her soft, toned body, his hands touching every sweet inch of her. His lips doing the same. Her intoxicating scent and delicious, sweet lips. Damn, this was a great place to be. "It's perfect here," he muttered.

"Good. Keep that place in your mind."

Not like he'd have a problem with that, although he'd prefer the real thing.

"Now we're going to do anchoring. I want you to put your thumb and forefinger together."

He did as he was asked, knowing this was important.

"Good. Now, anytime you use this exercise, your body will relax and take on the experience of your safe place. The more you practice it, the better you'll get at it."

He didn't have a problem with returning to that happy place at any time.

"We're going to begin the regressive therapy now. You might recall that on the phone I told you we tied it to an emotional state."

When he'd awakened in Colombia, he'd been bewildered. So he told her that. But that memory was after he was conscious, so he went to how he'd felt before he forgot everything. He and a few of his fellow agents were at a bar, and he'd been frustrated trying to fend off one prostitute after another. "I was frustrated before it all began."

"Good," she said in that still hypnotic voice. "Now, imagine we're going to journey between consciousness and subconscious. We must cross a bridge to get there. The planks in the bridge are thoughts, feelings, words, and experiences that we have. Let's go to the most recent time you were frustrated."

He automatically jumped back to when Madison left his bed in Vegas. That might not have been the most recent time he was frustrated, but it was strong. "A woman—my woman," he clarified, "left my bed without a word or backward glance." A realization that he'd said it out loud and hadn't worried about what the therapist said calmed him even more.

"Hold on to that a minute." She paused, and he frowned. "Now, go back to that significant time in your life when you felt that same level of frustration."

Going back to Colombia before he blacked out was the easy part. He remembered that daily. But the memory still wasn't there. Then, he saw a flash. "I've a flash of being at the bar after we'd fended off the prostitutes."

"Flashes are good. What are you feeling right there when you have that flash?"

"Relief."

"Okay, now we're going to step right into the image of that flash. Walk right into that bar. Tell me what you see. What do you hear?"

Anxiety tried to rip through his body and take him away from where he wanted to be, but he pushed most of it off. She'd told him he'd feel some anxiety, so he figured it was futile to lose it all.

"Some agents and I were at the bar. It smelled of cigarette smoke and sweaty bodies, like they might not clean the place often. But the dive was close to our hotel rooms and reasonably cheap for beer."

"Who was there with you?"

"My supervisor and two other agents. We're at the bar toasting to our ability to clear the way for the president in record time."

"What happens next? Are you still there? Does anything change?"

Although relaxed, he felt his brows draw down in concentration. She'd said it might not come today, but he wouldn't give up on the chance. What had happened?

"I needed to take a piss, so I walked toward the crappy bathrooms in the place." He paused, imagining himself walking past the bar and the other agents toward where tables and booths had been set up for maximum capacity. "It was slow and pretty quiet in there. There wasn't any background music or televisions over the bar to make more noise. It was mostly agents in there...and prostitutes."

"Tell me about your walk to the bathroom."

"My feet suctioned off the floor, telling me they didn't clean them often enough. I was just about to enter the hallway when I noticed one of my shoes was untied, so I kneeled down beside a booth that led into the hallways and—"

She didn't prod him any further. She'd promised to guide him, not push him to recall something that might not be fact. So, he waited and tried again to picture himself kneeling down on one knee to tie his black tennis shoes.

"I heard...." He trailed off, lost in the memory. He didn't speak out loud what he'd overheard two people discussing. It was a memory that would turn into a big scandal, and who would believe him—a now disgraced Secret Service agent? But someone's life could be in the balance. He had to come forward.

"I remember overhearing something I don't wish to repeat."

"That's fine. I told you in the beginning, you choose. Is that all you wish to recall?"

"No. I want to know about the prostitute."

"Okay. Slip into what you did after you overheard this conversation."

"I felt shaky and unnerved, but I reached the bathroom. By the time I returned, I was stronger, though still overwhelmed with what I should do. My supervisor handed me a beer when I returned, and I took it. A good cold beer helped to calm my mind.

"I drank about half and started to feel weird. Like I'd have felt if I'd been drugged. It must've occurred to me that something was wrong because I asked who bought the round, and when he told me, I looked toward the now empty booth. I'd known they'd drugged me, and I was scared of the reason why. I hurried from the bar before something could happen to me where I'd be incapable of caring for myself."

He took in a deep, steadying breath. "I made it to the hotel—it was within walking distance from the bar—and ensured my door was locked and my weapon handy. I couldn't say something would happen, but I wanted to be prepared.

"I got dizzy and lay down on the bed." He remembered toeing off his shoes and undressing for bed. "Then I woke in the morning with someone else in the room."

"When you were asleep, were you aware of anything around you? Feeling? Sounds? Tones of voices? Or were you in a deep sleep?"

"I was out cold. I don't even remember the door opening for someone to enter or anyone crawling into my bed. Wait," he said, his mind bringing everything together. "I left the bar alone, which means that I didn't take home a prostitute. I *was* set up to be disgraced. If I'd been killed, the president's visit would have been canceled, which would've opened a bigger problem."

"What about when you woke?"

"I remember that, and now I remember it all."

"Okay, let's bring you back. Go back to your safe place and tell me something you know is true about you."

This was where they entered the healing section, where they would correct his doubts about his memory or his behaviors. For him, though, all doubt was gone. "I know what I heard was true. And even while drugged, I'm an honorable man." He'd never doubt himself again.

"Brad, I'm going to count from one to five. At five, you'll return to the room feeling refreshed, relaxed, and empowered. One—feeling the energy coming back into your body. Two—lots and lots of energy. Three—wiggle your fingers and stretch your toes. Four—feel yourself coming back in. Five—eyes open and wide awake."

He suddenly felt the world's pull on him, yet he was relaxed and calm, ready to tackle anything that got in his path. But he wanted to see Madison even more.

"How do you feel?" Paula asked.

"Like the world's weight has been lifted off my shoulders," he answered. Yet he knew he had to act quickly. In light of recent events, he knew his memory was essential to the person it affected.

"Well, you were right about your willingness. It got you there, which is unlike most clients. Very few regressed and recalled in the first session. I should've asked you this before, but do you ever meditate?"

He did and didn't feel embarrassed to say. "I started a couple of years ago when my anger got the best of me."

"That's another factor that helped you. Never give meditation up."

He wouldn't lose this feeling of peace. His anger, which had once been at the world, had just transferred to a few people. He wouldn't allow them to ruin the peace he'd just embraced.

"I won't." Now to kick some ass and reinstate his good name.

Chapter Twenty-Four

During the drive home, Brad didn't discuss with Madison what had been revealed during his session. He needed to think it through. The revelation that he'd heard someone plotting murder stuck with him and set his anger to rising. Yet they hadn't committed murder. But he was more than aware now was the perfect time for them to do so.

At first, he wondered whether it was a true memory or something his psyche had dreamed up. Who would believe him? But, as the therapist had said, why would he make that up?

In Colombia, he'd heard Senator Brett Walden and his campaign manager, Thomas Hancock, discussing how the senator's wife—a new senator herself—had become more popular than her husband in her short time in office and how they could use that to their advantage. Since Senator Brett Walden had lost the bid to the presidency, they had come up with a plan for the next run. Have Senator Sharon Walden run and, when she got the ticket—and she probably would be popular and female—Senator Brett Walden would stay by her side—prime in the public eye. Then they'd have her killed, and with the outpouring of sympathy, Senator Brett Walden would assume her bid as the aggrieved husband taking up his wife's charge for the people she'd so full-heartedly represented.

A ludicrous plan. And risky. But people who weren't regular criminals couldn't be expected to make foolproof plans. And maybe it had only been the drink talking. They had been in a bar in Colombia. The Senator had come to try to one-up the incumbent president, who would arrive shortly. Yeah, it had to be the alcohol talking. No one would think up such a stupid plan. Would they?

The questions were: What was he to do with the information? And did they have something to do with trying to erase his memory and discredit him? It made sense that they had only two ways of handling him—besides ignoring it—kill him or discredit him so no one would believe whatever he said, thinking he was trying to worm himself out of whatever trouble they imparted upon him.

He guessed he should be thankful they didn't kill him, but damn if he'd tell them that.

His first instinct was to drive to Jesse's and tell him everything. Even with Madison with him and Ken and Sam following, it didn't stop him from making the drive to his brother's home. Jesse had a level head—when Kate's safety wasn't involved—and could help him figure out what to do with the information he now had.

"Where are we going?" Madison asked him from the passenger seat.

Realizing he hadn't shared his plan with her, he grimaced. "We're going to Jesse's. I need to go through what I learned with him."

"Are you going to share anything with me?" she asked.

He had no reason to keep it from her, so he told

her. "I overheard Senator Brett Walden and his campaign manager plotting to kill the senator's wife when she ran for president."

Struck speechless, Madison formed a big O. "Are you sure?"

Getting on the interstate, he nodded. "Very sure. It was right after the senator lost his party's presidential bid. Her popularity was so high that people were asking for her to run. That's what made them come up with a cockamamy plan."

"Why would they kill her? That doesn't make sense if she had a chance of winning. Think of it, the first woman president."

"Ah, see, there's the rub. Senator Brett Walden didn't want to be the first gentleman. He wanted to be president however he could get there. They figured once she was so popular that she'd sewn up the bid, they'd take her out and have him, as the grieving widower, slip into her slot and finally win the presidency."

"That doesn't make sense to me."

"It doesn't to me either because the scenario has too many what-ifs. But not all politicians are as sharp as my dad."

"So why aren't we going to the police with this?"

He hadn't thought police, only HIS, but she was right that they'd need to tell them, the Secret Service, and the FBI. But he had no idea if they'd even believe him. Would his word be enough to convict the two for planning the murder? They had to find evidence. Yet, he couldn't sit back and wait for them to make another move—the town car accident and shooting had already been an attempt on the senator's life. It would be months before the senator's wife could sew up the nomination. Brad couldn't stand it that long, always wondering if today would be the day.

Remembering she'd asked him a question, he glanced at her and smiled. "We will, but first, I want to go through it with Jesse."

"Why? If the police are who you need, why Jesse?"

Why indeed? Brad knew he was too emotionally charged with this and needed a level head to guide him through the bureaucracy of the government so he didn't lose his temper. "Because I trust Jesse to be objective. I don't think I can be. Plus, there's only my word. No evidence to support my claim."

"Of course you can trust yourself. Who'd expect otherwise?"

She was one hell of a woman. How did he get so lucky? "Well, I'm not very objective when you're involved."

She snorted, probably thinking of that day at the club when he'd gone all "alpha male," as she'd called it. Damn straight he had.

"They really want to kill her?" she asked.

"That's what they'd said. Whether they'd actually do it...I don't know, but that attempt on her life says someone is serious about it."

"I can't believe it." She folded her arms over her chest as if to ward off a chill. "It all sounds like a murder mystery."

He reached across the console and clasped her hand in his. "It does. A very bad one."

"At least you know you didn't take home a prostitute," she added.

There was that. That had been an enormous relief.

Although he couldn't remember the woman entering his room since he'd been out cold, he remembered making it to his room and crashing. "That's true." Had she ever doubted him on that score? He refused to ask the question because he might not like the answer.

Changing the subject, he asked, "What do you say to some steamed crabs and beer for dinner tonight? I know this great place to sit on the bay and enjoy a feast."

"Can I have wine instead?" she asked in a teasing tone.

Brad squeezed her hand. "Anything for you, princess."

"That reminds me. Where did you come up with princess for my nickname?"

He didn't have the slightest clue. It had just slipped out once, and he decided he liked it. "I'm not really sure where it came from, but now that I use it, I see you as the beautiful princess in the tower whose smile wins the hearts of her people."

She chuckled. "That's about the worst thing I've heard. Did you just make it up?"

"Well, yeah," he admitted with a laugh. "I don't know where it came from, but I like it for you. You're my princess."

"Does that make you my Prince Charming?"

He almost choked. No one had ever called him that before. Not even close. "I'll be whatever you want me to be."

Deep down, her laughter called to him lifting his spirit and easing the strain of the problem he needed to resolve.

They talked about inconsequential things for the

remainder of the drive to his brother's home. Jesse met them at the door and escorted them back to the war room, where some of the men and women were hanging out in shorts and sweaty T-shirts after what looked like a workout in the gym.

Sitting down together, Jesse started the conversation. "How'd it go?"

"I remember everything." He summarized what he'd remembered to Jesse. "The senator's life could still be on the line. I have to do something. Warn her at least."

"Tell me, why would she believe you? She might love her husband and believe the best of him. Don't you think this would sound outrageous to her?"

Brad sighed. He was right. The same thought dropped into his mind—Why would she believe a disgraced Secret Service agent? Someone whose word would be questioned even if he said the sky was blue. "She probably won't. But, still, I have to do something."

"I've got an idea," Jesse said. "Can you wait to tell her until I line this up? I may need Dad's clout."

"What are you thinking?"

"Are you ready to be bait?"

Chapter Twenty-Five

True to his word, Brad took Madison to Captain James Crab House for crabs and beer. She didn't say anything about preferring wine when he ordered a dozen jumbo steamed crabs and two Coronas. He had a lot on his mind and had obviously forgotten her preference. She hoped though that he had a big appetite, because that was a lot of food for two.

She'd been here before with Rylee and loved the place. It was a replica of a large boat on land, with an open deck where you could enjoy the breeze off the bay. Luckily, the crisp, salty scent of the air wasn't marred by any rotting fish or other foul pollution. She'd never tire of the smell and atmosphere that made her want to sit at the picnic bench for hours, eating crabs and reading a book on her tablet—two of her favorite things.

Feeling that he might need to address his worries now that he'd had time to process everything, she asked, "Are you okay with everything?" She couldn't imagine being sent into the lion's den and not being concerned.

He took a long draw from his beer. "Yeah. It'll be fine."

"But you argued the point on bringing a weapon pretty strongly." She'd thought during the conference call with the FBI and Secret Service that someone would've jumped through the phone and choked him for his insolence. But they needed him. Maybe not needed, but apparently, he was their best shot at getting the male Senator Walden to confess quickly.

"Of course I did. Who wants to walk into that type of situation unarmed?"

He asked like she should already know the answer, which was a stupid question. Okay, maybe it had been.

"How can I help?" she offered, wishing she was a real-life Nancy Drew and could be of use in resolving this issue.

"I don't think you can."

"You can talk to me, Brad."

He seemed to be mulling over his decision before he finally spoke. He set his beer down, probably a little harder than expected since he flinched a bit. "Okay, going in unarmed really does bother me. I get their reasoning for it, but going unprotected...."

"But won't you be wearing one of those bulletproof vests?"

"Not exactly bulletproof, especially at close range. And it doesn't cover my head."

The crabs arrived, and they let them sit for a minute to cool. It gave her a moment for her pulse to slow down from the worry about him being at risk—vest or not. Her head told her that everything would be done to keep him safe, but her heart couldn't help but be concerned for him being in potential harm's way.

"I'll be okay."

How many times had he said okay? Was he trying to convince himself or her?

"What do you think the senator will do?" They'd admitted it was a wildcard, a Hail Mary type of play, but the FBI and Secret Service wanted to try it. They didn't believe the senator would try to kill Brad. He hadn't thought that, but the risk had been greater since Brad could've had his memory intact. There'd been no guarantee that whatever they'd dosed him with would work that well as to wipe back for a few hours.

"Who knows? It depends on how backed into the corner he feels. My memory may not threaten him, but he went to a lot of trouble to help me lose it, so I don't think he's going to be happy I've recovered it. Of course, there's still the disgraced thing. I can't prove I didn't bring the prostitute to my room. I need her to clear me there. Unless the senator confesses to sending her, which I sincerely doubt he'd do."

"I'm surprised they're sending you in as a civilian." She'd been floored when it had been recommended by the Secret Service and echoed by the FBI. He was a civilian.

"Well, I've been in the Secret Service, and HIS has worked with the FBI." He shrugged. "Plus, I'm the only one who can confront him with my memory and have a rat's ass chance of gaining a confession."

"Do you have a plan?"

"No. And after we settle this tomorrow, we work on your problem," he said, testing the temperature of a crab. Seemingly satisfied, he ripped it apart, the top shell dropping to the table. He scooped out the guts, hurriedly set it down, and shook his hand when liquid hit it. "They're still a bit too hot," he told her unnecessarily.

Even though they were hot, he grabbed each one and ripped apart the shells so they would cool faster. She smiled at his thoughtfulness, which she doubted many people believed he possessed.

"What made you leave modeling and take up selling underwear?" he asked.

"It's lingerie," she corrected, and he grinned. "And it was time to leave. Younger models were starting to take my old contracts. There's a glass ceiling in modeling, and I broke it, but I couldn't stay there. Everyone wants young."

"You don't look old to me."

She considered patting him on the cheek and saying, "Aw, thank you, sweetie," but thought better of it. "Thanks" was all she said instead.

"Why lingerie?"

He got it right this time, whether by accident or on purpose, she didn't know. "It kind of found me. I was sketching some designs—I always have since I was a teenager—and Jacque saw the ones I'd done of lingerie and wanted to work with me to produce them." She took a drink of her cold beer and set the bottle down. "I was floored, of course, but the more he talked with me, the more I learned that high-end lingerie was a great place to be. So, I researched it and agreed."

"Is he helping you with your work?"

"He is." She beamed. "Only a few pieces and only in the shop to start, but once they grab hold, we'll expand."

"Doesn't it make more sense to go worldwide?"

She shrugged. It probably did, but that hadn't been her thought. "I guess I need to see that they're liked before I expand. We'll be selling it online, so it's kind of worldwide. But you can call it an apprehensive thing. I don't want to go worldwide—in stores—and fail. Too many designs do."

He picked up a crab and split it in half, handing her one half. "I don't know the first thing about it, so I'll leave it to you."

"Gee, thanks." She made a funny face at him, and he chuckled before he pulled off a leg with the rib meat attached. *Show off*, she thought. She may not be a novice card player, but she was with opening crabs. She didn't always grab them in the right place.

When she broke off the leg without the rib meat, Brad came to her rescue. He reached for her piece of crab. "Here, let me."

Then he cleanly pulled the legs off with the rib meat and laid them down for her before returning to his half crab. And so for the remainder of the dinner, he did that for her. He cleaned the shell for her when he didn't pull it out with the rib meat. Her chest expanded at his thoughtfulness.

On the drive to his house, they were silent, each lost in their thoughts. Her heart thrummed at the side of Brad she'd seen as he'd cleaned her crabs for her. So caring. He was so deep she wondered if she'd ever learn all the facets of the man. Her pulse increased at finding them out.

"Thanks for dinner." She patted her full belly. "That was magnificent." It had been more the company than the food—although that had been excellent—that made the dinner magnificent. Of course, any time with Brad was magnificent.

"It's nothing. We can go there anytime you want."

Her heart jumped in joy. They were planning future things together like that, and she couldn't be happier. So, when they arrived at his home, instead of going to the room she'd been staying in, she eagerly followed him to his room and enjoyed his attentive lovemaking, falling asleep, sated and well loved with the one thought of "Where would this lead?"

Chapter Twenty-Six

Brad still bristled at the microphone taped to his chest and that he was going into what could be dangerous without a weapon of any sort. He understood no handgun but hadn't realized that he couldn't even carry a knife for protection, or he might've backed out.

It was odd seeing the Secret Service work with the FBI. The line blurred a bit about who should handle this situation, so instead of flipping a coin, they pooled their resources.

After his experience in Colombia, it had been a tough call to trust the Secret Service, but he'd had to include them. One thing he was glad to occur was his old boss had been removed from the detail until they knew whether he was involved or not, considering he'd also been in Colombia at the time that Brad—confident now—had been drugged. He still couldn't believe it had happened to him, but his memory was clear that he hadn't drunk too much. Two beers and he'd been out of it.

"Are you ready?" FBI Special Agent Rose asked him.

Tense, he shrugged. "About as ready as I'll ever be. Do you think the senator will confess?"

The agent shook his head. "No, but it's worth a try."

The plan was for him to meet with the male

Senator Walden. Then, Brad would confront him with the knowledge he now held. His aim would be to get the female senator's husband to spill the beans. Brad wished he'd learned more from Matt on managing conversations. His twin could coax water from a desert.

The impromptu meeting was to take place at the residence rather than the political offices in DC. He was glad he didn't need to make that drive, but in DC concealed carry was prohibited so he'd feel safer. But would Senator Brett Walden carry a weapon or have one in his Baltimore home? With an internal nod, he answered his own question. Of course he would. The man was all about gun rights.

Getting in his vehicle, Brad glanced at Jesse, and with the confidence his big brother exuded, Brad's nervousness vanished. Jesse had been right to do it this way. If it worked, it was a much better plan than them taking action alone and not contacting the authorities. At least, not contacting them until things were settled.

The drive was short since his backup—not HIS, which bothered him—would be on the street near the residence so they could respond quickly. It wouldn't be quick enough if that asshole decided to shoot him. His thoughts on the drive over were of Madison and how she would be happy to see it vanquished if this was the big threat against them. Then he'd deal with Casden and Rogers. He'd already given a brief overview of what had been happening to them to their friend on the Baltimore PD, Lieutenant Dan Winters. He agreed to sit down with the authorities later and work out something. The police wanted Casden and Rogers also, but had failed each time they'd arrested them. Evidence tended to get lost, or witnesses disappeared.

Without a doubt, there were police in the department who were corrupt, and the police chief didn't tolerate it. Once he identified a crooked cop, he dealt harshly with the offender. Internal Affairs worked hard to keep the department clean, but there were some very slippery rotten apples on the force.

Brad strode up the walk to the front door of the Walden mansion. There was no better word for it. It was huge, with southern-style white columns on the front patio and chairs and lounges displayed in conversation and relaxation settings. At the dinner, Madison told him how she loved the porch and how it was set up. Maybe one day he could swing something like this for her. Not the home, but the outside setting. The new home she had offered didn't have this grand of a front patio, but she would have something to work with unlike his place.

When he rang the doorbell, the same butler who had greeted them at the dinner opened the door. "Mr. Hamilton, nice to have you visit again. The senator is waiting for you." He closed the door behind Brad. "Right this way." And he was gone, stopping suddenly in front of an open door that must serve as an office for one of the senators.

It was opulent, like the rest of the home. It also had the traditional look of floor-to-ceiling built-in bookshelves on one wall with a ladder on a rail to slide back and forth for books that were just out of reach. How often did they read any of those books? At a quick glance, they were primarily biographies and other boring subjects.

"Mr. Hamilton," the butler announced to the room and left.

"Come in," a deep male voice intoned.

A moment's hesitation, during which Brad's gut clenched, had the male voice calling him in again. Remembering the senator had been responsible for drugging him, ruining his career, and maybe trying to kill him on the road, his gumption grew, and he stepped smartly through the doorway to find Senator Brett Walden behind a large cherry wood desk with a computer monitor, keyboard, and stacks of papers in neat piles.

"It hasn't been long since the dinner, Brad. May I call you Brad?"

He didn't want the man to call him anything, but he saw no reason to anger him immediately. "That's fine."

"Good. Good. Have a seat." He gestured to the armchairs before his desk.

The senator's hands were on top of his desk. Relief swept through Brad; there was no weapon in hand. Brad sat, ignoring the urge to scratch where the tape stuck to his skin. He refrained and started the conversation before the senator even asked why he wanted the meeting.

"Funny thing," he began, "when I was drugged in Colombia, I lost my memory."

Senator Walden's jaw clenched. "I'm not sure why you're telling me this," he said carefully.

"It's interesting. I ignored it, not knowing what had happened to me or what had happened before I was drugged. Then someone gave me a brochure on hypnotherapy."

The senator visibly tensed, and his hands curled into fists. "Well, that's good for you. I still don't see why you wanted to meet with me."

"Well, with the hypnotherapy, I regained my memory. Or most of it, that is."

Sweat broke out on the senator's forehead, and his eyes shifted. Brad's pulse raced at the thought he might break the man.

"Thing is, you're one of the memories that resurfaced."

"Me?" He laughed, and the sound set Brad's nerves on edge. "Did you have some dream that I somehow appeared in?"

"I imagine you know the memory I have. Of you and your—at the time—campaign manager, Thomas Hancock."

"This meeting appears to be a waste of my time. I don't need to hear stories you have conjured and try to spout as a lost memory," he said dismissively.

"Don't you?" Brad had to do something to get the man to confess. "It involves your plans for your wife. It's terrible that you thought that many years ago, you could use her popularity for your own gain. Murder is a crime," he said as casually as possible, considering the subject matter.

The senator scoffed. "I haven't murdered my wife." His voice was laced with steel.

"But you and Hancock plan to." Brad knew he was grasping at straws. The conversation he'd overheard happened so long ago, but it was the only hand he could play. "And based on the conversation I heard, it will be soon. How do you think she's going to feel when she hears that? Not to mention how she'll connect the recent attempt on her life with you and this accusation."

It took Walden a moment to react. He wasn't as good a poker player as he might think. His emotions flowed over his face like a river. "No one will believe you. Your disgrace as a Secret Service agent will stand."

"But it will make her uncertain, wondering if what I told her was true." He needed the man to agree with him somehow. God, he wished Matt was talking in his ear. He wished he had an earpiece altogether, but the consensus was that if Walden saw it, all bets would be off.

"What do you want?"

Oh, so he wanted to pay him off. Funny, since most of their money came from his wife's inheritance from her parents. "I want my disgraced status removed from my Secret Service record. And I wanted to warn you. Give you a chance to do the right thing. I can't stand by, knowing someone may be murdered."

Suddenly, a side door he'd missed when he'd checked out the room briefly opened, and Thomas Hancock walked into the room, pointing a handgun at Brad's chest. His pulse rate skyrocketed at his new situation. *Fuck. Fuck. Fuck.*

"How inconvenient for you to have your memory returned," Hancock said. "We worked hard to ensure it faded along with your career so no one would believe your tale of possible murder."

A surge of fear and anger shot through him at his being unarmed. Brad sat very still while his chest beat a staccato rhythm. Thank God, he'd worn a vest. "You don't need to point that weapon at me, Hancock," he said plainly, so his backup would hear he was in trouble and alert them to another player in the room. How long would it take them, two or three minutes? His pulse thrummed at how long he'd deal with the situation alone. Once they arrived, his backup could spend another two or three minutes trying to find him in the home.

"Of course I do," Hancock said, stepping beside where the senator sat. "I knew once you began asking questions at the dinner that you'd be trouble. I sent someone to run you off the road—over the bridge, to be exact—but they failed. We should've killed you in Colombia and dealt with the political fallout."

Brad gulped. He'd wanted to hear the truth, and knowing it was his fault Madison had been hurt stirred his gut. "So you still plan to kill the senator's wife?" If the man answered, he had no plan to allow Brad to leave this situation. Where the hell was his backup?

"It is a grand plan. Once she has all the public votes, and with Brett by her side, she dies tragically, and Brett steps into her role to continue on the principles she stood on," Thomas sneered.

"You'd just let him kill your wife?" he asked the senator.

"She's a shoo-in for president. It should've been me who was president, not first gentleman. That isn't the role I was born into. President or bust. Any way I can get it."

"It seems like a big risk. What if the public opinion doesn't sway to you? You couldn't sway them four years ago."

These people were certifiable. The public might be sympathetic to the senator at the loss of his wife, but they wouldn't automatically vote for him. Hell, dozens of people in the primaries could bounce back up after she died. She couldn't die. He had to help stop it. Nerves began to assail him at the delay. Where the hell was his backup? He took a deep breath to keep himself from allowing fear to pervade his nerves. With another deep breath, he calmed that racing feeling along his spine so he could continue to deal with these two men and keep himself alive until someone arrived.

"He only lost by a small margin," Hancock said. "This time, we'll win it. No woman should be president. No matter how much the public loves her."

Brad felt the need to dropkick the sexist pig. He thought he had enough from them for a conviction, but since he had to wait for the cavalry, he decided to probe more. "Since you failed once already, how had you planned to kill her this time?"

Hancock smiled. "Yeah, she was supposed to have died in that accident, but you had to come along. But you won't be a problem this time," he sneered.

Brad gulped back the threat and secretly rejoiced that he'd got the admission on the attempt on the female senator's life. He still needed to push for time for his backup, so he sought more confessions. "So, how were you planning to do it this time?"

Hancock's smile turned sickly. "Intruder who got away, of course. Brett would be safely away—out of town—so no suspicion would befall him."

Brad heard the noise, slight though it was—someone was coming. His nerves eased a bit. Thank God.

"How had you planned to get rid of me?"

"Self-defense. You tried to attack the senator."

Fucker. He wanted to launch himself at the man and beat the shit out of Hancock for even thinking of killing him. Brad had too much to live for. Madison.

"FBI! Put the weapon down!"

Hallelujah. He wasn't completely safe as the handgun was still pointed at his chest. Brad wanted to close the distance between them and disarm the man responsible for his life and career troubles. He'd waited a long time to clear his name, and finally it was done. He felt a huge weight lifting from his body and soul even though he was still in danger while Hancock kept his weapon pointed at him. If only he were closer, Brad would attack the man. He'd love to take him down after the man had pulled a weapon on him.

"Put your weapon down," someone repeated to Hancock.

Hancock didn't obey. He held his weapon steady on Brad, and there was a frisson of fear that the man would actually shoot him with everyone present. Then he watched it as if in slow motion. Hancock brought the pistol to his temple. Brad called out and reached forward as if he could reach the gun before Hancock pulled the trigger. The man crumpled before Brad's eyes, with brain matter splattered near him.

Brad started. He wanted to lash out at Hancock for escaping justice, but he couldn't be sorry the man wasn't around to ruin any more lives.

The senator was pulled to a standing position and cuffed by Dan and another FBI agent. The man didn't speak, just looked at Hancock's body and, with his head down, was walked from the office by the police officer.

"Good job," Dan told him.

"Good? Where the fuck were you? The man was pointing a weapon at me!" he shouted.

"We got here in time, now didn't we?"

They had. He hated to admit it. "Yeah. Thanks."

After giving back the wire, he promised to come by

the FBI office later to make a complete statement. He needed to see Madison first. Although he never cowered from having a weapon pointed at him, the reality of it got beneath his skin and made him want what was important. And that was Madison Maxwell.

Still reeling from the accusations and all the dirty dealings of the senator and his deceased campaign manager, Brad drove home tense and eager to see Madison. It all seemed so anticlimactic. Then again, he didn't know what he really expected once confessions were dispensed. At least Senator Walden—the female one—would be safe.

Brad was desperate to hold Madison and know that all felt right in the world. She was his world, and her love could wash away all he'd witnessed. Did he have her love? He'd never wanted it before—from any woman—but now he craved it with every fiber of his being.

He knew he loved her and wanted to tell her, yet he worried what she'd say. *Pussy*, he called himself. The worst she could do was laugh in his face...or leave. "Christ!" he exclaimed in the rented SUV. "Why is this so fucking hard?" He knew better than to ask his brothers' advice on this topic, especially Devon and his sometimes good, and occasionally bad, advice. How the hell did he remain married to Rylee?

Well, he'd cleared the one threat to her...to them. The car accident wasn't Rogers and Casden, but Walden and Hancock. That meant the first two weren't escalating. But how did he get them to back off before they did? Maybe they'd do nothing, but he didn't want to let his guard down. Letting her go with just Ken and Sam had been tough, but he trusted his team leader.

Knowing they'd gone to the club, he thought to drive by there in case she was still there on the way home. He couldn't wait to see her. Couldn't wait to hear what she thought about it all. About him being set up. Of course, she'd attested her belief that he'd been set up from the beginning and not done something stupid. Having it validated felt right and had him standing taller and stronger.

Now, he needed his woman by his side.

Chapter Twenty-Seven

With Brad tied up with the Waldens and all that encompassed, Madison headed to the club to see the progress. Although Ken pushed them to wait for Brad, he reluctantly agreed that he and Sam would stay with Madison. The drive to the club was silent, and Madison felt a tension between Ken and Sam that she couldn't identify.

Arriving at the club, Ken led the way and told her to wait outside with Sam while he checked the place. There was only one car, which she guessed was the contractor's. A quick lance of concern stabbed her. The workers should be here. Surely, they hadn't taken a day off for the weather as she thought that, the sun dipped behind a dark cloud. Rain was on the way.

When Ken didn't return immediately, Sam tried to get her to retreat to the SUV. Before she could move either forward or back, Jeremy Rogers opened the door of the club and pointed a handgun at Sam, then removed another handgun from his waist and pointed it at Madison.

Her heart nearly stopped before blood rushed through her system in a wave of panic and fear.

"With two fingers, remove your weapon and place it out of arm's reach," he said to Sam. With murder in her eyes, she complied, and Jeremy waved one of the handguns, motioning them to enter the club. "Nice and quiet now," he said.

A lead weight settled in Madison's stomach, sending her senses reeling at the fact that the car in the parking lot hadn't been the contractor's. Unless—she gulped—they did something to him. And what about Ken?

Knowing she had no choice if she wanted to live—because with all she'd heard, she doubted Jeremy held her at gunpoint for the fun of it—she looked at Sam and stepped into the club. Once they'd both entered, she saw Ken—weaponless and with a handgun pointed at his temple—standing near Richard Casden. Ken's handgun was on the floor.

Madison's heart sank, and she fumed at the same moment. *The fuckers.* Brad was going to go ballistic. Her pulse thrummed in her ears at the thought of Brad on a rampage with these monsters—men she'd once thought harmless. Three people, three guns. No, it looked like Casden had another weapon. Had they planned on Brad being with her? Her skin crawled at the thought of them planning to hurt him—any of them.

"It's about time you arrived, Miss Maxwell," Richard said.

"I'm sorry I kept you waiting," she snapped, remembering how Brad thought she'd be too nice to the men. She almost snorted at how contradictory she'd been.

"Did you disarm her?" Richard asked Jeremy, nodding in Sam's direction.

Jeremy nodded. "Yeah."

Sam looked at Ken, and something silent passed between them. Whatever it was, it didn't change the dynamic of their situation.

A card table with two folding chairs had been set up in the middle of the club. Presumably, this is where the contractor spread out his plans and conducted any business. Now, there was a small stack of papers there.

Madison trembled with fear but worked to overcome it to think straight. What in the hell was going on? Did they plan to kill the three of them and leave them in the club? She swallowed hard. She didn't want to die. They still wouldn't get the club because Rylee wouldn't sell it to them, and Brad would hunt them down and kill them.

"Miss Maxwell," Richard said and motioned with his head to the card table, "if you please."

She saw Ken make a move, and Richard turned back to him and realigned his weapon with Ken's temple.

Once she sat at the table, the two men quickly adjusted their weapons. They had Ken move closer to Sam, and Jeremy covered each of them while Richard now held a handgun on her. *Good times,* she thought with an inappropriate internal laugh.

"Sign the papers, and you'll be free to go. You and your friends," Richard stated, but she didn't believe him. How could she believe someone who held you at gunpoint and had a reputation of murder?

With a will to live and trust in HIS, she hoped to stall until Ken and Sam could get something moving. She slowly perused the papers. They had to get them out of this because she'd never told Brad she loved him. She wanted a life with him, and these men would not deny her that.

Just as she thought, a bill of sale for the property was on top of the stack of papers. With full power of attorney, Rylee's signature wouldn't be necessary. What's worse was they also had a copy of the power of attorney on the table. Anger laced her spine at the fact they'd somehow gotten a copy. She couldn't worry about how right now because she had more important things to focus on.

"So, you want me to sign these without my partner knowing?" *Stall,* she thought. Ken and Sam looked intent. They had to be coming up with something.

"You can tell her later," Richard said.

"There's no notary here, and these need to be notarized." A slight relief hit her that the documents wouldn't be official.

Richard smiled, showing his teeth like a wolf. "Don't you worry about that. They'll get notarized fine."

Watching Ken for direction, she was astonished to see surprise and satisfaction on his usually stoic face. He gave her a slight smile and a barely noticeable nod.

Okay, so she was to sign. What if he and Sam couldn't help in time? She didn't want to sign the club away. Then again, she wanted them to live, so signing would be something she would do. She'd just take her time.

"I guess I need a pen."

Richard reached into his suit jacket and extracted one to hand to her. She'd remember that gold pen for the rest of her life. She'd never be able to hold one like it again and not recognize her fear...her will to live...and her despair at possibly dying without growing old with Brad.

Madison twisted the pen to showcase the writing tip. The paperwork had already been tabbed and highlighted for her to sign or initial in the appropriate places. Someone else had already filled in her name and the club information. *How thoughtful,* she mused sarcastically.

Making to drag it out longer, she checked every line, and when Richard saw what she was doing, he dug the gun into her temple. "Hurry."

Her blood ran cold. Would he really shoot her? She prayed not with everything inside her. She began on the first page, and the next thing she knew, Ken was tackling her, and all hell broke loose.

Something warm seeped across her belly. Oh God, had she been shot? She needed to tell Brad she loved him before she died. She needed to do so much, but somehow, she'd screwed up what would've been a good life for herself with a wonderful man.

When the stars floated before her eyes, the buzzing in her ears began, and then a blackness rimmed her eyes. She didn't fight her escape.

****

Brad pulled into the club's parking lot and saw Ken's SUV and another vehicle. Probably the contractor's. His blood ran cold when he didn't see Ken or Sam outside. One of them should have been outside checking the perimeter while one stayed with her. He parked and pulled his earpiece from the console between the seats. He'd removed it when confronting the senator and hadn't thought to replace it until now.

In his microphone, he called Ken's name twice, and fear crept up his spine when he didn't respond. He thought to jump from the SUV and rush in, but common sense slapped him across the face. He got on the phone, and instead of calling the police, he called

Devon, explained the situation, and gave the license plate so his brother could tell him who was here, even though he already had an idea. After that, an alert went out to the team, and he knew anyone nearby would be there within minutes to have his back. Thank God their departure to Belgium had been delayed by a day. Otherwise, he'd be screwed with manpower since Jesse lived so far away. He'd never make it in time. Actually, it was just that Brad wouldn't wait that long.

As it was, it felt like the most extended wait of his life, but he quietly updated Ken on what was occurring outside the club so he could be prepared. Ken's job was to protect Madison since Brad didn't know her location, and the men would be going in blind since Ken couldn't give them any information, but his inability to speak spoke volumes about the situation. There would be weapons involved, and more than likely, the three of them were being held at gunpoint. Anything less than that and Ken would've kicked ass. Brad still wanted to scream at the uncertainty of it. What if Ken couldn't get to her and protect her?

He wiped a hand down his tired face. He couldn't think like that. He trusted Ken with his life, which meant he trusted him with Madison's too. Still, so many dangerous scenarios ran through his mind, with Madison getting hurt in any crossfire that might occur. They planned to take the two men without firing their weapons—the police hated it when they did—and rescue his woman.

With six team members in place, including three of his brothers—AJ, Matt, and Jake—Rylee, and Rodney, Brad briefed them on the layout and what they could expect. Ready, they breached the club through the front and back door in single file. Angry at AJ and Matt for making him go last, he finally conceded that his head wasn't straight and he couldn't be objective. If they hurt Madison, he'd kill Casden and Rogers. He was thanking his fucking stars they allowed him to participate. Allowed? No, this was his mission. No one would kick him off it.

Coming in behind his brothers, in his peripheral, he watched Ken launch himself across the room and tackle someone sitting in a chair. He flew over the card table, and the two hit the ground with a thunk from the chair's frame as a weapon fired. He prayed it was to cover Madison because Brad had to pull Sam back from trying to kick Jeremy Rogers's ass.

Although he'd hoped for a quiet entry, several gunshots were fired, none by him, and both Casden and Rogers were down. Not caring the status of the men, he rushed to where Ken lay atop Madison. The poor woman spent more time beneath someone from HIS than anything else.

Blood, he smelled it…tasted the metallic tang in his mouth…saw it on her shirt when Ken moved off her and rolled to his back. Brad ripped her blouse from inside her jeans and frantically surveyed her belly. "Madison? Where are you hurt?" he asked her unconscious body. Blind panic and fury reached out to every nerve circuit in his body. He'd been too late to save her from being hurt…or maybe even dying if the wound was bad enough.

"It's me, man," Ken said. "I think she hit her head when I pushed her out of the way of the bullet that hit me."

His attention immediately turned to Ken. "Medic!"

he yelled to Rodney, who had been a military medic and breached through the back door with Jake and Rylee. Brad gulped past the lump in his throat. "Thank you." He cleared his throat and fought back the watering of his eyes. The man took a bullet for his woman. Brad would never be able to repay him. "Thank you for protecting her."

"Don't sweat it." His breathing became labored. "It's my job."

Job or not, the man still took a bullet. His stomach lurched at how Madison would be upset that someone was hurt protecting her. But Ken's quick moves potentially saved her life. Brad couldn't be more appreciative of the man who saved the woman he loved.

With Ken's bleeding staunched by Rodney and Sam at his side, Brad turned back to Madison. Sitting near her head, he pulled her head into his lap and ran his hands through her hair. She'd be all right. She had to. He couldn't live without her.

Chapter Twenty-Eight

"It's nothing but a slight concussion," Madison told Brad as they entered his home. "So you won't need to worry about me like before."

Worry about her? Was she out of her fucking mind? He'd worry about her to the ends of the earth. "Still. I think"—he winked at her—"that lying in my arms is what the doctor ordered." At least he should have ordered it.

"Oh, is that so?" She turned to face him, and he kicked the door closed with his foot while reaching his arms out to pull her close.

He could've lost her today, and that churned his gut. She probably would be dead if it hadn't been for Ken's quick action. He'd have to give the man a raise for taking a bullet in his hip to save Madison. Of course, he'd just say it was doing his job like he had said already. And it was, but still, he went above and beyond in trying to save not only Madison but Sam, who was still spitting mad at Rogers for pulling a weapon on her. Too bad he was dead.

AJ and Rob—the two who shot and killed Casden and Rogers—were at the police station with the HIS attorney. Brad had no doubt that it would be classified as self-defense, and the men would be back in the fold. They'd gone through that process more than once and knew when they were right in their shots. They'd deal with the anger of the police department for not calling them, and they'd survive.

Finally, there was no threat to Madison. She was free to return to her life. His heart clenched at the thought of losing her. He knew that the strength of his love could be enough to carry them, but he needed her love in return.

Focusing on the here and now, he lowered his head and touched his lips to hers, gently as if he might break her. She was fragile, even though she'd amazed him with her strength. Of course, her anger at the men doing what they did was stronger than her fear of when the handgun had been held to her temple.

He devoured her soft lips, tracing his tongue around them and then sliding it into her mouth where her tongue met his in a splash of erotic bliss.

Brad could kiss Madison all day and never get tired of her sweet taste.

Given all that had happened, he had to make love to her, let her know she was his, no matter what, and show her how precious she was.

Madly exploring her mouth, he grasped her ass and pulled her tight against him, his hardness firm on her belly. "I need you, Maddie," he said when he broke the kiss, but he kept his lips hovering over hers to let her know he wasn't finished kissing her.

"I need you, too."

His heart soared, and his dick hardened even more. It wasn't a devotion of love, but need was strong. "Let's kick off our shoes and head to the bedroom."

She had already toed off one shoe before he finished his sentence. He hurriedly removed his footwear and left them where they landed on the floor.

Grasping her hand, he pulled her to his bedroom and shut the door. He didn't expect anyone, but who knew if Matt would just show up. He still had a key to the house.

Pulling her to him, he tugged at the blood-soaked blouse tucked in her shirt while his mouth landed on hers, a hot, sexy kiss letting her know how much she was needed. He didn't think he could show her the need was stronger than just sex. It extended to everything in life. As he tasted her kiss, he knew he'd have to say something and take the hit to his heart and ego if she didn't love him back.

With her shirt up to her neck, he broke the kiss and pulled the blouse off and tossed it on the ground. He immediately reached around her for her pink, lacy bra. He'd mastered those things in college, and it only took a few seconds before he unhooked it and watched it fall off her shoulders and to the floor.

"This isn't fair," she said coyly, and reached for his T-shirt. He didn't stop her from undressing him, but he did take the shirt when she reached his neck. She was tall—and he liked that—but not tall enough to pull the shirt over his head unless he bent down. It was easier for him to take it off at that point.

Both of their hands went to exploring the other's chest. He had a mound in each hand, kneading and massaging before his thumbs flicked her erect nipples.

A shiver ran through him when she played with his nipple. He'd never realized how erotic that touch could be. It never had been. It was all Madison and her hands that did it for him. She made him want to break all his rules.

"Pants," he breathed after lifting his mouth. He slid

his lips to her throat and began undoing her pants while she undid his.

"Faster if we do our own," she said through breath, sounding like she'd just run a mile or two.

He didn't argue. He needed to be inside her, now. Needed to feel how alive she was.

In her hurried state, he barely had a moment to register the pink, lacy panties she wore that matched her bra. He'd see it on her again, because even though she didn't need to stay with him any longer, he expected her to be here a great deal.

"Do you need to grab the scarf?" she asked as she climbed on the bed.

No. He wanted her hands on him. Wanted the feelings that flowed through her. "No."

"Are you sure? The first time we were together, you told me it was the one rule you didn't break."

True. That was before he got to know Madison. "Well, I'm breaking it for good with you. I want your hands on me." Since he planned to remain honest with her, he saw no reason not to explain further.

"Then come here," she directed, lying in a sensual pose that made his dick pull him forward by need and desire.

God, he loved this woman, both in and out of his bed. She might have been stubborn and hardheaded, but that worked for him.

He pulled out a condom from his bedside table and put it on. Then he climbed on the mattress and lay beside her, propped up on an elbow. His free hand traced circles on her stomach, and he watched the goose bumps ripple across her skin.

Leaning his head down, he took a taut nipple into

his mouth and sucked and licked it until she mewed and moaned. She almost leaped off the bed when he caught it in his teeth.

The amber scent of her lotion lifted lightly to his nostrils, and the urge to take her almost drove him mad. He'd make sure she was ready for him.

Reaching his hand down between her legs, he leaned over and kissed her stomach. Hot, fiery kisses that trailed around in the same circles he'd made with his fingers. Damn, she was wet and ready for him.

"I want to taste you," he said, his breath blowing on her belly.

"Next time," she said. "I want you now, Brad."

Who was he to argue with that? He lifted himself over her and positioned his cock to her hot core. Leaning down, he took her lips with his and entered her slowly and steadily until he was fully seated. With the heat and tightness and her hands rubbing up and down his back, he might just come on the spot.

Football stats, he reminded himself. If this problem kept occurring with Madison, he would be a genius on football stats because he always wanted to come as soon as he entered her, but he preferred to remain there, sheltered in her warm heat.

They moved at a slow rhythm, lost in their sensual kiss. After a few minutes, he broke the kiss and attacked her throat with his mouth and tongue. He loved her taste. So sensual yet feminine.

"Faster, Brad."

Again, who was he to argue? He increased the rhythm until he found the speed at which she moaned and arched her back. She was close. Knowing she could come so fast with him set his spirit—and ego—afire with delight.

Reaching a hand down, he touched her nub, and she almost came off the bed. Blatantly watching her now, he rubbed it in a circular motion and looked for clues as to what felt the best. When she gasped in pleasure, her body straining against his, he gave it all he had with the motion of his hips and the movement of his hand.

When his balls drew up and that tingling at the base of his spine started, he knew he wouldn't last much longer.

"Oh, Brad, I'm going to come."

Thank God. "Me, too."

They came together—or close enough—and the world tilted off its axis momentarily. Aware he was crushing Madison where he'd just fallen, having lost control of his muscles, he shifted off her and the bed with wobbly legs to dispose of the condom.

When he returned, she still lay on the bed with that "just fucked" look—her face flushed with a hint of a satisfied smile on her swollen lips and her body glistening. It was sexy as hell.

He had to tell her he loved her before she was good and away from him. He was a big boy; he could suffer the hurt. Not that he believed that, but he had to tell himself that, or he wouldn't have the courage to say those three little words.

Standing by the bed, naked, he called to her, "Maddie."

She turned her head to him and smiled. "Yes?"

"Maddie—" He gulped against the nervousness in his throat. "Maddie, I love you." He'd said it for the first time in his life to a woman who wasn't his sister or mother.

It took a moment for her to grasp his words, and those were some of the worst seconds of his life. But he knew he'd been right to tell her when she caught them.

She sat up in bed, then stood before him, her naked body still glistening from their lovemaking. She placed a hand on his cheek and whispered, "I love you, too." Then she kissed him tenderly. After too many years of being empty, Brad felt whole again.

Chapter Twenty-Nine

Brad shook his head. He was right where his other brothers were at one time when he'd made fun of them. Standing at the altar of a church he'd attended once to marry the love of his life, was more peaceful than he thought it would be. Madison would be his forever.

They'd spent the last five months getting to know each other. With her support and help, he'd lost his anger at the world and had dropped all the pain and misery he'd heaped on himself after the incident in Colombia. He'd cleared his name. Yet he'd said no when the Secret Service offered him a job again. He was settled with his brothers, and there was no place he'd rather be.

He rarely listened when his brothers told him he'd gone over the top with something, but his Maddie had no trouble telling him. And he listened. It didn't stop fights between the two of them. They were both too hardheaded, but the makeup sex was always great. They even brought out the scarf from time to time. Well worth getting angry for that brief time. They never went to bed angry. That had been a rule they'd established up front.

Madison closed on her new home, and he would move in with her—officially—after the wedding. Instead of selling his home, he rented it to two HIS team members at a low rate. Enough to cover the mortgage was all he wanted.

Looking out to the crowd, he saw his family with a fully recovered Ken. Besides them, quite a few tough men dressed smartly in suits and sports coats sitting on one side. Virtually all were turned and drooling at the abundance of gorgeous models dressed to the nines with broad smiles who sat on the other side. The reception was going to be very interesting. Even so, he and Madison would be slipping out as soon as possible. They were eager to have their first sex as husband and wife.

The church had been decorated with white flowers. Some he knew were roses, but he had no clue what the others were. But he liked it. Clean and simple yet elegant. His fiancée had great taste. He grinned to himself. Of course, she did choose him.

"The last man standing takes a fall," he heard AJ say from within the line of groomsmen. He'd planned to have only Matt stand up for him, but Maddie had Rylee and some model friends she'd asked to be bridesmaids. So he had Matt, Jesse, Devon, and AJ standing up with him, all dressed in their tuxedos.

"And he said it would never happen," Devon laughed.

Fuckers.

"We knew it would happen, and when we saw him with Madison, it was obvious he was a goner," Jesse said to the group, as if Brad wasn't there.

And he had been and wouldn't have it any other way. He understood his brothers and their wives' relationships better now. His heart beat for the love he had for his family. "No matter, I'm glad I'm here," he said to them. This was important for him to say, but it took swallowing hard past a lump in his throat to do it. He'd never spoken such words from his heart before to his brothers, but he had to say this. "I now know what you felt with Caitlyn, Kate, Rylee, and Megan. You can't let her go for anything in life."

Matt slapped him on the back. "Things will only get better after this."

He couldn't imagine them getting any better, but he wouldn't argue with the men who'd married that one special woman and were still in love to this day.

Music began to play, and the group turned toward the church doors. Reagan and Amber, in their cute little white dresses, carried baskets of white rose petals that they dropped on the ground to their special seat on the front pew. The two would never remain still during the ceremony if they had to stand. As it was, everyone knew the two would be squirming around and probably talking, but no one cared.

One by one, he watched the bridesmaid models walk up the aisle toward him before they turned to the bride's side of the altar. Then the music changed, and he held his breath, waiting for the vision of his soon-to-be wife.

She stepped into the doorway and took his breath away. She was wearing a full-length gown covered in lace, cut in a V-shape on the front and form-fitting where her beautiful figure showed before it fanned out loosely below the waist. A small train, or whatever they called it, marked it off as the perfect dress.

As she neared, he saw the bit of lace that covered most of her face—a veil. Like the lace on her dress, the lace had flowers in it for design. He loved the look on her, although he wanted to rip the veil off and kiss her hard. He swallowed back the urge. His nieces weren't the only ones who had to promise to behave today.

"Dearly beloved...."

He tuned out the words the minister was saying. He'd heard them repeatedly while his brothers had married. He just had to be ready for his part. Matt had the ring. He was relatively sure of it. Shit. He should've checked. No. He could depend on his twin.

He was about to be a married man, and he felt a responsibility to take care of his wife. It was an old-fashioned value, but he didn't discount they were partners, and as strong as she was, there was no denying she would stand beside him. Even so, he wanted to be that rock for the two of them and any children they were blessed with having.

Financially, she'd never need him. La Belle was up and running, and based upon the hours she happily spent there, things were going well. He'd visit her at the store, and she'd be swamped with customers. He had no clue people would spend that much on underwear. Yet it was quality, so he guessed that mattered.

But still, not being able to support her financially since she made more than him hurt his pride. She didn't flaunt it in his face, so he'd learned to deal with it. Hell, they would live in a house she bought and wanted no contribution from him in return. That had been one hell of an argument where they'd had makeup sex for days. Finally, he'd caved. He made good money, but he could also be a kept man. He laughed inwardly at that. His brothers would have a field day with that one, especially since he'd given Jesse such a hard time about Kate and her millionaire status.

The girls were squirming in their seats, as

expected. He imagined their mothers were itching to move to that pew and correct them. Mothers always did. It didn't bother him, though; it made him smile. One day he and Maddie would have children of their own. They'd talked about it. Before, he'd never seen himself as a father, but with Madison the dream was all too real. Thankfully, they hadn't argued over that topic. They just wanted however many children they were blessed with, and be it boy or girl, they didn't care as long as they were healthy.

Matt nudged him and brought him out of his reverie. "I will," he said quickly, hoping that was what was needed at the moment.

The minister smiled, so he had gotten it right. Thank goodness. He'd have hated to mess up their special day.

He paid attention through the rest of the vows and ring exchanges, knowing these were the critical parts.

His heart beat fast when he was told he could kiss the bride. This was the final step, and she was his forever.

Facing each other, he lifted her veil and leaned his lips down to her. He only meant to give her a chaste kiss—they were in church, for Christ's sake. But well-laid plans could have a monkey wrench put in them. She kissed him back with gusto, and he couldn't let go. He had to deepen the kiss until he tasted her thoroughly and branded the kiss in her memory.

After the clearing of a throat, he pulled back slowly and watched the darkening of her eyes. He wondered if they could skip the picture taking and reception altogether.

They were told to turn and face the crowd with

their hands still entwined.

"I present Mr. and Mrs. Bradley Hamilton," the minister said to the crowd.

Brad's heart swelled. So, he might have been the last man standing. But Madison Maxwell was well worth his fall.

Epilogue

Since it was cold in the early evening, Brad grasped Madison's hand as they strolled up the walkway to his father's home and hurried her steps. He'd forgotten his gloves, and his hands were already freezing. December in Silver Spring was just downright frigid.

"Is this a tradition for your family?" Madison asked.

This was the first time all of his brothers and sisters had been together with their father on Christmas Eve since they were boys. He wasn't sure if they'd make this a tradition, but he liked the idea. Even Matt and Trent flew in with their families and newborn babies.

That was why he figured his father had invited everyone—all the little ones who called him Poppy and whom he spoiled. He had ten grandchildren, none from him and Madison—yet.

They'd just had confirmation right before the holiday that she was two months pregnant. She wasn't ready to tell everyone, saying much could happen that early in pregnancy. They would wait until she was three months along before they spilled the beans. Of course, they might notice she wouldn't drink anything alcoholic tonight. His sister and sisters-in-law were sharp. Not much got by them. But he also knew they wouldn't say anything if Madison didn't. They understood discretion.

Opening the front door decorated with greenery outlining it and a wreath on each door, the warmth hit him in the face, and the smell of Christmas—pine, cedar, cinnamon, and baked apples—was in the air.

He couldn't wait to dive into the feast his father's cook had prepared. The woman was a genius in the kitchen. When they were little, she'd always had some cookies made for them when they got home from school.

Brad and Madison removed their coats and handed them to a man Brad had never met, who took them away. His father must've hired help for the big family gathering. Including the children, there were now twenty-six of them. How was his dad going to feed them all? The table, while large, wouldn't hold that many. Of course, he told himself, his father knew that and surely made some accommodation for it.

Walking into the family room, he quickly scanned the area, counting brothers, and realized they were the last to arrive. He couldn't help it if he'd had to have his woman while she'd tried to dress for tonight.

The women sat in the chairs and on the couches while the men stood, keeping a post near their family while the kids played in the middle of the room where a coffee table had been removed for space.

Madison leaned to him and raised her hand as if to cover the words. "I think we're late."

He clasped her and squeezed tight. "We're right on time," he responded.

"I have sitters for the newborns so parents can eat without worry," his dad said. Boy did he think of everything. "And Jason has volunteered to sit at the kids' table so you won't have to worry."

Jason beamed with pride at his selfless act. He might have bitten off more than he could chew with the six young ones.

"Now Brad and Madison are here, we can go in to eat. Take your children and get them settled."

"Daddy, how come I can't eat with you?" Reagan asked Jesse. "I'm a big girl now. I know how to behave."

Her heartfelt plea got a few "aahs" from the group. But Jesse didn't fall for it. "See, I need you to sit at the kids' table. Jason can't watch all the little ones by himself. He'll need your help."

She looked at Jason, who was smiling at his sister. "You bet I do." He held out his hand, and she took it and followed him out of the room.

AJ and Megan took Alex, who bounced in his seat. Jake and Emily carried Amber and Leslie, settling the latter in a highchair that was also lower than usual. Devon and Rylee got Mitch settled. Then, Trent brought Ashley into the room while Kelly reluctantly handed Roger over to a sitter. Matt and Caitlyn gladly released their twins—Travis and Scott—for what he suspected was much-needed peace.

After it was just adults—who kept glancing toward the kids' table and upstairs where the infants went—the sixteen adults sat at the table built for twenty and set with fine, white pieces of china, a miniature Christmas tree decorated with small glass bulbs sat as the centerpiece. Its low height didn't prevent anyone from seeing another. Threaded down the center of the table to the end was fresh greenery with bulbs decorating it here and there. So fresh you could still smell it as if it had just been cut. And there was a magic marker at each place. Odd.

"I want to thank you all for coming tonight. I know being away from home at Christmas with kids is a challenge," Blake said to Trent and Matt, who nodded. "I hope we've got you settled for tomorrow so the kids don't miss a thing." Both of his brothers from out of town were staying with their father so the kids could have a stable Christmas in the morning, even though not all were old enough to notice it.

"The last time we were all together," he said, "you saved Elizabeth's life. I can't thank you enough for that. My goal tonight was to be together without a crisis worse than diaper rash."

Chuckles erupted from the table, but Matt and Caitlyn only grimaced. That must be a problem for them with the twins.

Twins. He couldn't even imagine. He hoped he and Madison only had one because from what he'd learned from his brothers, one was enough to drive you crazy. How did Matt handle two?

"Since the kids will get older and Christmas at home will be a big deal, I'd like to start this tradition, but Elizabeth and I would like to start it on Thanksgiving of each year. We didn't this year because Caitlyn and Kelly were too close to delivering. And we didn't want another year to go by without all of us getting together. So, I propose we do this every year on Thanksgiving. What do you think?"

That sounded good to Brad. Less food they'd have to cook. Less work for Madison as she tended to shoo him out of the kitchen when she got into a cooking mood.

Everyone nodded. Why wouldn't they? A reason to

get together and have some of the best food around? It was a done deal.

"That's one tradition we'll have. Another tradition that we'll do is being thankful. This tablecloth will be used for our holiday dinners year after year. You have a magic marker in front of you. I propose that you write something you are thankful for this year on the tablecloth and then share it with us. Every year, you add to it and reflect on all you've been blessed with. What do you say?"

There was some apprehension, but everyone nodded. It wasn't a tough request, just odd. But he liked the idea if they continued to use this tablecloth. Each year passed, he could see what he'd been thankful for. He figured it'd be Madison every year. Then his kids.

People began moving their plates forward to bare the cloth before them, and the women began to write. Glancing around, Brad noticed his brothers were looking at what their women were writing, but one by one, they began to write themselves.

Brad's was straightforward and took no time to write. He couldn't see it changing over the years.

Once everyone put their markers down, his dad asked Jesse, as the eldest, to begin.

Jesse cleared his throat and didn't look down at his writing. "I'm thankful for my wife, children, family, and friends."

Just as simple as Brad's, yet he hadn't added children.

As they went around the room, laughter broke out. Everyone had written something similar to—if not exactly the same—as Jesse's thankful statement.

Midway through the group, his dad asked, "Did

anyone write anything different?"

No one commented or raised their hand.

"Well, it appears I have raised fine, upstanding men, and you have chosen the right women to complement you. My thankfulness is very similar but includes grandchildren."

Dinner was served with the traditional turkey and ham with stuffing, mashed potatoes, green beans, cranberry sauce, and rolls. Brad ate until he couldn't move. His dad's chef had outdone himself. When pumpkin, apple pie, and a plate of chocolate chip cookies made their way to the table, he wondered if anyone would notice him loosening the button on his pants.

Most of the group left the dessert for later. Like him, they'd overdone it on the main course. When the talking died down, and the last bite had been taken, Blake ushered everyone into the family room where Jason and Reagan were keeping the smaller kids busy.

The young ones who understood Christmas were excited, as they knew they had to open a present from their grandfather that night before Santa Claus came to visit them.

The man who'd taken their coats walked into the room, holding a box and gingerly setting it under the tree. Brad smiled.

He and Madison were exchanging gifts tomorrow, but he couldn't wait on one and had convinced his dad to let him exchange it there. They hadn't wanted others to feel they should've done the same. After getting agreement from the family, he selected her gift. He prayed she liked it. She'd said she wanted one. Hopefully, she hadn't meant only the one she chose.

He left her in an armchair and picked up the box, then walked back to her. "Maddie," he said to get her attention, realizing it also got everyone else's attention since he stood there with a present. "I have a present for you that couldn't wait until tomorrow."

"Brad, I didn't bring you anything." They'd agreed to exchange gifts at home, but this one couldn't wait.

"It's not like that. This just couldn't wait another day." He handed her the box, and she looked at it, narrowing her eyes when she saw the little holes poked into the decorated box. "Brad?" she questioned before lifting the lid off.

Her face lit up, and she looked at him with watery eyes. She stood to kiss him but was hampered by the box between them. Instead, she looked down at the box and set it and the lid on the chair. Reaching in, she pulled out a calico kitten of about six weeks old. That age was the animal shelter's best guess.

"You said you wanted one and were the only Hamilton wife without a pet...."

She laughed as she cuddled the now-awake kitten to her chest. "This is perfect." Leaning toward him, she told him she loved him before kissing him.

The kids had all circled around her, their own presents to be opened forgotten. "What's its name?" Reagan asked.

"It's a girl," Brad told her.

"I think...Princess." She cast Brad a sly smile. "What do you think?" she asked the kids.

"Princess is a good name," Amber stated.

"Can we pet her?" was repeated by the little ones.

"I'll tell you what," Brad said, "after you open your presents, you can pet her. Right now though, your

Poppy has something special for each of you."

The kids raced to the tree where his dad was waiting to hand out presents.

"Are you sure it's okay I picked her out without you?" Worry laced his words.

"I'm positive. This way is better." She walked into his open arms, and he held her.

Looking around the room, he took in the couples' dynamics—all touching in some way—and the kids. He was damn lucky to have the family and wife that he had. They adopted a cat and soon would have a child of their own. Yeah, life didn't get any better than being a Hamilton.

A Note From Sheila

Thank you for reading *His Fantasy*! If you enjoyed reading Brad and Madison's story, I would appreciate it if you would help others enjoy this book, too. You can recommend it to friends, readers' groups, and discussion boards. It would mean a great deal to me if you'd take a moment to write a review and share how you feel about my story so others may find my work. Honest reviews help bring my books to the attention of other readers. The best news is that only a few words are needed.

A word about the author...

Sheila Kell writes about the romantic men who leave women's hearts pounding with a happily ever after built on memorable, adrenaline-pumping stories. Her debut novel, *His Desire* (HIS Series #1), launched as an Amazon #1 romantic suspense bestseller, later winning the Readers' Favorite award for best romantic suspense novel.

As a Southern girl who has left behind her days with the U.S. Air Force, and as a University Vice President, she can usually be found nestled in the family home in Florida, where she lives with her cats. When she isn't writing, she has her nose in a good book, or is wishing she had a genie to do her bidding.

https://www.sheilakell.com

Thank you for purchasing
this publication of The Wild Rose Press, Inc.

For questions or more information
contact us at
info@thewildrosepress.com.

The Wild Rose Press, Inc.
www.thewildrosepress.com